At the end of the meal they left the restaurant hand in hand. 'This way,' he said suddenly, leading her down one of the quaint little alleyways lined with smart shops and tubs of flowers. It was also deserted.

She was taken aback when he suddenly gathered her into his arms. As he kissed her he slipped a hand into the front of her dress. Warm fingers teased one pert nipple, then closed on her full breast, sending shivers of excitement shooting through her. Somehow both breasts were now exposed to the warm night air and he stroked and kissed them until her legs threatened to give way beneath her.

'What if someone comes?' she moaned.

'That's never worried you before,' he said as he lifted her skirt and began to stroke her delicately between her legs, over her satin panties . . .

Also available from Headline Delta

Undercover

Felice Ash

HEADLINE
DELTA

First published in 1994
by HEADLINE BOOK PUBLISHING

A HEADLINE DELTA paperback

10 9 8 7 6 5 4 3 2

ISBN 0 7472 4499 5

Phototypeset by Intype, London
Printed and bound in Great Britain by
Cox & Wyman Ltd, Reading, Berks

HEADLINE BOOK PUBLISHING
A division of Hodder Headline PLC
338 Euston Road
London NW1 3BH

Undercover

Chapter One

Tim Preece reassembled the telephone, now complete with bugging device, and replaced it on the small walnut table. He walked down the hallway and entered the opulent drawing room.

The secretary was arranging some papers neatly on the desk in the corner and it was a few seconds before she noticed him. It gave him time to admire her slender body, her curves only partially concealed by a severe grey wool suit worn over a crisp white blouse. Her sleek dark hair was cut in a smooth bob framing delicate, patrician features.

'You shouldn't have any more trouble with the phones, love, but if you do just report it,' he told her. He was American but nobody would have guessed, his accent was decidedly East End.

The secretary's upper-class background, on the other hand, was immediately obvious when she spoke.

'Thank you so much.' She paused, then indicated the Georgian silver coffee pot on the table. 'Would you like a cup of coffee before you go?' Common sense told Tim to leave, now he'd accomplished his mission and bugged the phones. Instead he heard himself accepting.

Glancing around the expensively decorated room, furnished with what he knew to be some very valuable antiques, he marvelled at how easily he'd been able to gain entry. The house had an elaborate state-of-the-art security system and if he'd decided to break in he'd have had his work cut out.

As it was he'd presented himself on the doorstep saying he was a BT engineer and had come to repair the fault on the line. She'd picked up the phone in the hall, satisfied herself that it was dead and let him in.

Perched on the edge of the desk opposite him, her cool grey eyes swept over his body as she asked, 'What's your name?'

'Bill,' he replied, mentally undressing her.

'Should I ask for you if the line goes dead again?'

'No point. They'll just send whoever's available.'

'Pity.'

To Tim's surprise he saw her eyes lingering on his groin. Had she guessed he was imagining her naked? Or perhaps just in the string of pearls she was wearing around her slender neck – and maybe the high-heeled shoes.

Her legs were crossed and her grey skirt had ridden up to reveal several inches of shapely thigh. As he watched she ran her hand down over her hip, then uncrossed and recrossed her legs.

'I know what you're thinking,' she told him.

'Do you?' he said blankly.

'You're thinking you'd like to throw me on the desk and fuck me,' she said softly. 'Actually, you can if you want to. I find men like you exciting once in a while.'

Tim's dick, which had been stirring slightly as he looked at her, leapt eagerly upwards at her unexpected words. He'd lived in England long enough to have picked up a few things about the class system. This ex-debutante obviously enjoyed what she no doubt thought of as 'a bit of rough' in the sack.

Who was he to disappoint her?

The fact that he was a middle-class, college

educated American was irrelevant as far as he was concerned.

Rising to his feet he swiftly undid the buttons on her crisp white blouse, revealing a pristine, plain white bra. Deftly unclipping it he uncovered small, ivory-skinned breasts with pointed rose-pink nipples and cupped them with the palms of his hands.

She sighed and closed her eyes, then made a little mewing noise as he ran his thumb over one nipple until it hardened. He bent his head and took it in his mouth, his tongue flickering over it until she moaned.

Suddenly, at the sound of a car door slamming in the square outside, her body went rigid and she turned her head to look out of the window. A second later she pushed Tim away and began hastily fastening her bra, hissing, 'It's Sir John – my boss. Quickly, you'll have to leave! Go out the back way!'

Glancing out of the window Tim saw the man he had under surveillance and whose phone he'd just bugged, giving some instructions to his chauffeur.

'Don't just stand there! Hurry up!' she urged him.

Mentally cursing Sir John for his untimely arrival, Tim headed swiftly towards the door.

Once back at the office of his private investigation agency, Tim sat at his desk gulping coffee and trying to make some inroads into the stack of paperwork awaiting his attention.

He wished that Alexa, the best operative on his payroll, hadn't chosen this of all weeks to take a holiday when they were snowed under with work. She'd said she had a very good reason, but declined to tell him what it was.

The agency specialised in corporate and industrial work and was one of the most successful in that area. He really needed to take on another operative, but people of the right calibre were hard to find.

His staff needed to be bright, resourceful and possessed of a chameleon-like ability to blend in anywhere. They also needed a fairly comprehensive knowledge of computers, as most investigation in the post-chip age was carried out at a computer terminal. There wasn't much you couldn't find out about anyone if you could tap into the right information systems.

Martha, Tim's secretary, appeared in the doorway at that moment. She hesitated, then in response to his enquiring expression came into the room and closed the door behind her.

'There's a Mrs Halliday to see you.'

'Who?' he demanded laconically.

'A potential client, I gather.'

'Does she have an appointment?' Tim had reverted to his normal American accent.

'No. Actually she's phoned a couple of times this week – she wants you to handle a personal investigation for her. I told her that the agency only operates in the commercial sector but she says you were highly recommended by a friend. I've just told her the same thing again, but she insists on seeing you personally.'

'Can't you get rid of her?' he groaned.

'She says she's going to sit in reception until she's seen you.'

'I suppose you'd better wheel the lady in, then. If I haven't managed to get rid of her in five minutes could you ring through and say there's an urgent call for me?'

Mrs Halliday wasn't what Tim had expected at all. When a married woman wanted a personal investigation handling, it usually meant that she suspected her husband of extra-marital activities and wanted him following.

If Mr Halliday was involved in any hanky-panky with a woman other than his wife, he must be a madman.

From her baby blonde hair down to her high-heeled shoes, Mrs Halliday was simply one of the most luscious females Tim had ever set eyes on.

She looked to be in her early twenties and was possessed of the sort of figure which made strong men turn to jelly. She was wearing a low cut, pink angora dress which was jacked in around her tiny waist with a wide leather belt. A pair of magnificent breasts strained against the soft pink wool of the dress, which also clung closely to the traffic-stopping curves of her gorgeous backside.

Tim passed the back of his hand over his suddenly damp brow as he went through the motions of holding out a chair for her.

She smiled at him beguilingly, her pouting rosebud mouth painted with lipstick the same shade of pink as her dress. Her round china-blue eyes were fringed by improbably thick, dark lashes which she batted at him as she smiled.

She appeared to like what she saw, which was a tall, good looking man with a rangy body, tow-coloured hair and hazel eyes.

Instead of launching into a terse explanation of why the agency never touched personal investigation cases, Tim found himself saying charmingly, 'What can I do for you, Mrs Halliday?'

She batted her eyelashes at him again.

'Please call me Serena.' She paused for a moment, then continued, 'I'm afraid I've been a naughty girl and I've got myself in a teensy-weensy bit of a mess.'

'What sort of a mess?'

She looked him up and down then smiled another smile which played havoc with his hormones. He brushed the back of his hand over his brow again, pushing back a lock of wayward fair hair.

'I've been a little bit indiscreet.'

'Why don't you tell me about it?'

Tim had absolutely no intention of taking the case on, but he was quite happy to sit and feast his eyes on the gorgeous creature on the other side of his desk for a while longer.

'My husband's much older than me and he's very . . . jealous and possessive.'

Tim could imagine.

'He's also away a lot on business and I get . . . lonely.'

Tim could imagine that too.

'I was very foolish and had a sort of . . . fling.'

Tim didn't need her to spell out what sort of fling she meant.

She settled herself further back in her chair with a seductive little wriggle.

'He's called Sean Hesketh and now he's black-mailing me. He's got photos and he says he'll send them to my husband one at a time unless I pay him.' She took out a tiny lace-edged handkerchief and dabbed at her eyes.

'How compromising are the photos?' he asked.

She dabbed at her eyes again, then reached into her bag.

'This compromising,' she said, passing one over to him.

A strong desire to see her naked, or perhaps just in a suspender belt, stockings and high heels had been flickering through Tim's overheated brain since she'd sashayed in through the door, so this just seemed too good to be true.

If only all his desires were gratified so readily.

He tried to keep his expression neutral as he

studied the photo and felt the blood drain from his face and straight to his already hard dick.

It was quite an effort not to let his jaw drop. Like most men he'd seen his share of pornographic photos, but this was in another league.

Serena and her lover were engaged in the sort of sexual scenario many men fantasise about but never get remotely close to in reality.

Tim was transfixed.

When he could tear his eyes away from Serena's lovely form, captured so graphically on celluloid, he studied her blackmailing sexual partner. If his expression was anything to judge by, Sean Hesketh was enjoying the fuck of his life.

'Are they all like this?' he enquired hoarsely.

'Some of them are even a little bit naughtier, I'm afraid,' she murmured, her eyes downcast.

Tim could easily imagine the effect receiving such a photo in the post would have on her husband. If he was quite old, or had a weak heart, it would probably be enough to finish the old man off.

'How much is he asking?'

'Fifty thousand per photograph.'

'How many photographs are there?'

'Around twenty.'

Tim whistled silently. Some people were just greedy. Imagine having the pleasure of Serena Halliday and then turning round and asking for money. He'd never understand how some men's minds worked.

'How can he do this to me?' demanded Serena tearfully. 'And I thought he was such a nice man.'

Tim flashed her a sceptical look.

'Does your friend Sean have any reason to think you can afford to pay him?'

'Only that my husband's a multi-millionaire, but I don't have any money of my own at all.'

He sat and looked at her, discreetly admiring her shapely legs. Was that a glimpse of stocking top or was it just wishful thinking on his part?

The door opened at that moment and his secretary appeared.

'Tim, there's an urgent call for you on line one.'

'Yeah ... thanks, Martha honey. Could you take the details and say I'll call them back, please?' Smiling knowingly and rather grimly Martha pulled the door to behind her.

Her interruption reminded Tim of just how busy he was. He could have sat and admired Serena Halliday all day, but there was that pressing pile of paperwork.

Reaching for a pad, he scribbled down the name and address of an agency which he knew specialised in cases of this sort. He tore off the sheet of paper and handed it to her together, regretfully, with the incriminating photo.

'As I believe my secretary explained to you, we only work in the commercial sector, but this firm will probably be able to help you.'

She stared at him beseechingly, her lower lip trembling, her blue eyes swimming with unshed tears.

'I don't want them, I want you. Please say you'll take the case – I feel I can trust you.'

Tim Preece was a tough man. Ex-CIA, he'd withstood torture, been shot three times and held hostage for over a year in appalling conditions in the Middle East. But he had one weakness.

Beautiful women.

And they didn't come much more beautiful than Serena Halliday.

Stalling, he asked, 'What is it you're hoping I can do exactly?'

'Get hold of the negatives and any further sets of prints and return them to me,' she replied promptly.

'Where are the negatives?'

'I can't be sure but probably in the safe in Sean's bedroom. You will help me, won't you, Tim?' She rose to her feet with fluid grace and came to sit on the edge of the desk in front of him. He could smell her musky perfume and see the rise and fall of her breasts under the clinging dress.

He made one last attempt to refuse.

'Serena, this isn't my area. I specialise in corporate or industrial investigations – I don't have the necessary skills or back-up for such an assignment.'

She pouted at him prettily. 'When you started out you used to handle cases like this.'

She was certainly well informed. When he'd opened the agency Tim took anything he could get. He had bills to pay, after all. But cases like this were always messy and rarely paid enough to justify taking them on.

She leant forward and coiled her arms around his neck, pressing her breasts against him as she murmured huskily, 'I'd be so grateful and I'd make it well worth your while.'

Her tone of voice promised untold sensual delights.

He knew damn well he was being manipulated in the most fundamental way possible, so why then did he find himself saying, 'Where does your blackmailing friend live?'

She delved into her bag, took out a card and handed it to him. 'It's the flat on the top floor. I'm so grateful you're going to sort this out for me.'

'I'll need as much information on him as you've got. What does he do for a living? What are his habits? How does he spend his time?'

Serena answered his questions rather vaguely but Tim was able to build up a reasonable picture.

When they'd finished she stood on tiptoe and kissed

him on the cheek, making sweat spring out on his brow again, then undulated towards the door, her back view as sensational as her front.

'I'll be waiting to hear from you.'

She turned and blew him a kiss before leaving the office.

It was raining hard and the traffic on the M6 was particularly heavy. The windscreen wipers on Jess's Fiat Uno just couldn't cope with the torrential rain deluging down and the filthy spray thrown up by the lorries thundering past – she felt as if she was trying to drive through a washing machine.

The journey from her home in Cheshire to her destination in Leicestershire should have taken her only two hours, instead it looked like it was going to take over three.

She sighed as she joined a long tailback of traffic waiting to enter yet another contraflow system – the whole motorway seemed to be up. Thankfully she was leaving at the next exit.

Jess wondered if Alexa would arrive before her, or if her sister's journey from London would be as problematic as her own.

She had mixed emotions about their forthcoming reunion. It would be nice to see Alexa again for the first time in over a year, but on the other hand her glamorous twin sister always made her feel dull and dowdy – and her self-esteem was quite low enough at the moment.

When Alexa had phoned the week before, Jess had been at a particularly low ebb. The summer stretched out in front of her long and empty, with nothing to fill it except preparing her lectures for the next academic year – and she'd already done most of that.

She found herself telling her sister how down she

felt, with the result that Alexa proposed that the two of them should go away together for a few days.

Jess was hesitant at first, she wasn't exactly in a holiday mood. But when Alexa suggested a week of being pampered and cosseted at Blydean Hall, one of the country's most exclusive health farms, she allowed herself to be talked into it.

But now she was having second thoughts.

She loved her sister dearly and when they were younger they'd been inseparable, but Alexa was so beautiful, so sexy and so full of life, that beside her Jess always felt plain and insignificant. Now she was worried that after a week together she'd feel even more depressed having compared her twin's exciting, colourful life with her own.

Signalling in plenty of time, Jess manoeuvred her way into the left-hand lane and prepared to leave the motorway.

Alexa looked appreciatively around the spacious bedroom.

'Hmm, not bad,' was her verdict.

'Where do you want this case?' enquired her companion, a good looking man in his early thirties.

'Just toss it on the bed for now, Ned,' she returned, briefly inspecting herself in the mirror.

'Does this room have a mini-bar?' he asked. 'I could use a drink.' Alexa was busy tidying her red-gold hair and didn't reply, so he began opening cupboards, but was unable to find one.

Walking over to where she stood in front of the dressing table, Ned slipped his arms around her waist from behind and ran his hands down over her hips.

'Do you really have to stay here?' he murmured in her ear, nuzzling her neck. 'Come up to Glasgow with me for the week instead.'

She leant back against him, feeling the hardness of his erection against the small of her back.

'We've been into that, Ned. Jess sounded very depressed when I spoke to her and I'm here to cheer her up if I possibly can. And anyway I need her to do something for me.'

'Your twin sister – does she look like you?'

'Well, she does and she doesn't.'

'I'd like to meet her – it could be interesting.'

Alexa's green eyes with their unusual yellow flecks met his dark ones in the mirror. She chuckled when she saw the expression on his face.

'Don't even think about it – Jess isn't at all like me except for the way she looks. She'd be horrified by such an idea. You'll have to make do with just one of me.'

'Talking of which . . .'

He walked over to the door and locked it, came back to her and then slowly slipped his hands up beneath the skirt of her cream linen suit. Their eyes were locked in the mirror as he found the soft skin between her stocking top and panties and caressed it gently.

She leant her head back on his shoulder and continued to look at his reflection as he slid his hands further upwards, smoothing over the firm globes of her satin-covered bottom, tracing the cleft between them with his thumbs.

His fingertips found the top of her panties and he began to ease them down, sliding his hands around her to stroke first her stomach, then the silken fuzz of her bush. Alexa's satin panties slithered down around her ankles and, stepping out of them, she kicked them to one side.

Ned brushed his fingertips lightly between her legs, feeling that the soft wisps of pubic hair concealing her labia were already damp.

12

Probing gently, he parted the outer lips and slipped his forefinger inside her slick, warm folds.

In the mirror he saw that her eyelids were half closed, veiling the hot, excited glitter of her green eyes. With his other hand he undid the buttons of her jacket revealing that underneath she wore only a front-fastening cream satin bra. He undid it deftly, releasing firm, high breasts with creamy skin and coral-pink nipples.

He held one full breast, savouring the weight of it, then caressed the nipple, enjoying the sensation of the crinkled nub jutting even more sharply outwards as he touched it.

His forefinger was still delicately exploring her tight wetness. When he began to slowly rub the most sensitive point, Alexa inhaled sharply and her legs opened, slightly at first, then wider as he intensified the pressure.

Reaching behind her she undid his belt then slowly unzipped his trousers. She gripped his cock through the soft cotton of his underwear and squeezed it firmly, then pulled it free from the restricting briefs.

It sprang eagerly out and she guided it to the right place between her quivering thighs where it forged swiftly upwards, making her gasp with pleasure.

Ned clasped her breasts and bent to kiss her neck and shoulders as they moved against each other. She bent forwards over the dressing table, reaching behind her to pull him closer, grinding her bottom against him as he thrust faster and faster, her skirt crushed up between them.

At last, with a shuddering sigh, Ned made one final determined thrust, then came with a long-drawn-out groan of release.

It was still sheeting down as Jess drove along the winding Leicestershire lanes beneath windswept, dripping trees. It felt more like March than July – she hoped that Blydean Hall was well heated.

Hoping to lighten her mood she pushed a cassette into the slot, then winced as the soulful tones of Dusty Springfield filled the car singing 'I Only Want to be With You'. It was Ralph's favourite and the one he used to refer to as 'our song'.

In a sudden rage she ejected it and smashed it against the dashboard. Opening the window a crack she threw it out, then spent the rest of the drive feeling guilty because she'd despoiled a country lane with non-biodegradable litter.

When she eventually drew to a halt on the gravel driveway in front of the elegant Georgian mansion, Jess was wishing she hadn't come. She sat disconsolately in her seat for a couple of minutes before forcing herself to grab her small suitcase and run quickly up the flight of shallow steps in the driving rain.

A pretty girl in a white uniform showed her to the room. It was immediately obvious that Alexa had already arrived because every available surface was littered with her twin's clothes and cosmetics and she could smell her distinctive perfume.

Jess was just hanging her own clothes in the wardrobe when the door flew open and there was Alexa standing in the doorway, one hand on her hip, a quizzical expression on her face.

'Hi sis,' she greeted her. 'How's it going?'

Looking at her twin's lovely heart-shaped face framed by wavy red-gold hair, Jess was suddenly glad she'd come. Alexa was the one person in the world she might be able to confide in. Perhaps she could unburden herself at last.

She hurried across the room and hugged her, saying, 'Alexa! It's so good to see you again. How long have you been here?'

'About an hour. I've just been having a look around.'

When they separated Alexa moved over to the mirror and began to touch up her make-up, telling Jess about her journey and lamenting the terrible weather. Perched on the end of one of the twin beds Jess watched her sister affectionately. Alexa was wearing a simple cream suit which was elegant and understated but which somehow drew attention to the lovely figure beneath it.

Jess felt dowdy in comparison in her sweater and trousers. They were identical twins but she'd never been more aware of the difference between them than at that moment.

Alexa's hair was a stunning red-gold, where her own was a dull mouse with just a few sandy highlights. They were the same height and measurements, but Alexa moved with an unselfconscious grace which drew attention to the curves of her lithe, alluring body.

Jess herself had a habit of hunching her shoulders and looking downwards as she moved; unattractive she knew, but she couldn't help it.

'So what do you think of this place?' asked Alexa, putting her powder compact down on the dressing table.

'It's lovely,' returned Jess, glancing around at the luxuriously appointed room with its pretty furnishings.

'It's not one of those places where they starve you – at least not if you're not overweight – so we can actually look forward to our meals. And there's a bar,' Alexa told her. 'Well, I think it's time for our appraisal.' She began to strip off her clothes, tossing them carelessly onto a chair.

'What's that?' asked Jess.

'Oh, we go downstairs and get weighed, measured and asked which of the treatments we want, then they make out a schedule for us. I'm not planning anything too energetic myself – I need a rest.'

She looked so gorgeous in her cream satin bra, panties and suspender belt that Jess felt momentarily ashamed of her own plain white cotton bra and pants. She turned her back to undress and shrugged hastily into the spotless white towelling robe provided.

The afternoon passed quickly as she decided which of the treatments she wanted, or rather Alexa decided for her. Of the two of them her twin had always been the leader and she hadn't changed.

They just had time for a swim before dinner. Physical activity was the one area where Jess outshone Alexa. She was a strong and confident swimmer and forged up and down the pool doing length after length.

Alexa, on the other hand, was nervous in deep water. She swam backwards and forwards across the shallow end a couple of times, then sat on the steps watching Jess until it was time to return to their room to shower and dress.

'It's given me an appetite just watching you,' she teased her twin as she climbed out of the water.

Jess wished she could say the same.

Chapter Two

Over dinner in the conservatory restaurant with the rain drumming monotonously on the glass above their heads, Jess and Alexa chatted about their respective jobs.

'So how's the exciting world of undercover investigation?' teased Jess.

'Tiring at the moment. Tim, my boss, isn't too pleased with me for taking a week off. How about you – still happy with the academic life?'

'I'd hardly call teaching English at a college of further education an academic life,' commented Jess wryly, 'but it's okay, I suppose.'

'And how's Ralph?'

'Okay I suppose.'

Alexa shot her a surprised look from beneath her dark brows, her green eyes questioning.

'You don't sound very enthusiastic. What's wrong?'

Jess sighed and poured them both another glass of wine.

'Well, if you must know, I recently found out Ralph's been having an affair with his secretary.' She pushed her plate away, her meal unfinished.

'Tell me about it.'

'It was the usual story. He started working late a lot, had a sudden spate of conferences he had to attend and he never wanted to make love.'

17

Jess's voice shook on the last few words and she took another gulp of her drink before continuing, 'He came home reeking of perfume a couple of times and then I found his Access bill on the dressing table showing meals in expensive restaurants he'd certainly never taken me to.'

'What did you do?'

'Nothing, I'm ashamed to say. You know how I hate scenes, it would probably still be going on now if Pru, the secretary, hadn't come round to see me.'

Alexa pushed a wayward tendril of hair back from her face. 'And what did she have to say?'

'That Ralph wanted to leave me for her, but hadn't got round to telling me yet. It was really awful. I telephoned Ralph and demanded he come home immediately, then Pru and I sat in uncomfortable silence until he arrived and I asked her to repeat what she'd said to me. Actually, it was almost funny. His mouth opened and closed like a landed fish and it soon became obvious that he'd never really had any intention of leaving me and was annoyed with Pru for forcing the issue. Anyway, to cut a long story short, it's over, he's got a new secretary and we're supposedly as we were – except . . .'

'Except what?'

'Except I can't stop thinking about it,' wailed Jess, 'and I'm just so angry with him.'

'Well, that's hardly surprising,' commented Alexa sympathetically. 'How long have you been together?'

'Seven years.'

Alexa and Jess had been to Manchester University together. They'd both taken English but they'd led very different lives. Alexa, always poised and confident, had thrown herself into a hectic social life. She had so many boyfriends that Jess soon gave up any attempt to remember their names.

Jess concentrated on her course, spending long hours in the library, and her boyfriends were few and far between. She met Ralph at a party Alexa dragged her to after their finals and continued to see him after she returned to Manchester in the autumn to do a teaching course.

Alexa moved to London and worked for a time as an assistant editor for a publishing company, but she found it dull and decided to try journalism.

She proved to be very good at following up leads, making enquiries and obtaining information, but disliked actually writing up the stories. The move from journalism to private investigation seemed to be a logical step after that.

Jess and Ralph moved in together at the end of her teaching year. She liked him, he was kind and humorous and if she sometimes thought he was too involved with his work – he owned a small company which designed computer software – she couldn't really blame him for that, he was operating in a very competitive market.

But for the last couple of years whenever he was home he seemed to spend most of his time sitting at his computer in the office upstairs, emerging only briefly for meals. Discovering that he'd been having an affair for the last few months hadn't helped. Jess was unhappy and dissatisfied with their relationship, but didn't know what to do about it.

It was a relief to tell Alexa.

'So what happens next?' questioned her sister.

'I don't know. Everything just seems so flat and I feel down all the time.'

'Do you want to finish it?'

'I don't think so, but I'm not sure.'

'How's the sex?'

Jess blushed and lowered her eyes.

19

'Practically non-existent and even when we do have it I don't particularly enjoy it.'

'Was it ever any good?' There was a pause. The rain drummed on the roof even harder.

'I'm not sure, I don't have much to compare it to. I think it was okay for the first few years. Never earth-shattering, but okay.'

Alexa grimaced. She couldn't imagine ever settling for sex which was only okay. The session with Ned just before Jess arrived had been great. They'd ended up doing it again, this time with her seated on the dressing table, her legs around his waist. She'd parted from him with regret – in all probability it would be the last sex she'd have for a week.

But it would probably be as well for her to have no distractions while she worked on Jess.

Aloud she said, 'Jess, by the time we leave here I promise that you'll be feeling much better.'

Jess was tired and went to bed early, but Alexa was restless and told Jess she'd be up later. If it hadn't been raining so hard she'd have gone for a stroll in the gardens, as it was she wandered around the various lounges before deciding to go and take a late-night jacuzzi.

The jacuzzi room was deserted. Alexa didn't want to disturb Jess by going up to their room and fetching her swimming costume. Thinking that she was unlikely to be joined at this time of night, she stripped off her clothes and lowered herself into the gently steaming water.

Resting her head on the side she closed her eyes and thought about her sister's situation.

Jess had always lacked self-confidence and never more so than in her dealings with the opposite sex. The twins hadn't spent much time together since leaving university – the years had just flown by – but

Alexa had always meant to take her siste[r] some day.

The ideal opportunity had now presented itself. [She] could do Jess a favour by helping her to make th[e] best of her looks and try to instil some self-confidence into her at the same time. Then Jess could do her a favour in return, one which she would hopefully enjoy very much.

As Alexa's body moved around slightly in the churning jacuzzi, a jet of warm bubbling water caught her squarely between the legs. The sensation was so delicious that she parted them and held herself in that position.

She wondered what Ned was doing up in Glasgow. Was he having an early night alone, or had he found company? She didn't mind if he had – he was just one of several of her casual lovers. She always enjoyed seeing him but didn't lose any sleep if he didn't call her for a while.

The jet of water between her legs was making her feel aroused – what a pity that Ned wasn't there now. It had been extremely erotic watching him screwing her in the mirror that afternoon, knowing that they could be interrupted at any time if Jess arrived.

The memory of it caused her to slip a hand between her slim thighs and touch herself.

And later, sitting on the dressing table with Ned's cock embedded deep within her, her skirt hoisted up around her hips and her bare bum sliding backwards and forwards on the highly polished surface . . .

A faint noise made her eyes fly open and she saw a tall, fair haired man in a pair of brief swimming trunks standing by the side of the jacuzzi. She hastily removed her hand from between her legs and hoped that in the foaming water he hadn't seen what she was doing.

'Do you mind if I join you?' he asked, his voice

.ep and gravelly, 'or were you hoping to be undisturbed?'

'No, do join me.' The words were out of her mouth before she remembered she was completely naked. She could only hope that his stay wouldn't be a long one. She sank further under the water so it came up to the tops of her creamy shoulders and looked at him appraisingly.

He was really very attractive. He was young, had a good fit body which was muscular but not overly so, and his face was pleasant without being too handsome.

'Are you staying here?' she asked.

He shook his head. 'No, I'm Sam. I work here. I'm the masseur.'

This was interesting.

Alexa had booked a daily massage for the duration of her stay but she'd assumed it would be with a woman. Well, she certainly wouldn't object to this man's large capable hands kneading her body. What woman in her right mind would?

'You're a guest and you've arrived today – right?'

'That's right, I'm Alexa and I'm here with my sister. Do you think we'll enjoy our stay?' she asked demurely.

'We're not doing our jobs right if you don't. I try to make every woman who goes through my hands feel like a million dollars.'

'And how do you do that?'

'By finding her points of tension and relieving them.' His eyes wandered lazily and appreciatively over her bare shoulders.

'Where do you think mine are?'

'I don't know, but I'll look forward to finding out.'

Alexa lifted one shapely leg out of the water and offered him a slim foot. 'What about my feet?'

He took it between his hands and massaged it gently. Alexa leant back against the side of the jacuzzi and closed her eyes. It felt so good that she let out a little murmur of pleasure. Sam began to knead the ball of her foot, then the surrounding area until the whole of the sole was a tingling mass of pleasure.

A feeling of wellbeing stole up her leg, adding to the arousal she already felt. When he'd finished with her foot he reached for the other one, working on it until every muscle and sinew felt relaxed and revitalised.

She was disappointed when he stopped.

'Is that all I get?' she asked.

'Do you want more?'

She looked at him from under her long lashes.

'Maybe a little more would help me sleep,' she suggested. He moved across the jacuzzi and sat next to her on the ledge which ran around the side, a couple of feet below the surface.

'Turn round,' he ordered her.

Obediently she presented him with her back. He ran his hands over it but made no comment on the fact that beneath the foaming bubbles she was obviously naked. He began to massage her, working his way down her spine, then concentrating on the area between her shoulder blades.

'You need a lot of work here,' he commented, digging the balls of his thumbs into her flesh, 'you're much too tense.'

'I know. I intend to spend the next week unwinding completely.'

He worked on her back in silence for a time. On a couple of occasions his fingers strayed under her arms, almost, but not quite, brushing over the swell of her breasts.

She wished he would touch her breasts. Her nipples

23

were hard with anticipation. Eventually he stopped and hauled himself out of the water.

'Time for me to go. I'll look forward to seeing you tomorrow when I'll be able to give you a thorough going over.'

'Is that a promise?' she asked sweetly.

He grinned at her. 'You bet. And incidentally . . .' He reached out and turned the jacuzzi off so the bubbles subsided and her naked form was revealed beneath the surface of the water.

'What?' she asked, smiling up at him.

'The management frown on skinny dipping. You'll need a costume – at least when there's anyone else around.'

'I'll try to remember.'

Alexa took Jess in hand the day after their arrival.

In the morning she accompanied her to Blydean Hall's hairdressing salon to have Jess's hair tinted to the same rich red-gold shade as her own and cut in the identical style. The first in a series of lessons in how to apply make-up followed.

'We haven't looked so much alike since we were children,' commented Jess dazedly. They now looked like the identical twins they were. Both of them had heart-shaped faces, small noses and full lips, but Alexa still projected self-confidence and sex appeal while Jess looked nervous and uncertain.

Not bad for a beginning, thought Alexa, as they enjoyed a light lunch in the conservatory dining room.

In the afternoon Alexa handed her sister over to the dance instructress with a request that she teach Jess to walk and hold herself more confidently. She watched critically for a while, then, satisfied that her sister was in good hands, strolled off for her massage, which she'd been looking forward to all day.

Sam was wearing a white T-shirt and a pair of white trousers which emphasised his excellent physique. He greeted her pleasantly and soon she was stretched out on the massage table on her stomach, with a towel wrapped loosely around her waist.

It was absolute heaven.

Sam massaged his way over her body leaving her feeling wonderful. Last night's session in the jacuzzi had been just a small foretaste of what was to come. Alexa had half expected it to be uncomfortable, but it was an extremely sensual experience. Her arms, legs and back all benefited from Sam's expert ministrations.

As he slid his hands up and down her spine, spreading more oil around, Alexa wondered if all the women he massaged found it as much of a turn-on as she was doing.

Wherever he touched her there seemed to be a direct nerve leading to her groin.

A thin sheen of sweat broke out on her back in the warm room and she found herself pressing her pelvis unobtrusively against the towel-covered massage table.

The heat in her loins continued to build as he massaged the lower part of her thighs. She was mentally willing him to work his way further upwards, but he restricted his attentions to just above her knees, handling her as impersonally as a doctor would.

Alexa's breathing was becoming ragged and she tried to control it with some difficulty. She was starting to find the sexual tension unbearable when he said, 'You have a choice now. You can rearrange that towel so you're decent, then turn over and I'll do your front, or . . .'

'Or what?' she prompted, her voice husky with suppressed lust.

'Or you can take it off and I'll do the bit I've missed.'

In reply, Alexa twitched the towel from around her waist and threw it onto a chair.

She felt a dribble of warm oil trickling over her, then his hands closed on the firm globes of her backside, cupping them briefly before beginning to knead them.

If Alexa had been aroused before, now she was molten.

Sam parted her buttocks and rotated them, first one way, then the other. His thumbs slipped fleetingly into the cleft between them, just brushing over the tight circle of her anus.

Alexa caught her lower lip between her teeth and tried not to gasp with pleasure. She could feel her private parts, hidden in their nest of silky pubic hair, moistening and unfurling in preparation for sex and was unable to stop herself parting her thighs a little.

He slid his hands between them, but didn't touch her intimately. Instead he massaged the top half of her thighs.

'Good?' he asked, his deep voice solicitous.

'Very,' she managed to reply, pressing her pelvis downwards even harder. He positioned her thighs wider apart and began to rub the smooth skin just a couple of inches away from the slick entrance to her honeypot. She groaned aloud and wriggled down the table, thrusting herself against his hand.

'Do you want the special?' he asked her softly.

'What's that?' she gasped.

In reply he brushed his fingers between her legs, lingering briefly on the sensitive bud of her clitoris. It was like a volt of electricity running through her body leaving her panting with need.

'Yes!' she exclaimed.

'Okay. Just relax now.'

He resumed massaging her backside and thighs but now he let his hand drift gently between her legs at the end of each stroke. Eventually he worked his way inwards and upwards until he was concentrating his attention on the outer regions of her pussy.

His touch there was sensitive but sure, parting the slick folds and stimulating her skilfully until she stopped trying to hide her excitement and moaned aloud.

His fingers moved inside her and he massaged her internally in a way she'd never experienced before. She pressed down against the hand buried within her while his other hand roamed caressingly over her backside.

A wave of sheer erotic heat rushed over Alexa, then her body shook in a series of spasms which left her wet, weak and shaking.

The special massage was certainly that.

When she returned to her room she found Jess studying her reflection bemusedly in the mirror.

'I can't get over it,' her sister announced. 'For the first time since we were about eleven someone might mistake me for you – however briefly. I'll never have your poise, though,' she added gloomily. 'In fact look at you now – you're glowing with health and vitality, while despite the hair and make-up I look like I'm recovering from a long illness.'

Sprawled elegantly on the bed, Alexa knew that the glow she had at the moment was simply the aftermath of sexual euphoria.

'It's not that difficult,' she said lazily. 'It's just a matter of projection – like being an actress. Look, over the next few days just pretend you're me. Copy my mannerisms and let's see if we can have some fun

27

when people get us confused.'

'I can try,' said Jess doubtfully, 'but it would only work with strangers, we wouldn't fool anyone who knew us for a minute.'

'You never know,' murmured Alexa.

Later that evening over drinks in the bar, Alexa began to talk about her job as a private investigator. In the past she'd always seemed reluctant to discuss it, but now she chatted about it quite openly.

Jess was fascinated. Alexa also mentioned several of her men friends, entertaining her sister with amusing and sometimes wicked stories about them. Jess couldn't help but feel a twinge of envy – it would be wonderful to lead such a glamorous and cosmopolitan lifestyle.

If only she were more like Alexa.

Jess glanced across the table at her sister, struck by the elegance of her sister's sitting position.

'Just look at the difference in the way we're sitting,' she pointed out, 'it says it all, really.'

Alexa had her legs crossed and at a slight angle. She was sitting casually back, one hand negligently along the arm of the small sofa.

Jess on the other hand had her knees together and her feet flat on the floor and was slumped inelegantly in her chair.

'It's easy,' Alexa told her. 'Always keep your spine straight, your legs crossed at the knee and your hands relaxed. Everything else just follows naturally.' Jess tried it, it seemed to work.

'Sometime this week we must go shopping,' said Alexa. 'Your wardrobe is long overdue for a revamp.' She glanced dismissively at Jess's calf-length cotton skirt and shapeless blouse. 'You've got a good figure – why hide it?'

'I don't like men looking at me,' muttered Jess defensively.

'I wouldn't like it if they didn't,' said Alexa airily. Jess went over to the bar to get another drink.

'How was your massage, by the way?' she asked when she returned.

'*Very* enjoyable,' replied her twin.

'I've one booked tomorrow. I'm a bit nervous about it, actually, I understand the masseur is male. What did you wear?'

'Just a towel.'

'Did . . . did you find it embarrassing at all – having a strange man touching you?'

'Not at all,' answered Alexa truthfully. 'He was pleasant and attractive – just relax and enjoy it. I felt great afterwards.'

Jess fished the slice of lemon out of her drink and sucked it reflectively. 'I wonder what Ralph's doing now?'

'Sitting at his computer, I should imagine. Why, are you missing him?'

'No, I'm glad to be spending some time apart, actually. Things were very strained between us. Maybe I'll feel better about everything after a week's separation.'

Tim was relieved to discover that Sean Hesketh's safe was a fairly basic model. It hadn't taken more than a few discreet enquiries to find out that he was away for a few days – a lucky break if ever there was one. Tim had accordingly broken into his flat without too much trouble, then cracked the safe with disdainful ease.

He knew from Serena's description that he was roughly the same height and build as the blackmailer. A dark wig and moustache together with a pair of aviator sunglasses of the type worn by Sean meant that from a distance he looked like him.

At least enough for it to cause no comment if anyone saw him going into the flat.

The safe contained about a thousand pounds in cash, some jewellery and an envelope containing a set of the prints he was looking for. Unfortunately there was no sign of the negatives. Tucked away at the back of the safe however was a key, which Tim suspected was for a safety deposit box.

Taking the photos and the key he let himself out of the flat and went to phone Serena.

She knew which bank Sean used and gave Tim the address. It wasn't difficult for him to gain access to the deposit box by the simple expedient of impersonating Sean Hesketh and forging his signature.

Bingo!

The negatives were there together with another set of prints. There was also roughly ten thousand pounds in cash and several sealed bags of white powder which he guessed to be cocaine. Rather regretfully he took only the negatives and prints, then bought a sandwich and returned to the office.

He planned to take a leisurely look at the prints while he ate his lunch, but he only got as far as having one bite. Once he'd started going through them his sandwich lay forgotten on his desk.

Man, she was hot.

She'd been right when she'd indicated that the other photos were even more damning than the one he'd already seen. He could feel the blood pounding through his body at twice its normal rate. The lady was a walking, talking sex bomb.

And she owed him.

She owed him big.

In fact she owed him mega.

He dialled her number with a sense of erotic anticipation he hadn't experienced since high school back in North Carolina.

'Serena? Hi, it's Tim Preece.'

'Tim, I've been hoping you'd call all morning.' Her voice was like golden syrup. 'Do you have any good news? All this is making little me just an itsy-witsy bit edgy.'

'I've got the negatives.'

'Ooh, you wonderful man. When can I have them?

'Any time you like.'

'How about tonight?' Her voice dropped to an even more seductive pitch.

'Tonight would be fine. Where shall we meet?'

'Would you mind coming here? Harold's away at the moment so I'm all on my lonesome. Say about eight?'

That was fine by Tim.

'Okay. See you then, Serena.'

'Bye, Tim.'

Chapter Three

Alexa spent the day in a fever of erotic anticipation of her second massage.

This time she didn't bother with the towel, she just stretched out lithely on the table, completely naked.

'You've got a beautiful body,' Sam commented as he trickled oil onto her back. He began to stroke her shoulders, gently at first, then with deeper strokes. He took a long time over it, manipulating every inch of her skin from the tips of her toes up to her slender white neck.

Then he turned her over, dribbled oil into the hollow of her cleavage and started on her front. He handled her generous breasts gently, cupping them with his big hands, then stroking them seductively until the nipples hardened like small, glistening acorns.

As he worked his way down her stomach towards her mound, Alexa lay with her eyes half closed, her breathing ragged. When he'd massaged his way up her legs he arranged them with the knees bent and wide apart.

'That's one place you don't need any oil,' he commented, running the tips of his fingers over her slippery labia. As he stroked and delved his way into her heated honeypot she mewed with pleasure and parted her legs even further. She came quickly, her back arching and her head falling backwards.

'What do you get out of this?' she asked him curiously while he was washing his hands.

He turned to grin at her. 'Are you kidding?' he asked teasingly.

She smiled back as she sat up and reached for her towel.

'It's rather one-way traffic,' she commented.

'That's a situation I'll be happy to remedy.'

Sam came to stand in front of her. She reached for his zip and drew it slowly down to reveal a pair of briefs as spotlessly white as his outer garments. She could see the outline of his cock as it strained against the constricting cotton. It sprang eagerly free as she peeled the briefs down over his muscular buttocks and strong thighs.

Perched on the edge of the massage table, Alexa grasped his cock firmly by the shaft, running the fingers of her other hand up and down the full length. Leaning forward she took the tip into her mouth and flicked her tongue over it. She teased it for a while, then slowly began to draw more of him in, exerting an erotic suction with her full lips.

She heard him exhale with pleasure and redoubled her efforts. When she'd taken as much of him as she could, she let him slip out, kissing and licking her way along the underside of the rock-hard shaft.

The only sound in the room was of Sam's harsh breathing and the tick of an old-fashioned clock on the wall over the massage table.

Moving forward to the very edge of the table Alexa opened her legs and used the end of his cock to stimulate herself. He placed his hands on her breasts and stroked them as she wound her legs around his waist and pulled him closer.

He slipped inside her and forged upwards in a leisurely fashion until he was buried up to the hilt in her warm, welcoming pussy.

They began to move together, keeping the rhythm slow to begin with, soon establishing a seductive rocking motion. As their mutual excitement mounted they quickened the pace, Sam still caressing her oiled breasts.

Sliding his hands beneath her firm round bum, he lifted her so he was supporting all her weight. In this position he could manoeuvre himself even deeper inside her and she clung to his neck as she moved her hips eagerly against him.

After three last thrusts he let out a hoarse cry and came, jerking convulsively as he filled her up.

While Sam was adjusting his clothes Alexa said lazily, 'I'd better warn you that my twin sister has a massage booked with you later this afternoon. Don't get her confused with me and think I've come back for a repeat performance. She's very shy – she'd be horrified if you offered her one of your specials. In fact I doubt if she'd know what you meant.'

He grinned at her.

'Don't worry. I can always read the signs. I never make the offer unless I'm sure it'll be well received.'

'You must make a lot of women very happy,' she teased.

'That's what I'm here for.'

'Do many women suggest returning the favour by offering you their fair white bodies?' Alexa asked interestedly.

'Some. Or at the end of their stay they buy me a little present. Either way I'm just happy to be of service.'

Alexa wound the towel firmly around herself.

'See you tomorrow.'

The sun came out that evening so Alexa and Jess were able to enjoy their pre-dinner drinks outside.

'This feels good after all that rain,' commented Alexa, closing her eyes and turning her face towards the warmth of the setting sun.

'Perhaps we'll be able to go for a walk tomorrow,' suggested Jess.

They could see the countryside surrounding Blydean Hall quite clearly for the first time, instead of through a veil of rain and mist. Built at the top of a gentle incline, the house was surrounded by parklands, meadows and copses. In the evening sunshine it looked lush and verdant after all the recent rain.

'Maybe,' said Alexa, who if she was going to walk anywhere liked it to be while shopping, preferably for expensive clothes.

'How did you like your massage with Sam?'

'It was good. I was a bit tense for a while, but once he'd started I became so relaxed that I nearly fell asleep.'

Sleep had been the last thing on Alexa's mind once Sam had begun work, but she and Jess had always reacted differently to similar situations.

Alexa had persuaded Jess to borrow one of her outfits for the evening, a simple pale green dress which set off her twin's newly tinted hair and deepened the colour of her yellow-green eyes.

'You look great,' she told her suddenly. 'Really great.'

Jess blushed. It was rarely anyone paid her a compliment. Ralph certainly never spontaneously said she looked great – but that was probably because she never did. If they were ever going out somewhere and she asked him how she looked, his invariable response was, 'Fine.'

Finding out he'd been having an affair had made her feel like the most unattractive woman on earth, so it was good to be told she looked great, even if only by her own sister.

Tim gulped when he saw what Serena was wearing.

A transparent fondant-pink chiffon robe covered a flimsy little shortie nightie in the same material. Both garments were so low cut that they swooped virtually down to her navel and he could see her stunning breasts through the two layers of gauze.

In the hallway she took the proffered envelope from him eagerly, checking the contents before turning to him with a grateful smile.

'Thank you. I don't know how I'm ever going to repay you.'

Tim could think of several ways, but he settled for saying, 'A drink would be a good start.'

To his delight she led the way upstairs, her backside swaying alluringly in front of him. She was wearing a pair of panties so tiny that they only covered a very small area of her bottom. The cleft between her buttocks was clearly visible, a darker shadow beneath her provocative attire.

Pink was obviously her favourite colour. The bedroom was a mass of sugar-pink frills and flounces, billowing in all directions. Tim sat gingerly on a small rose-coloured sofa, pushing aside a couple of be-ribboned satin cushions.

He felt as out of place in there as a nun in a brothel but it was, he supposed, the perfect setting for Serena's pink and white prettiness.

'What do you think of my boudoir?' she asked as she poured him a drink.

'Very, uh . . . feminine,' he said.

'Harold hates it. He won't even sleep in here, he says he feels as if he's smothering in candy-floss.'

Glancing at the tent-like folds of pink silk which cascaded down over the bed from above, Tim felt a spark of fellow feeling for the man he was hoping to cuckold.

Serena came and sat on his lap, enveloping him in a wave of her heady perfume. She felt wonderful, her backside soft and yielding against his groin, one generous breast resting against his chest.

'How much do I owe you?' she murmured, wriggling against him in a way which almost deprived him of the power of speech.

'Uh, I'll have my secretary send you a bill.'

She sat with her eyes downcast, her rosebud mouth pouting.

'The thing is ... I can't actually pay you. I don't have any money of my own, I just buy what I want on credit cards and Harold pays the bills. He likes to keep ... tabs on me.'

Tim could see why. She obviously led Harold one hell of a dance.

She hung her head and peeped at him from behind her long lashes.

'Are you very angry?' she asked at last.

He found it hard to be angry when he had a hard-on which felt like it was going to bust open his zipper. Slipping a hand up her milky thigh under her robe, he followed the curve of it up to her hip.

'Maybe we can come to some other arrangement,' he suggested, bending his head and kissing his way down her cleavage.

'I'm sure we can,' she agreed huskily.

Tim knew quite well that she was taking him for a ride but as long as it was the right sort of ride, he was prepared to write off the agency fee. 'No' wasn't really a word in his vocabulary where desirable women were concerned.

'I know I've been a naughty girl,' she continued winsomely, 'so naughty that I think I deserve a spanking.'

She slipped off his lap and bent over the back of an overstuffed pink armchair just in front of him, flipping her robe up as she did so. She had the most gorgeous butt he'd ever seen in his life. In that position the shortie nightie had ridden up to her waist and the tiny pink panties had tightened over the bottom half of her delectable creamy globes.

Tim gulped and swallowed hard. He wasn't a man who often found himself at a loss but he was now. He could think of various things he'd like to do to her gorgeous little ass, but spanking it wasn't one of them.

She wriggled it enticingly in his direction as he rose slowly to his feet and shrugged off his battered leather jacket. Her legs were long and shapely and her small feet were thrust into a ridiculous pair of high-heeled slippers which had ostrich feather puffs on the front.

He stood behind her and ran his hand over her backside, caressing and stroking it, exploring every contour.

'Spank me!' she invited him playfully, raising herself onto her tiptoes and pressing her bottom against his hand.

Tim found himself in a quandary; he'd never hit a woman in his life and despised men who did. On the other hand he was always prepared to put himself out to oblige a lady.

'Spank me!' she repeated. Swallowing again, he tapped her gently on the seat of her panties a couple of times. She wriggled with delight. 'More! On my bare bottom!' she urged him.

He eased the panties down her thighs to her knees. He could see the soft floss of a few wisps of pubic hair peeping from between her parted legs and had to suppress an urge to slide his hand up there.

She wriggled her bottom provocatively again and he delivered a few more half-hearted taps onto the smooth white skin.

It seemed to satisfy her because she stood upright and leant back against him. He removed her robe then slipped his hands inside her shortie nightie and cupped her breasts. They overflowed pleasingly from his hands and he stroked them feverishly as she ground her backside against his denim-covered dick.

He caressed his way over her gorgeous body before pushing an exploratory hand between her thighs.

She was hot, wet and ready.

Unzipping his jeans he peeled them off, then arranged her over the back of the chair – it was a position she seemed to like, after all – and entered her with a slow, controlled thrust.

She moaned, gasped and pushed back against him, her backside rotating as she impaled herself on his iron-hard member. As he shafted her he thought fleetingly he'd never known a woman with such a wonderful backside. She rolled and wriggled it against him, now withdrawing so he slipped partially out of her, now jamming it back hard against him.

He lasted as long as he could but since he'd first set eyes on Serena his mind had been working over-time with visions of screwing her. The photos he'd spent most of the afternoon studying hadn't helped.

After he'd come he pulled her back with him and sat on the sofa with her on his knee, his dick still firmly embedded deep within her. She wound her arms around his neck and snuggled up to him. He lay back with his eyes closed for a few minutes until the blood pounding through his body had slowed a little.

When he opened his eyes, the sight of her breasts half escaping from their pink chiffon covering prompted him to slip the thin straps of the nightie down to her waist. He feasted his eyes on the perfect milky orbs tipped by crinkled marzipan-pink nipples.

It was a supremely stirring sight.

He caressed them reverently, lifting them slightly so he could savour their weight, then running the palms of his hands over the jutting nipples.

Slowly, he felt himself grow hard again within her and feeling it she knelt astride him and began to rise and fall on his rearing shaft. She started slowly, teasing him with little squeezes of her internal muscles, then moved to a slightly faster tempo.

He reached between her legs and felt for the engorged sliver of slippery flesh which was the centre of her sexuality. He manipulated it skilfully as she rode him, making her cry out with pleasure.

Faster and faster she rode him, the sound of flesh slapping against flesh clearly audible as her bottom smacked against his thighs again and again. When she came, her cries echoed around the room accompanied by a half-strangled, long-drawn-out groan of his own.

A few seconds later Tim was startled to hear the sound of the front door banging then a man's voice calling, 'Where's my precious little girl, then?'

They both froze, then Serena leapt off his lap as if on a powerful spring. Tim was sure that the sound they made as they separated, like a cork coming out of a bottle, must have been audible downstairs.

Tim gave Serena full marks for acting quickly. She ran over to the door and called, 'Your little girl's up here, darling. No, don't come up, I look a fright. I'll be down in a few minutes when I've made myself pretty for you.'

She locked the bedroom door and flashed past him into the bathroom as he tried to scramble hastily into his jeans. He could hear the sound of water splashing, then she emerged in the doorway drying herself between the legs with a towel.

She'd just readjusted her nightie and shrugged herself back into her robe when there was a tap on the door.

'I'm impatient to see my little girl.'

Grabbing a bottle of scent, Serena sprayed it frantically into the air, shouting, 'Coming.'

In his panic Tim found himself unable to get his jeans on the right way round. He dragged them off again just as she threw open the door to a small ornate balcony.

'Stay out there until I've got him downstairs,' she hissed. In a daze he grabbed his jeans and jacket and stepped outside. Serena glanced around and threw his shoes and socks after him. Unfortunately, one shoe went sailing past his ear to land in the road below with a clunk.

As he struggled into his jeans Tim glanced down at the quiet and thankfully deserted road. He could do without some neighbour or passer-by letting Serena's husband know there was a half-dressed intruder on his balcony.

It wasn't that he was physically afraid of Harold – Tim was well able to take care of himself. It was sheer embarrassment at the prospect of coming face to face with a man whose much younger wife he'd just screwed.

Once in his jeans he peered through a crack in the flounced pink curtains to see Serena kissing a short, bald and very old man. After what seemed an endless kiss she took his hand and led him towards the door. He heard her say, 'I'm going to fix you a nice big drink, then you can tell me all about your trip.'

Tim gave it five minutes then stealthily opened the balcony door and re-entered the room. He crept over to the bedroom door and listened, then, satisfied that the pair weren't still in the hallway, left the room and silently descended the stairs, carrying the one shoe still in his possession.

A trill of laughter from one of the downstairs rooms indicated their whereabouts. As he passed the door, which was slightly ajar, he couldn't resist a quick look through the crack.

Serena was perched on her husband's knee with her arms around his neck, the personification of the adoring wife. Harold had a drink in one hand and with the other he caressed one of her ample breasts.

Tim just hoped she hadn't left the photos lying around.

The week at Blydean Hall was passing too quickly for Jess. She was enjoying herself more than she had in years. Days spent in a pleasant regime of beauty treatments, exercise and relaxation resulted in her looking a hundred times better than the despondent creature who'd arrived several days ago.

The weather turned warm and she spent a couple of hours a day lying in the sun which imparted a warm glow to her pale skin.

One afternoon Alexa took her shopping and she purchased several new outfits. As a present her twin bought her a set of alluring silk underwear, which included a suspender belt. Jess had never worn stockings in her life, considering tights more practical. But even she had to admit that she looked good as she paraded around their bedroom in the luxurious lingerie.

Another thing which she found gratifying was that she had an admirer. His name was Ben, he was eighteen years old and he was staying at Blydean Hall with an elderly aunt. The old lady hadn't wanted to come alone without someone to dance attendance on her, so her favourite nephew had been heavily bribed by his mother to fill this role.

She and Ben swam, played tennis and went for long walks together, none of which Alexa particularly wanted to do. Usually shy with men, Jess found Ben too young to be intimidating. He was the same age as many of her students so she found him easy to talk to.

She also thought it was nice that he was solicitous of his aunt, always ensuring she was happily occupied before joining Jess. The old lady tended to go to bed early and as Alexa usually mysteriously vanished after dinner, Jess was happy to have his light-hearted company.

Alexa teased her about it, but Jess didn't care. She was tired of being dull, drab Jess – she wanted to enjoy herself for a change.

She dreaded the week being over and having to return to her old life.

Lying among a tangle of damp sheets in Sam's room, Alexa lay on her side, idly caressing his cock. They'd been in there over two hours and were just taking a break between bouts of very pleasurable sex.

'Where's your sister tonight?' asked Sam, who was stretched out on his back with his hands behind his head.

'Playing backgammon with her admirer when I last saw her,' returned Alexa, running the tip of her fingernail down the length of his shaft. 'And good luck to her, it's doing wonders for her self-esteem to have him obviously besotted by her.'

'Do you think he's getting his leg over?'

'No,' said Alexa decidedly. 'Why, do you have any reason to think he is?' When he didn't reply she tugged gently at his cock. 'Don't tell me that you've been giving her your special massages too?' she said, amused.

'No, it was difficult enough getting her to relax for the straightforward one. I can always tell the ladies who'd appreciate more.'

'How did you know I would?'

'All the signs were there that you found the massage sexually exciting. You were flushed, short of breath and took me up on my offer to massage your luscious backside. Then you parted your legs perceptibly when I was touching you. Besides, I already knew you were a highly sexed woman.'

'How did you know that?'

'I'd been watching you masturbate for a minute or so in the jacuzzi room before you opened your eyes and saw me.'

Alexa stopped playing with his cock and punched him lightly on the shoulder.

'You should have let me know you were there – or been really gentlemanly and left silently. Do you often play voyeur?'

'I don't often get the chance,' he returned, rubbing his shoulder ruefully. 'I think I was pretty restrained given the circumstances. I know what I'd like to have done.'

'What?' she challenged him.

He reached between her legs.

'This for a start . . . then this . . .'

Alexa sighed with pleasure.

'What a pity you didn't.'

It was the day before they were due to leave that Alexa dropped her bombshell.

The two women were having coffee on the terrace overlooking the garden.

'I wish we didn't have to go tomorrow,' said Jess wistfully.

'Is that because you want to stay here or because you don't want to go back to Ralph?' asked Alexa.

'The latter, I think.'

'What, no regrets at leaving Ben? The boy's got it bad for you.'

'Don't be silly,' protested Jess, blushing, 'I'm just someone for him to play tennis with and talk to while his aunt's otherwise occupied. Besides, I'm practically old enough to be his mother.'

'You're only ten years older than he is. And anyway that excuse has never washed, age has nothing to do with sexual attraction.'

'I like Ben a lot but I don't think of him in that way. And you needn't look at me like that, Alexa,' she added as her twin grinned knowingly. 'Anyway,' she said, changing the subject, 'what about you? I'd have to be stupid not to guess that you're off seeing someone in the evenings. Who is it? The chartered accountant from Basingstoke? Surely not the married music professor? Whoever it is I know you're sleeping with him, you only have that "cat that got the cream" look when you're in the throes of an affair.'

'Hardly an affair,' said Alexa, stretching then pouring them both more coffee, 'more of a pleasant interlude. To return to my original question, if you don't want to go back to Ralph just yet, why don't you come and stay with me in London for a few weeks?'

Alexa had often issued casual invitations in the past and occasionally Jess had accepted them, but she'd always taken Ralph. Previously the idea of going away without him had seemed unthinkable, now it seemed very desirable.

'College doesn't start again until late September, does it?' went on Alexa. 'It's only July now. You could have a wonderful time in London for a few weeks.'

Jess thought about it. The more she thought about it the more she liked the idea.

'Are you sure you wouldn't mind?' she asked at last.

'Actually, you'd be doing me a favour,' said Alexa slowly. 'Or rather there is a favour I want to ask of you . . .'

'What's that?'

'I want you to pretend you're me for a few weeks.'

Chapter Four

'You want me to do *what*?' gasped Jess, thinking she must have misheard.

Alexa stirred her coffee and repeated, 'I want you to pretend to be me for a few weeks.' Jess stared at her as if she'd suddenly grown two heads. Alexa burst out laughing at the shocked expression on her twin's face.

'Whatever for?' demanded Jess at last, completely bemused.

'Because I need to be in two places at once.'

'How come?'

Sitting back in her chair and tilting her face towards the sun Alexa said, 'It's work. I'm involved in two cases at the moment and one of them needs me to go abroad for a few weeks.

'It's an investigation I'm doing for a company called Hodder-Denstein. One of the board of directors, Will Harper, vanished a few weeks ago taking most of the company's funds with him. Under normal circumstances he wouldn't have been able to get at the money, but the company will be going public in a couple of months and has been undergoing financial restructuring.

'The situation is an extremely delicate one,' Alexa continued. 'While there's any chance at all of getting the money back and resolving the situation quietly,

Hodder-Denstein doesn't want the police called in. It's essential the theft is kept quiet and the money retrieved or the flotation can't go ahead.'

'Is there any chance of getting the money back?' interjected Jess, who'd been listening fascinated.

'Yes – but only if I can locate Will Harper and persuade him to give back the money voluntarily, in return for the company not pressing charges.'

'That doesn't sound very likely,' said Jess sceptically.

'You're probably right. I do have one thing on my side though.'

'What's that?'

'Will and I had an affair a few years ago, before I became a private investigator. We parted amicably, but with some regret on his side. If I appear to run into him by chance wherever he is, I may be able to get close to him again which will give me a huge advantage.'

Jess could see that it might. Alexa was wearing a pale yellow sun-top and a pair of shorts in a darker shade. Her slender but curvaceous body was accentuated by the skimpy clothing and her long shapely legs seemed to go on for ever.

Quite honestly, Jess didn't see how any man would be able to resist her if she set out to attract him. But there was a difference between getting close to a man and parting him from a huge amount of money.

'What's the other case?' she asked.

'A fairly routine insurance fraud,' replied Alexa. 'But the head of the company, Daniel Moult, has used me in the past on several other cases. When I told him that one of the other operatives was going to take over from me, he practically blew a gasket and said that if I didn't continue with it personally, he'd take his company's business elsewhere. They put a lot of work our way so he needs to be kept happy and it's true that I do know a lot more about insurance fraud than any of my colleagues.'

'Which is where I come in,' said Jess slowly.

'That's right. As far as Daniel is concerned I'm still working on the case.'

'But I don't know anything about private investigation,' protested Jess, 'and even less about insurance.'

'You don't need to. It's really just a case of checking in with Daniel every few days, and keeping things ticking over until I get back,' Alexa told her. 'I'll brief you on the background before I leave and Tim will tell you what to do after I've gone. Most of the work's done on computer and that isn't a problem because you're more computer literate than I am.'

Jess didn't know whether that was true or not, but certainly after eight years of living with Ralph her knowledge was fairly wide-ranging.

'So it's just a case of convincing one man that I'm you, and I need only see him for a few brief meetings?'

'Well, actually it's slightly more complicated than that,' admitted Alexa. 'Unfortunately Daniel Moult's sister moves in the same social circles as I do. Which means that you also have to be me as far as all my friends are concerned, or it could get back to him.'

'Alexa, I just couldn't carry it off, I know I couldn't.'

'Of course you could, we're identical twins. No one could tell us apart if you just continue to dress and do your make-up like me. You're even starting to walk and sit like me.'

Ben appeared at that moment carrying his tennis racket.

'Here comes your youthful admirer,' Alexa teased her. 'Think about my suggestion. It could work out well for both of us. You need a breathing space from Ralph and I need you to pretend to be me.'

Ben joined them at that moment.

'Hi, Ben,' Jess greeted him. 'Is it time for our game?'

He smiled shyly at them both.

'In about ten minutes.'

Alexa rose sinuously to her feet.

'And I'm due for a facial. Think about it, Jess. We'll talk it over again later.'

Jess couldn't concentrate on her game and Ben won every set. Pretend to be Alexa? Live her fascinating, glamorous life for a few weeks? The idea had a certain appeal, but surely she'd never be able to carry it off?

Alexa thought she could.

No, the idea was ridiculous.

Or was it?

Later that day she and Ben went for a long walk. For a lot of the time they walked in companionable silence. Ben appeared to have something on his mind and Jess was mulling over Alexa's outrageous proposal.

They paused to rest under the spreading boughs of an oak tree. Ben chivalrously threw his jacket on the ground for Jess to sit on and she sank thankfully onto it. It was very hot and no breeze stirred the leaves above their head. The Leicestershire countryside shimmered under a heat haze, the only sound was the occasional moo from some cows in a nearby field.

Ben began to talk haltingly. Jess was so preoccupied that she only paid desultory attention to what he was saying. She registered that it was about a girl he was keen on but beyond that didn't take much notice.

Eventually he stopped talking and she became aware that he was waiting for her to say something.

'Sorry, what was that, Ben?'

'I said, do you think I should do anything about it?' he repeated patiently.

'Yes, yes you should,' she answered at random.

She was taken aback when he seized her hand and said fervently, 'Jess, I adore you. Can we continue to see each other? I'm only going to be in Birmingham, after all – that's not very far from Manchester.'

She knew he was starting at Birmingham University in September, but what exactly was he suggesting? It soon became very clear. Without waiting for her to reply he leant across and pressed his lips hesitantly to hers.

Jess didn't know what to do – if only she'd listened to what he'd been saying, she'd surely have picked up on the fact that it was her he was talking about. As it was he'd obviously taken her silence for encouragement.

She didn't have the heart to reject him outright so she allowed him to kiss her, thinking that when it ended she'd let him down gently.

He knew she was living with someone but she'd probably said enough to indicate that all was not well between them. He could easily have taken that as gentle encouragement.

If only she'd listened to Alexa.

But it made her uncomfortable to think of a boy as young as Ben having a thing for her, so she'd ignored the signs.

He continued to kiss her, his mouth gentle but questioning on her own. It was a sweet kiss and she couldn't help but enjoy it. She could smell the clean scent of his hair and feel his sun-warmed skin against hers as he tightened his arms around her and pulled her closer.

She placed her hands on his chest prior to pushing him away gently. Unfortunately he misread the gesture as a caress and pulled her down onto the ground, deepening the kiss and beginning to stroke her shoulders.

He continued to kiss and touch her so tenderly that

she still couldn't bring herself to call a halt to the proceedings. The hot sunlight filtering down through the leafy branches interwoven above them made her feel languid and added an air of unreality to the situation.

She couldn't remember the last time anyone other than Ralph had kissed her – it must have been while she was at college. In fact, come to think of it, she couldn't remember the last time Ralph had kissed her, other than a brief peck on the cheek as she'd left home last week.

The memory of Ralph, and how uninterested he'd been in her sexually for a long time, suddenly made her glad that Ben found her attractive.

His hesitant caresses were evoking a warmth which spread over her body making her very aware of how long it had been since she'd last had sex. When the tips of his fingers passed tentatively over her breast, a shiver of pleasure passed through her. She could feel the hard muscles of his back through his thin cotton shirt and ran her hands over them appreciatively.

The feeling of heady languor which suffused her increased. She really should stop him but it was all so very pleasurable.

Jess was wearing a couple of her new purchases, a beige wrap-around skirt and a short-sleeved black linen blouse. The blouse must have come adrift from the waistband of the skirt because she suddenly felt Ben's warm hand on her bare back.

It felt good.

So did the hand which had now closed on her breast over the linen blouse. She could feel a hardness pressing against her hip and knew that he had a massive erection. In the heat of the afternoon he continued to kiss and caress, her arousing her until all she was aware of was a liquid heat, warm and demanding, in her groin.

He shifted position above her so she could feel his hardness pressing against her mound through their clothing. He raised himself slightly and undid her blouse, his fingers clumsy in their haste. She heard him gulp when he saw her breasts, only thinly covered by another new purchase, a sheer black bra.

He bent his head and fastened his mouth over one nipple through the flimsy fabric. His mouth felt hot and urgent as he tugged gently with his lips, causing the point to harden and jut upwards. He sucked on it with a contented sigh before turning his attention to the other.

When both nipples were tingling pleasurably he reverently undid the catch of the front-fastening bra, exposing her breasts to his hungry gaze.

Jess found it very erotic to be lying there virtually naked from the waist up in the open air.

He slipped his hand into her wrap-around skirt and began to caress her bare thighs, paying particular attention to the soft skin at the top. Then somehow her skirt was lying open around her, revealing a pair of sheer black panties which matched the bra.

The touch of his fingers between her legs was electrifying, sending a tremor through her, leaving her feeling molten inside.

She wanted more.

Opening her legs to him she moaned softly as he stroked her over her panties, sometimes feathering over the fuzz of her bush, sometimes rubbing directly between her legs. She could feel herself becoming wet and made no objection when he slipped exploring fingers under the elastic and touched her directly.

She felt as if she was going to explode.

Tentatively she reached for his belt and undid the

buckle, then the zip of his jeans. He rolled off her and dragged off both his jeans and underpants at the same time, pausing to struggle briefly with his shoes before tearing them off too.

Jess closed her eyes after catching a glimpse of his cock. It looked so big and hard that she gulped before she reached out for it. Clasping it in both her hands she drew him down on top of her again. He continued to caress her between the thighs, until the crotch of her panties was wringing wet. Only then did he kneel above her and ease them down her long slim legs.

He paused for a few moments gazing down at her naked body in awe.

'You're beautiful,' he breathed. The creamy orbs of her breasts were tipped with coral-coloured nipples and a fuzz of silken red-gold hair concealed the entrance to her honeypot.

He lowered himself onto her and she felt the end of his cock nudging between her thighs. She helped guide him to the right place and he entered her, slowly at first, then as if reassured by the copiousness of her creamy juices, faster.

They moved together in the still, silent afternoon, continuing to explore each other's bodies with their hands and mouths. It was the most erotic encounter of Jess's limited experience – she'd never made love anywhere except in a bedroom and the outdoor setting made her feel heady and reckless.

It didn't last long – Ben was young, ardent and very aroused. He went rigid in her arms then climaxed in a series of shuddering thrusts, crying out so loudly that the birds flew out of the tree above their heads, their wings flapping wildly in panic.

When Jess returned to their shared bedroom she

found Alexa stretched out on her bed in a silk robe sipping a glass of chilled white wine, looking cool and lovely.

Jess had done her best to repair her appearance but it hadn't been easy without the aid of a mirror or comb. She'd been hoping Alexa wouldn't be there – she wanted to shower and change before seeing her.

'Hi,' her twin greeted her casually. 'Pour yourself a glass of wine. I told you it was too hot for walking – you look frazzled.'

There was a pause while Alexa took in the full extent of her dishevelled appearance, then she said slowly, 'Well now – what *have* you been up to?'

Jess could see her reflection in the full-length mirror. Her hair was a wild tangle of undisciplined curls, her beige skirt crumpled and grass-stained and she saw to her dismay that her blouse was buttoned up incorrectly.

A knowing smile curved Alexa's full, red lips.

'A dispassionate observer might think you'd just been enjoying a roll in the hay. Ben, I presume?'

Jess stood there completely at a loss, then she bolted into the bathroom and locked the door. Sinking onto the side of the bath she asked herself what she'd done.

She'd only just parted from Ben and until Alexa looked at her so knowingly she'd still been in an erotic haze.

Had she really let a boy she'd known for less than a week make love to her in the dappled shade of an oak tree in full view of anyone who might have walked past?

Yes she had.

She sat there for a long time until Alexa tapped on the bathroom door.

'Jess, are you okay?'

Pulling herself together she managed to call, 'Yes thanks.'

'I'm going downstairs, see you at dinner.'

Jess ran herself a deep bath and lay up to her chin in soapy bubbles.

What had she done?

When she slid into her seat opposite Alexa in the restaurant Jess refused to meet her twin's eyes. She'd considered skipping dinner, packing her suitcase and leaving so she needn't see either Alexa or Ben again. But where would she go? The way she was feeling at the moment she couldn't face going back to Altrincham and Ralph.

She went for a walk in the grounds after her bath, slipping out of a side door and hurriedly vanishing into the shrubbery before anyone spotted her – she needed time to calm down.

She was in a state of total confusion. Too much had happened today. First there was Alexa's startling proposition that she should move into her flat and pretend to be her. Then as if that wasn't enough, the walk with Ben culminating in a sexual encounter as abandoned as it was unexpected.

Where did all this leave her?

She didn't know.

It was a relief when she joined Alexa at dinner to have her sister make no reference to their last exchange. When they'd finished eating they had their coffee outside. The evening was warm and scented and they sat in silence for a while before Alexa said, 'Well then, are you coming back with me tomorrow – or is it home to Ralph?'

Jess shuddered.

'I don't know,' she confessed miserably, then, unable to keep quiet about what was uppermost in

her mind she said, 'Alexa ... about this afternoon ...'
She stopped, uncertain of how to continue.

'Now don't get it out of proportion, Jess,' Alexa
told her lightly. 'You enjoyed yourself for a couple of
hours with an attractive young man? It's no big deal,
so don't make it into one. I know how your mind
works, you'll drive yourself into a frenzy over something which should just be an inconsequential,
pleasant interlude. There's no harm done, you hardly
owe Ralph any fidelity after his affair with his
secretary. Let me ask you just one question – did you
enjoy it?'

'Very much,' admitted Jess.

'Well then, it was worth it. Now put it out of your
mind and think about what you're going to do tomorrow. London with me? Or Cheshire with Ralph?'

'Alexa, I'd like to stay with you for a while,' said
Jess wretchedly, 'but I don't know if I'm capable of
impersonating you.'

'Then come down for a few days while you think
about it. If you decide against the idea you can just
go back home and forget about it. You don't have to
decide now – I won't be leaving for a week or so. Is
that settled, then?'

'I suppose so,' replied Jess uncertainly.

'Good, you can drive us both down, it'll save me
having to get the train – I left my car in London
because I got a lift up here. Now I think I'd better
leave you, because here comes Ben.'

With a cheerful wave of her hand Alexa strolled
off into the night and no doubt to a last rendezvous
with her mysterious lover, thought Jess, envying her
sister's insouciance.

She was glad it was going dark, she was embarrassed to see Ben after this afternoon and she knew
she was blushing. How could she have allowed such

a thing to happen? She was the one at fault. She was a mature woman in her late twenties, Ben was a young boy who'd just left school.

She should never have allowed him to kiss her, then the situation wouldn't have got out of hand.

But there was a barely acknowledged part of Jess which was glad. Finding out about Ralph's affair had undermined her self-esteem and made her feel sexually undesirable.

Sex had never been a particularly important part of their relationship, even in the early days. It tended to take place in bed late at night before they went to sleep, or on Sunday morning before they got up.

But it was always pretty much the same and although pleasant enough, not very exciting. Even so it had made her feel bad when Ralph's interest had waned.

She had been mildly flattered that Ben had appeared to enjoy her company over the last week, and what had happened between them this afternoon had made it obvious that he found her very attractive. Which, she had to admit, made her feel better about herself.

And it had been extremely erotic.

The next half-hour was going to be very difficult. She knew he wanted them to arrange to meet again soon and was convinced that this afternoon had been just the start of a long-term affair.

She had to tell him as gently as possible that it had been a one-off and that it wasn't going to happen again.

It wasn't going to be easy.

Alexa and Sam decided to go for a swim in the deserted pool. They didn't put the lights on and Sam swam up and down in the darkness, the only illumination the moonlight spilling in through the glass sides of the pool room.

Alexa was wearing a black bikini which clung tightly to the curves of her breasts and hips. She sat on the side watching Sam do a powerful crawl up and down the dark water, the ripples he made glinting silver in the pale moonlight.

'Come on in – the water's lovely,' he teased her.

'In a minute,' she returned lazily. He coaxed her in and pulled her against him in the water. She felt how hard he was and slipped a hand inside his swimming trunks.

'My, my,' she commented, 'I thought men shrivelled in cold water.'

'Not when they're being fondled by a red-haired beauty with a knock-out figure,' he grinned.

She removed her hand and swam over to the side. He followed her and lifted her so her long legs were wound around his lean waist. She could feel the length of his cock pressing against her mound and murmured, 'Dare we?'

In reply he slipped his thumbs under the stretchy black material of her bikini pants and touched her intimately, feeling how hot and wet she was. She squirmed with pleasure and unwound her legs for long enough for him to strip the panties off.

He lifted her again and she lowered herself a tantalising inch at a time onto his straining rod, holding onto his shoulders for support. In contrast to the cool water his cock felt red-hot inside her as he filled her up and she began to move against him.

His hands were beneath the luscious mounds of her undulating buttocks, helping support her as she rode him. He removed one hand for long enough to unclasp her bikini top, freeing her perfect breasts from the constraining fabric.

He feasted his eyes on them as they bobbed seductively up and down in time to her erotic rhythm. In the moonlight they looked like cool marble and he bent his head to take one water-stiffened nipple in his mouth.

Like his cock, his mouth felt red-hot to Alexa as he flickered his tongue over the hard nub of flesh, teasing and coaxing until it swelled under his ministrations. He turned his attention to the other pert nipple, sucking and tugging at it, tracing circles and arabesques with the tip of his tongue.

She continued to rise and fall on his rock-hard shaft, loving the feeling as she bore down and buried him inside her up to the hilt, then raised herself so he almost slipped out.

His hands moved to her hips, helping lift her higher with each rhythmic movement, then pulling her down demandingly again for maximum penetration.

As their excitement mounted they moved faster and faster, each giving and taking gasping, panting pleasure from the encounter.

Alexa came first, her low, long-drawn-out moan coming from deep within as she tightened her legs convulsively around Sam's waist and bore down on him.

Her internal muscles squeezed him spasmodically as a series of orgasmic shudders passed through her slender body. The additional stimulation made Sam unable to stop the climax he'd been striving to hold back. Groaning loudly, he pumped his juices into her in several strong, conclusive thrusts.

Bending her head Alexa kissed him lingeringly.

'You're really something, you know – I'm going to miss our little interludes. Not many men know their way around a woman's body the way you do.'

'Practice makes perfect,' he returned, kissing her

cleavage, then lowering her to her feet in the waist-high water. She shivered suddenly.

'Brr! I feel quite chilly.'

'How about a hot shower?'

'That sounds like a good idea.'

Hand in hand they left the pool and went into the women's changing rooms. In the shower cubicle Sam worked up a rich lather with a tablet of scented soap and, starting at Alexa's shoulders, began to work his way down her body.

He soaped her breasts with sensual circular movements, grazing the palms of his hands over the nipples, until the whole area was a mass of soapsuds. He washed his way down to her narrow waist then outwards over the curve of her hips.

When he came to the silken fuzz of her bush he toyed with the soft curls, brushing over them with his fingertips, pushing aside the fine fronds which lay over the outer lips of her honeypot.

She opened her legs to him and he traced the shaft of her clit with one finger, then lifted the shower head out of its wall bracket and directed it at the sliver of soft sensitive flesh. He held her outer lips open so the needles of water rained down diagonally onto it.

She was so aroused that she came again very quickly, arching her spine and throwing her head back, her eyes closed, her mouth forming a silent ooh of pleasure.

Before the last spasm finished, Sam reached between her parted legs and skilfully manipulated her swollen clit for a few seconds. The pleasure was so intense that it was almost painful and she tried to push his hand away.

Another orgasm swept over her followed by another as he repeated the procedure until she gasped, 'No more!'

She leant against the wall, shaking, as he lathered his way down her shapely thighs and calves, then carefully rinsed her off.

When it was her turn to wash him, Alexa took a long time over it, splaying her fingers over his broad back as she worked up a lather. She traced the line of his backbone, soaping him thoroughly, then washed the bubbles away with the hand-held shower spray.

When she came to his cock she worked up so much lather it completely hid his massively rearing column. She massaged and squeezed it lovingly, then closed her hand over it and began to masturbate him.

Sam loved it, she could tell, the thick soapsuds rendering it a slippery, sensual experience. She had to work at it. She could tell he was holding back to prolong the pleasure.

Smiling wickedly she began to soap her own breasts with her other hand.

It was too much for Sam.

His hot juices spurted strongly upwards, splattering all over her breasts. She massaged the creamy liquid in so it mingled with the soapy lather and ran down towards her stomach, washed away by the warm water cascading down on them from the shower.

Chapter Five

The following day Alexa and Jess left Blydean Hall, waved off by Ben and Sam. Ben was disconsolate but Jess was sure he'd soon get over her, particularly if he met someone else.

Alexa parted from Sam without regret – they'd had a great time but she'd already spotted him surveying the new arrivals with interest. She'd have put money on it that he'd be satisfying another woman before the day was out.

Before they left, Jess was again seized by doubt and wondered aloud whether she should go back home to tell Ralph she'd be staying with Alexa for a while.

'Phone him from London,' was Alexa's brief advice.

'I should really pick up some more clothes – I know I've bought some but I don't have anything like enough.'

'Your own clothes will be of no earthly use to you if you're pretending to be me.' Alexa pointed out. 'Besides, I've far more than I ever wear – you can borrow anything you want.'

Jess had allowed herself to be persuaded.

The journey down the motorway was uneventful. Alexa spent most of the time telling Jess about her work and friends, filling her in on the people she knew and the places she went.

Jess was amused. Alexa wasn't wasting any time in

beginning her briefing, even though Jess hadn't yet agreed to take her place.

They eventually arrived at Alexa's flat in Hampstead at around two o'clock. It wasn't very large – the second bedroom had barely enough room for a bed and a chest of drawers – but it was attractively decorated and well furnished with simple modern furniture.

It was immaculately tidy, but Jess knew that was because a cleaner came in a couple of times a week and not because her sister was remotely domesticated.

Alexa kicked off her shoes, put her feet up on the sofa and began to open her mail while Jess unpacked. When Jess had finished she went back into the sitting room and found her twin playing back the messages on her answering machine, most of which were from men.

'I suppose I ought to go and buy some groceries,' said Alexa, looking at her watch and yawning.

'Why don't I go and do that?' asked Jess. 'You must have lots to do.' Alexa was more than happy with the idea so Jess spent a pleasant hour shopping for food. She loved the shops in Hampstead and bought a range of continental cheeses and cooked meats as well as more basic provisions, thinking they would have an indoor picnic that evening instead of cooking.

Alexa dismissed the idea.

'What! Stay in on Saturday evening?' she exclaimed, breaking off a chunk of white stilton and popping it into her mouth. 'Not likely. You and I are going to have a night on the town. We can eat the food you bought tomorrow.'

Jess wasn't sure she felt like a night on the town and said so. When it became obvious that Alexa was determined to have her own way, Jess took refuge in an unanswerable argument.

'Surely you don't want everyone to know you have an identical twin sister if I'm supposed to be pretending to be you for a few weeks? Wouldn't it be safer for me to lie low and not let anyone see us together?'

'You've got a point,' returned Alexa, 'but I don't want to leave you here alone.'

'I'll be fine,' Jess assured her. 'I'll have something to eat, then read or watch TV.'

Alexa allowed herself to be persuaded. When one of her male friends came to pick her up around eight, Jess stayed in the bedroom until they'd left.

Later she phoned Ralph.

She told him that she was staying with Alexa for a while but was deliberately vague about her plans. He seemed perturbed and tried to get her to say when she'd be back but she wouldn't commit herself and the conversation ended uncomfortably.

The following day Alexa took her into the agency.

'The first thing you need to know is how we operate,' she explained.

'I still haven't decided I'm going to do it,' protested Jess, worried she'd get in deeper and deeper to the point where she might find it hard to say no.

'It doesn't matter,' Alexa assured her breezily, 'aren't you interested anyway?'

'Yes,' replied Jess guardedly, 'but . . .'

'Then let's go.'

The agency was situated in a quiet mews off Kensington High Street. The place was deserted when they arrived and Alexa sat Jess at one of the computer terminals and left her to familiarise herself with it while she went off to look for a file.

Jess was poring over the manual when a deep voice with an American accent said from behind her, 'Hi honey – good holiday?'

She turned round on the swivel chair and saw a tall, broad-shouldered man with tousled fair hair. Before she could speak he continued, 'It's obviously done you good – you look like a million dollars. But then, when don't you?'

Jess was wearing a short, pale blue-and-white striped dress with a scooped neckline. She'd borrowed a pair of cream suede high-heeled shoes from Alexa and knew she looked very different from the way she had only a short week ago.

Unsure what to say she smiled but remained silent while he went on, 'Am I glad you're back. What a time to take a holiday – we're even busier than we were last week. Now, have you thought about the . . .'

He trailed off, his expression one of sheer astonishment, his attention obviously distracted by something behind Jess. Turning her head she saw Alexa leaning against the door.

He made a swift recovery, lounging on the end of one of the desks, his hands in his pockets while he looked from one to the other.

'You told me that you had a sister, but not that she looked just like you,' he said slowly, his eyes on Jess. 'Aren't you going to introduce me?'

'Whatever makes you think you know which one of us is which?' asked Alexa from the doorway.

'You're Alexa,' he said to Jess.

'Well, so much for your powers of observation, Tim,' Alexa chided him. 'Jess, this is my boss, Tim Preece. Tim, meet my twin sister Jess.'

He leant forward looking bemused and shook her hand, saying, 'I'm delighted to meet you, Jess – how come I haven't met you before?'

'I'm not down here very often,' explained Jess. 'I live in Cheshire.'

She looked up and saw that Alexa had an

expression of mocking triumph on her face. She knew quite well that her twin was thinking that if they could fool someone who saw her every day, they could fool absolutely anyone.

Wednesday was a particularly frantic day. At around seven o'clock Tim sat at his desk drinking a glass of imported Bourbon and planning his next move in a particularly complex case he was investigating.

The phone on his desk rang and kept on ringing, which meant that everyone else had left for the night. When he picked it up he immediately recognised the voice of his ex-wife, Sherry.

His stomach lurched and he felt the familiar tight feeling in his chest that any contact with her always evoked.

He'd been half expecting to hear from her. He knew that her alimony cheque was a few days late, but although the agency was doing well it also had occasional cash flow problems.

'Tim, I need you to come over right away,' she greeted him without preamble. Her voice was low-pitched and husky, with an American accent redolent of the deep south and *Gone With the Wind*. It was a voice which conjured up images of mint juleps and hot, steamy nights.

'Why, what's up?' he asked, taking another gulp of his Bourbon and trying to subdue the vague stirring of excitement she could still arouse five years after their divorce.

'I've been mugged.'

'Are you hurt?' he asked in alarm. 'Where are you?'

'Not badly, just shaken. I'm at home – can you come over right away?'

'Sure, honey, I'll be right there.'

'Oh and Tim . . .'

'Yeah?'

'Bring your tool kit – I need you to put some new locks on the doors for me.'

Hurriedly draining his drink Tim shrugged into his battered old leather jacket and left, the investigation he was working on forgotten.

When he arrived at the small but elegant town house in Fulham, Tim found two policemen drinking coffee and staring at his ex-wife in a mutual state of besotted lust.

He could see why.

Reclining on a small sofa in a silk robe, Sherry managed to look both fragile and delicate, while still projecting the luscious desirability which over the years had brought men on two continents to their knees.

Born in South Carolina, Sherry was the original southern belle, an infuriating mixture of beguiling vulnerability and diamond-hard determination to get her own way.

Her dark hair, slanting smoke-blue eyes and magnolia skin were enough on their own to turn men's heads. Combined with a gorgeous, curvaceous body and a way of moving which was as provocative as it was graceful, she still had the power to get to Tim, even though he was under no illusions about her.

She was an actress, and just about scraped a living with bit parts on TV and the occasional minor role in a feature film. Most of the money for her comfortable lifestyle was provided by Tim, who continued voluntarily to pay her alimony, even though they had no children.

He knew quite well that if it went to court he'd be unlikely to have to pay her anything at all, but he continued to do so. Whenever he baulked at her regular demands for an increase, she painted such a harrowing picture of the poverty that this would force

70

her to endure that he always ended up writing the cheque.

'What happened?' he asked her. One of the policemen cleared his throat. He looked very red in the face and as if his collar was too tight.

'May I ask who you are, sir?'

'This is my ex-husband come to look after me,' Sherry informed them, stretching out one of her slender hands to Tim, then pulling him towards her for a kiss when he took it. The two policemen stared at him with ill-concealed envy.

'What happened?' repeated Tim, then, as she didn't seem inclined to let go of his hand, sank down next to her on the edge of the sofa.

'I was just having a drink with a friend outside Pepe's, when a vicious thug snatched my bag and ran off with it. And do you know, *nobody* did a thing to stop him.'

The two policemen shuffled uncomfortably as if somehow they were personally responsible.

'Did he hurt you?' Tim asked, running his eyes over her for any sign of injury.

'No, not really, but I was very frightened.'

'What did he do? Knock you down? Have you been to hospital for a check-up?'

'Well, he didn't actually touch me, just grabbed my bag from the chair next to me and ran off,' she admitted.

Tim exhaled with relief. He should have realised that if the mugger had as much as broken one of Sherry's perfectly manicured nails, she would have dramatised it into a broken arm at least.

'But my address and house keys were in the bag, so I'm terrified of being alone here,' she continued. 'That's why these two nice men were real kind and stayed with me until you arrived.'

Taking their cue, the two policemen rose to their feet and after much throat-clearing and mumbled thanks for the coffee, took their leave.

As soon as Tim had seen them to the door he returned to the sitting room and opened his tool kit.

'Is it just the front door locks they have the keys for?'

Sherry looked piqued.

'Aren't you going to come and hold me after all I've been through?' she demanded, shooting him a provocative glance through her long lashes.

Tim looked at her warily. Sometimes a suggestion like that constituted an invitation to bed, often it didn't and there was hell to pay if he misread the signs.

'Sure, honey,' he said cautiously, putting his arms around her and hugging her briefly and impersonally – no easy task. He could feel the soft pressure of her ripe breasts through the thin silk of her robe and smell her seductive perfume as she wound her arms around his neck and rubbed her peach-like cheek against his rough stubble. He swallowed, then gently disentangled himself.

'I'll get the locks changed. Don't worry – you'll be quite safe. Even I'd have difficulty breaking in here by the time I'm through.'

'Hurry back, I'll be lonesome on my own,' she told him, arranging her lovely limbs in an even more seductive position on the sofa.

Tim changed the locks and added a stronger safety chain and two bolts. He then checked the locks on the back door and all the windows, replacing a couple of faulty catches.

Although he was fairly handy with a tool kit, it still took him a while because his mind wasn't on the job – it was on his ex-wife's delectable body. As a result, he gouged a lump out of his hand with the screwdriver and dropped his heavy metal tool kit on one foot.

When he'd finished he limped back into the sitting room to find Sherry still reclining on the sofa and watching a soap on TV.

'It took you long enough,' she said, without looking up. Pouting disconsolately at the TV she continued, 'I was up for that role – that bitch only got it because she slept with the producer.'

As the actress in question was a respected star of both stage and screen with a track record which far outstripped Sherry's, Tim thought it best not to comment.

'The front door's secure now and I've checked the locks in the rest of the house,' he told her. 'Anything else I can do before I go?'

'Yes, you can open a bottle of wine, I need a drink – today's been very traumatic.'

Tim obligingly opened a bottle of her favourite Chablis, poured her a glass, then picked up his jacket.

'You're not going, are you?' she wailed, her expression heart-rendingly pathetic. 'How can you be such a brute as to leave me at a time like this? Have you got a date – is that it? Well don't let me keep you – you go and enjoy yourself while I stay here alone and get murdered in my bed.'

Sighing, Tim poured himself a glass of wine and sank into a chair. He knew he was a fool for staying, but Sherry had always had an infinite capacity for making him feel guilty.

Even during their marriage when he had ample evidence that a succession of other men were sharing her bed, he always ended up feeling like it was his fault. Being married to a government agent was no picnic for a woman. Particularly not a beautiful, sensual woman like Sherry, who needed a lot of attention.

He spent most of his time working abroad, his life

was often in danger and for one terrible year he'd been held political hostage in a filthy cellar in the Middle East.

Sherry had made it quite clear that any infidelity on her part came from the strain of having a husband in the CIA who was never at home, and that *she* wasn't to blame. Even he couldn't really bring himself to blame her. Men became like dogs on heat around her, himself included. She must have been very lonely with him away so much of the time.

Eventually, it became politically expedient for him to leave both the CIA and the USA after he made some particularly powerful enemies. They moved to London and he opened the investigation agency while Sherry pursued her career with as little real success as she'd had in America.

It soon became clear that having him around all the time wasn't going to stop Sherry from indulging her amorous appetites where, when and with whom she chose. She still regarded extra-marital affairs the way a woman on a diet might regard chocolates in a box. Naughty but irresistible.

In the end he walked out, but Sherry could never bear to let a man leave her. Even after all this time she still called him whenever she wanted anything, whether it was to have him dance attendance on her or something more practical like putting up a set of shelves.

And he put up with it.

The reason was very simple.

He'd never met another woman who made him so hot.

Her capacity for sexual pleasure was infinite. Even now as he sat opposite her in the pretty sitting room of the house he paid for, she kept shifting position on the sofa, offering him alluring glimpses of her gorgeous body.

She sat up and swung her feet in their high-heeled slippers back onto the floor. Her robe had parted at the front showing a generous amount of shadowy cleavage. She was wearing a lace slip underneath it and, he suspected, not much else. He could see that she was wearing stockings in an ivory shade which drew attention to the smooth, rounded contours of her calves. But whether they were held up by a suspender belt or a pair of the lacy garters she sometimes wore, he couldn't tell.

She saw his eyes lingering speculatively on her legs and moved slightly so that her robe fell open, showing most of her thighs. He caught a glimpse of stocking top but still couldn't tell what was holding them up.

She ran a hand caressingly up her own leg, pushing the edges of the robe further apart to reveal a pair of lacy garters, each one around the top of a sheer stocking with three or four inches of bare thigh above it.

She continued to stroke herself, her slanting eyes half closed, her full lips curved in a slight smile. Her fingers played lightly on the bare skin above the stockings while Tim watched mesmerised.

Her hands moved to her breasts and she opened the robe from the waist up, revealing a lace slip with three tiny pearl buttons down the cleavage. She undid them slowly, then drew out first one full, perfect breast, then the other. Her nipples were a deep rose-pink and she toyed with them as he watched her with mounting excitement.

She caressed them for a long time until he was worked up to a fever pitch. He was careful to keep his face expressionless, if he appeared too easily aroused she might very well stop the show prematurely.

Unfortunately he couldn't conceal his massive erection.

When her nipples were thrusting outwards like

small, ripe raspberries her hands moved to undo the belt of the silk robe. It fell apart revealing the whole of the short lacy slip, which only just covered the tops of her creamy thighs.

Slowly she pulled it up while he held his breath in anticipation.

There it was, the naked perfection of her shaven mound.

When they were first married he used to shave it for her, sitting her on a towel and working up a soapy lather with an old-fashioned shaving brush. She'd sit there, leaning back on her elbows with her legs apart, enjoying his attentions. When he'd finished and rinsed away the soap, he'd test the shaven area for perfect smoothness with his fingertips and then his tongue.

Without a covering of hair, her cleft was completely exposed to him. She opened her legs slightly so he could just see the moist tip of her clitoris protruding from between her labia. She trailed her fingers between her thighs and dabbled them lazily into the glistening folds of flesh.

With a sultry, inviting smile she lay back on the sofa.

Like a man in a trance Tim crossed the room and knelt between her parted thighs.

At first he ran his tongue over the whole of the shaven area and found it satin-smooth as usual. Then he flickered the tip between her legs, carefully avoiding her clit as he licked and probed his way along the slippery folds of flesh he found there.

When he'd explored the whole area thoroughly, delving into every last hidden crevice, he probed as far as he could into her warm, welcoming interior. She moaned and pushed her pelvis forwards so his face was completely buried in her heated private parts.

He knew she wanted him to pay some attention to

her clit but he ignored it, continuing to tease and tantalise his way around it with his tongue. She spread her legs even wider, moaning and turning her head from side to side.

Sitting up, he substituted his fingers for his tongue, deftly holding her wide open so he could admire the slick folds of welcoming pussy – hot, wet and waiting for him.

He could see she was flooded with creamy juices and more than ready for him, but still he held back. Slipping two fingers inside her he rotated them gently, pressing against the velvet-lined walls of her interior.

She was moaning in earnest now, her eyes closed, her lips half parted. She tried to reach between her legs to give herself the release she craved, but he caught her wrists and held her hands away.

At last he touched her clit.

The result was devastating.

A shudder passed through her slender frame and she moved her hips in a demanding movement. He intensified the pressure, stroking deftly along the shaft, and within a few seconds she came.

Her whole body shook with the intensity of the climax, then she reached out and pulled him hungrily down on top of her.

He unzipped his jeans and entered her in one smooth, easy movement, supporting his weight on his elbows. He began a series of deep, smooth thrusts while she lifted her hips to meet each upward push, gasping with pleasure as he shafted her tirelessly.

Making love to Sherry was the nearest Tim ever came to pure contentment.

It was different every time.

She kept him constantly off balance by offering or denying him different sexual stimulation as the whim took her. Often he wished he could say no to her, but he never could – however infuriatingly she behaved.

What man could deny himself so much pleasure, however high the price?

The week passed quickly for Jess. She spent a lot of time at the agency and met Alexa's other colleagues. She was thoroughly briefed on the job her twin wanted her to take over and quickly familiarised herself with the computing system.

Alexa told her about all her friends in detail, particularly her male friends, and prepared a reference book for her with names and vital information.

When she wasn't busy, Jess wandered around London, visiting museums and art galleries or going shopping. She enjoyed herself very much and was glad she'd accepted Alexa's invitation.

The sisters were careful not to be seen in each other's company anywhere Alexa might bump into people she knew, but they spent a lot of time together.

Ralph phoned several times and after the first couple of calls Jess told Alexa to say she was out – she wanted a break from him. She didn't know what her plans were and didn't want him to keep asking when she was going home when she didn't know herself.

On Wednesday evening the doorbell rang and as Alexa was in the bath Jess answered it.

Ralph stood there on the doorstep.

'Hello, Alexa,' he greeted her, 'I've come to see Jess. Is she in?'

Jess was completely nonplussed. This was the man she'd been living with for seven years and he didn't even recognise her. Briefly she considered pretending to be her sister and sending him away, saying she wasn't staying here any more. But she rejected the idea immediately.

'Ralph, I'm not Alexa, I'm Jess – you'd better come in.'

He followed her into the flat saying, 'What have you done to yourself? You look just like Alexa.'

'You don't sound very pleased about it. Don't you think I look attractive?' she demanded accusingly. He seemed taken aback by her response and said hurriedly, 'Yes, very nice. It's just a bit of a shock, that's all.'

Alexa appeared at that moment and kissed him on the cheek.

'Hello, Ralph. Doesn't Jess look great?'

He stared from one to the other then said slowly, 'I'd never really noticed just how alike you are.'

The next hour was strained. Jess got Alexa alone and begged her not to let Ralph stay the night. Whenever they'd both stayed at the flat in the past Alexa had given them the double bed in her room and slept in the spare room herself.

Jess had moved out of the bedroom she shared with Ralph at home as soon as she'd found out about his affair with Pru. She didn't want to have to spend the night with him tonight, particularly not so soon after Ben.

'And please don't leave me alone with him,' she begged.

'Okay, if that's what you want,' agreed Alexa blithely.

The three of them sat uncomfortably in the sitting room – at least Jess and Ralph were uncomfortable. Alexa sat and made endless light, inconsequential conversation until Jess found it hard not to laugh.

Ralph politely tried to join in but eventually he said, 'Jess, can we go somewhere for a drink? I need to talk to you alone.'

'I'm sorry, Ralph, but I don't want to talk to you.

I don't even know why you're here.'

'I'm here because I want you to come home.'

'And I've already told you that I don't know when that will be. Please go, Ralph.'

'Jess, we need to talk about this. Please come for a drink, or a walk, or whatever you like,' he begged. When she didn't reply he turned to Alexa. 'Would you give us a few minutes alone, please?' he appealed to her. Alexa looked enquiringly at Jess who rose to her feet.

'Please go, Ralph – you're just making things worse. At the moment what I need is a break from you. Don't call me and don't come here again.'

She left the sitting room and went into her bedroom, closing the door firmly behind her.

Chapter Six

After Ralph's visit Jess threw herself into learning what she could about Alexa's life with renewed vigour. She hadn't definitely decided to do what her sister asked, she told herself, but just in case she decided to . . .

She had to admit that she found the job fascinating. She discussed the cases Alexa was working on with her and successfully followed up a couple of simple leads on her behalf. She was also good on the computer.

Alexa told Tim about her idea that Jess should replace her temporarily. At first he was sceptical, but she talked him round.

'All she has to do is make regular reports to the insurance company as if she was me,' she argued. 'Someone else can actually take over the investigation. Just give Jess some of the routine stuff to do – but don't overwork her because she's supposed to be on holiday.'

'I don't like it,' he protested. 'Jess hasn't had your training or your years of experience and presumably she doesn't know anything about insurance fraud. What if she slips up?'

'We're no worse off if she does. Daniel said he'd give the investigation to another agency anyway if I wasn't working on it. With a bit of luck I'll be able to track down Will Harper, embezzler of this parish, very quickly, wrap the case up and be back within a couple of weeks. I already have several leads as to his whereabouts – I'm planning to leave on Sunday.'

Tim wasn't a hundred per cent sold on the idea but he acquiesced. As Alexa pointed out, they didn't really have anything to lose.

He found the idea that Alexa had an identical twin fascinating and covertly studied the two women together. Whenever he saw one of them alone he tried to decide which of them it was with varying degrees of success.

It was much easier to tell if the one he was watching was moving around the office rather than sitting at a desk. Alexa still projected more self-confidence in her movements, but in repose they were difficult to tell apart – particularly since they even shared several of the same mannerisms.

At least watching the sisters took his mind off Sherry.

She'd insisted he stay the night on Wednesday, but he'd pretended reluctance for the pleasure of having her seduce him all over again. They'd made love three more times and he'd left in the morning a sated, if not happy man.

That was the way it was with her. If he made it clear he wanted to screw her she retreated, but if he seemed indifferent she had to prove to both of them all over again that she could have him at any time she chose.

If only it worked the other way round.

But he knew better than that.

If he was the one who tried to take her to bed, she refused. She had to be the one to initiate it.

She hadn't forgotten his late alimony cheque either. He'd found himself signing away an even larger amount than usual, an amount which he knew would make his accountant blanch.

The worst thing was that whenever he did screw her he spent the next few days wanting to do it again.

And again.

And again.

He didn't know when he'd next hear from her – it could be in a few days.

Or weeks.

Or even months.

On Friday evening Alexa insisted on taking Jess out for a meal. When Jess made her point again about them not being seen together, Alexa vanished into her bedroom and came out wearing a brown wig and a pair of glasses with plain glass lenses.

'I'm unrecognisable when I've changed my make-up too,' she told Jess. 'I often wear a wig if I need to be unobtrusive when I'm working. There's some foot-slogging even in a high-tech operation like ours and red hair is just too memorable.'

They went to a small Italian restaurant in Highgate where to their mutual amusement the waiters paid much more attention to Jess than Alexa.

'This is a first,' commented Jess wonderingly. 'You've always been the one men fell over themselves to impress.'

'Only because I chose that they should. You could have done the same any time, you just decided not to until now.'

Over pasta and a bottle of Barolo, Alexa broached the subject which had been hanging between them all week.

'I'm leaving on Sunday. You are going to become me until I get back, aren't you, Jess?'

Jess hesitated then took a gulp of her wine to nerve herself to reply.

'Okay, I'll do it.'

Alexa smiled. 'Thanks, sis. And do you know something? You're going to love being me. Probably so

much that when I come back you won't want to stop.'
She paused while the waiter topped up their wine.

'Talking of which, feel free to sleep with any of my male friends that you like. I can recommend all of them highly – I don't sleep with men who're useless in bed. Though bed is often the last place that my myriad hot and breathless couplings take place,' she ended airily.

Jess found herself giggling reluctantly.

'Alexa, you're completely shameless. I think I can safely say that I won't be taking you up on your kind offer.'

'Don't make any rash decisions at this stage – you haven't even met any of them yet. At least go out with a couple of them and have a good time.'

'I don't think I know how to have a good time,' pointed out Jess mildly.

'Exactly. Take a look at your life, Jess. You didn't go out much when we were at school because you spent all your time studying for 'O' and 'A' levels. Once at university you spent all your time studying for a degree, then you met and moved in with Ralph.

'From what you've said I gather that your life since then revolves pretty much around your job. Do you ever go out and have fun together? Because it's news to me if you do. I agree that work is very important but life's short and it's important to get the most out of it that you can.'

Jess had been thoughtfully running the tip of her index finger around the rim of her wine glass while Alexa spoke. It was true that she lived a rather dry academic life in which fun didn't play much of a part. Occasionally they socialised with Ralph's clients but that certainly couldn't be classified as fun.

'You're probably right,' she agreed eventually. 'I'm in a rut, I suppose.'

'Well, now's your time to get out of it. Take full advantage of the situation. Don't just pretend to be me while I'm away – *be me*.'

The flat felt empty after Alexa left on Sunday. Jess did some tidying up, then moved her things into Alexa's bedroom. Her twin had invited her to do so and it was true that the spare room was very cramped.

She felt at a loose end and went for a walk on Hampstead Heath. She was feeling apprehensive. Would she be able to convince all Alexa's friends and, most importantly, the head of the insurance company, that she was in fact her sister?

She'd at least try.

The phone was ringing when she let herself back into the flat.

'Hi, Alexa, it's Bob.'

'Hello, Bob, how are you?' asked Jess, trying to emulate Alexa's breezy telephone manner, while frantically flicking through the notebook which held details of all Alexa's friends. Where there was a photo it was clipped to the opposite page and Jess had studied them all carefully in case anyone who obviously knew Alexa greeted her while she was out.

Bob . . . Bob . . . which one was he? Here it was – Bob Beswick, creative director at one of London's leading advertising agencies. Thirty-one, attractive, amusing . . . what did that next bit say? Something about any time, any place. She couldn't quite decipher Alexa's scrawl.

Luckily there was a photo which showed an extremely good looking man with dark hair, aquiline features and a rather sardonic curve to his mouth.

She became aware that Bob had just asked her something, but she wasn't sure what.

'Sorry, Bob, what did you just say?'

'I said, are you still okay for tonight? You asked me to ring and check when we spoke on Thursday. I've made the reservations at the Conservatory. Shall I pick you up at eight?'

Jess smiled wryly to herself. Trust Alexa. Her sister was obviously determined that Jess wasn't going to sit in the flat alone at night. She wondered how many other dates had been made on her behalf.

Perhaps it wasn't such a bad idea. If she could get one of Alexa's men friends to accept her as her twin, it would be a boost to her confidence for when she had to meet the person it was most important to convince – the head of the insurance company.

'Eight's fine, Bob,' she found herself saying, 'see you then.'

Jess wasn't sure what to wear, she didn't know whether the Conservatory was smart or not. She spent a pleasant hour rifling through Alexa's wardrobe and trying on her clothes, before deciding on a simple, bright pink silk dress.

It wasn't a colour she would ever have chosen – it made such a flamboyant contrast to her red-gold hair, but it did look stunning on.

Short and close fitting, it seemed to accentuate curves she didn't even know she had. She wore her new cream satin underwear underneath it and borrowed a pair of mole-grey suede high-heeled shoes and a matching bag.

By seven-fifty-five Jess was pacing the sitting room nervously, trying to talk herself into the light-hearted frame of mind she imagined Alexa would be in before a date.

When the bell went she almost jumped out of her skin. Taking a deep breath to steady herself she pasted a smile on her face and went to open the door.

Jess knew from his photo that Bob Beswick was attractive, but nothing had prepared her for the sheer animal sexuality he exuded.

He walked past her into the sitting room then turned to survey her from head to foot, his eyes lingering on her breasts and hips. The way he looked at her made Jess's legs turn to jelly.

It was a look which said quite clearly that he and Alexa had been sexually intimate and if he had anything to do with it, would soon be again.

Without speaking he approached her, pulled her into his arms and kissed her. Jess was completely unprepared and didn't know what to do. His hands roamed over her back, stroking her over the thin silk, then moved down to her backside, holding her tightly against him.

She could feel how hard he was against her and her face flooded with warm colour. He kissed his way around her neck, nuzzling her ear in a way which left her breathless.

At last he moved away. Jess didn't know whether to be glad or sorry.

'I don't need to ask how you are this evening,' he told her, flopping down in an armchair and stretching out his long legs in front of him. 'Good enough to eat, as usual. Tell you what – shall I cancel the table and we'll send out for something?'

Jess moved over to the drinks tray, trying to emulate Alexa's sinuous walk.

'No don't do that – I feel like going out. Have we time for a drink?'

He glanced at his watch.

'Yes, I should think so. The usual please.'

Jess hesitated, her hand fluttering uncertainly above the bottles.

'Vodka and tonic,' he prompted her, grinning, the

sardonic twist to his mouth much in evidence. 'That's just dealt a hefty blow to my ego – you don't remember what I drink.'

She shot him a sidelong glance.

'The heat of our embrace must have driven it out of my mind,' she said lightly.

She congratulated herself.

That was exactly the sort of thing Alexa would have said.

The Conservatory turned out to be a casual but expensive restaurant in Hampstead. Jess remembered now that she'd walked past it when she was shopping. The rear half of the restaurant opened out into a walled garden. A riot of roses, clematis and sweet peas swarmed up the crumbling walls, filling the evening air with scent.

Jess was about to exclaim with delight when she remembered that Alexa would undoubtedly have been here before. Besides, her twin wasn't really given to exclaiming over anything.

Bob ordered champagne without consulting her. She tried to sip it insouciantly – it was Alexa's favourite wine, she knew, but it seemed like a very sophisticated thing to be doing.

She really ought to face it – she was completely out of her depth.

She was dining with a devastatingly attractive man who obviously expected sex to be on the agenda and she didn't have a clue how she was going to handle that.

He was also so witty and acerbic that conversationally she was out of her depth too.

There wasn't a hope she was going to enjoy the evening.

Jess went to pieces when presented with the extensive menu and just couldn't decide what to order. Eventually as the waiter stood with his pen poised over his pad her mind went a complete blank.

'I'll have what you're having,' she blurted out to Bob at last.

He raised an enquiring eyebrow. 'I thought you particularly liked the lamb with wild mushrooms here? And haven't you noticed the asparagus among the specials?'

'Oh . . . yes. I'll have both those please.'

When the waiter had gone Bob looked at her quizzically.

'What's the matter with you tonight, Alexa? You seem on edge and some of my best *bon mots* have barely raised a smile.'

Jess took a frantic, nerve-steadying gulp of champagne.

'I'm even more overwhelmed by your animal magnetism than usual,' she managed to quip.

He grinned at her wolfishly. 'If I'd realised that I'd have . . . overwhelmed you before we left your flat. It's been a couple of weeks and I've missed you.'

He put his hand on her stocking-clad knee under cover of the tablecloth as he spoke. Jess jumped and nearly let out a yelp. He patted her knee soothingly then began to stroke it.

'You're very tense. Are you still under a lot of pressure at work?'

'Yes . . . yes I am.'

'We'll have to see what we can do about that later – I know exactly what to do to relieve your tension.' His hand crept under her skirt and up her thigh, stroking the bare skin below her satin panties.

Jess's mouth went dry and she took another steadying gulp of champagne.

This couldn't be happening.

But it was.

'Or maybe I should do something about it now?' he murmured, slipping his hand between her thighs and pushing them apart. 'Relax, no one can see us.'

The tips of his fingers grazed over her satin-covered private parts, sending shuddering tingles of lust through her.

'Stop that, Bob – or I won't be able to eat,' she admonished him, striving for Alexa's light tone. The fingers paused, brushed over her one more time, then thankfully stopped their arousing movements.

'It would be a waste of money, I suppose,' he admitted. 'Okay, we'll wait till later.'

Jess decided that there was no way she was going to invite Bob back to the flat at the end of the evening. She'd just have to feign illness. He was obviously the type of man who'd have her out of her clothes before she'd finished closing the front door, and she really didn't want that.

Or did she?

After a couple of glasses of champagne she relaxed enough to enjoy the food. Now she knew how she was going to handle him she could try to enjoy herself. He was, after all, very amusing company.

After the meal they lingered over coffee, enjoying the warm breeze which meandered in through the open doors. Jess rarely drank and the champagne made her feel slightly giddy. It helped in a way. She was able to laugh quite naturally at his witty conversation and even venture a couple of mild jokes herself.

At the end of the meal they left the restaurant hand in hand and headed back towards the car, parked a couple of streets away. Jess planned to tell him that she wasn't feeling well as soon as they reached the car, then get him to drop her off at the flat saying she needed to go to bed.

'This way,' he said suddenly, leading her down one of the quaint little alleyways which abounded in Hampstead. Thinking it was a short cut Jess followed him. The alleyway led behind some smart shops and had pretty tubs and pots filled with flowers at intervals along its length.

It was also deserted.

She was taken aback when Bob stopped suddenly and gathered her into his arms. She was even more taken aback when he kissed her and slipped a hand into the front of her dress, finding his way unerringly inside her bra.

Warm fingers teased one pert little nipple, then closed on her full breast, stroking it seductively and sending shivers of excitement shooting down to her groin.

Trying to avoid his demanding lips she tipped her head back, but he simply trailed kisses down her neck towards what she now realised was a naked breast.

Swiftly he released it from its satin cradle and took full advantage of the fact by fastening his lips to it and tugging gently.

Then somehow both breasts were exposed to the warm night air and he stroked and kissed them until she was trembling and her legs threatened to give way beneath her.

He drew her over to a wide window ledge which projected from the back of an expensive clothes shop. Lifting her by the waist he sat her on it and stood between her parted legs, continuing to kiss and caress her naked, tingling breasts.

'Bob, I . . .' she gasped, her head dropping backwards again as his fingers stroked their way seductively downwards over her stomach.

'Mmm?'

Instead of telling him to stop as she intended to,

Jess found herself saying breathlessly, 'What if some-one comes?'

'That's never worried you before.' He lifted her skirt as he spoke, pushing it up around her waist so he could see her panties, suspenders and stockings.

He ran a finger up her thigh under the elastic of one of the suspenders, then stroked her delicately between her legs, over her satin panties.

Part of Jess wanted to expire from embarrassment at the situation she found herself in – sitting, legs spread, in a back alleyway, her skirt up around her waist, while a man she'd met for the first time only a couple of hours before touched her intimately.

But part of her was desperately aroused.

In fact she'd been aroused since he'd first kissed her after arriving at the flat, and he'd kept the fire stoked by fondling her under cover of the tablecloth in the restaurant.

Part of her wanted him to stop.

But part of her wanted him to carry on.

It seemed to Jess that the situation was well out of her control. There was a fire burning in her loins as he continued to caress her satin-covered crotch and she could feel a small patch of dampness spreading outwards, silent testimony to her arousal.

Bob took her hand and guided it to his groin, laying it flat against the huge hardness she felt there. She snatched it away in a reflex action and saw his surprise.

'What . . .'

Voices a few yards away made him turn his head, then he swiftly pulled her down from the window ledge as a couple came out of the back door of one of the shops and began to water the plants in the tubs.

Bob put his arm around her shoulders and they walked away, back towards where the car was parked.

'That was close,' he commented, obviously not particularly perturbed. Jess was too confused to reply.

Once in the car he kissed her hungrily and she didn't feel she had the strength to resist. Her limbs felt weak and her head was spinning.

It had never been this way with Ralph.

When his hand found its way between her legs again she parted them with a sigh which was half pleasure, half resignation. His probing fingers slid beneath the loose-fitting satin and pushed inside her. She could tell from how easily he gained entry that she was dripping wet.

A group of youths walked towards the car jostling and pushing each other noisily. Reluctantly, Bob released her and started the engine. He drove the short distance to Alexa's flat with his hand between her legs, keeping her in a state of quivering expectation.

By the time they entered the flat Jess was molten inside and just wanted him to finish what he'd started and damn the consequences. She'd worry about the shamelessness of her behaviour tomorrow.

She started to lead him towards the bedroom but he pulled her against him and kissed her. Before she realised what was happening she heard the sound of a zip going down, then felt his cock determinedly nudging against the elastic of her satin panties.

He was inside her a few seconds later, sliding into her velvet tunnel, filling her up completely. She gasped with surprise as he screwed her up against the closed front door with vigorous expertise, making her cry out with breathless pleasure.

Jess had been expecting that they'd retire to the bedroom where he'd undress her slowly, then make prolonged, sensual love to her. Instead she found herself pushed back against the door with her legs wide apart and her pink silk dress in disarray.

The door banged rhythmically in its frame as he shafted her expertly.

Jess had never had sex like that before and found it wildly exciting. She slammed her hips forward into him to meet each thrust, gasping and moaning abandonedly.

When at last it was over and he withdrew from her she felt so weak that she almost slid down the door to slump against it in a sated daze. He sat down next to her and cradled her head on his chest, kissing and stroking her hair.

'Alexa, darling,' he murmured, 'you're the most exciting woman I've ever met. Why can't we move in together?'

Without having to think about it Jess said huskily, 'And lose the thrill? It's better the way it is, Bob. Now, can we make it to the bedroom, do you think?'

Chapter Seven

Alexa caught an afternoon flight to Malaga where she hired a car and drove west along the coastal highway to Marbella.

It was stiflingly hot and unfortunately she'd been unable to hire a car with air conditioning. She could feel her back and thighs sticking to the fine fabric of her sundress and opened the window a few inches. But the air which blew into the baking interior of the car was hot, dusty and laden with petrol fumes so she soon closed it again.

She kept seeing the Mediterranean, unbelievably blue, on her left as she drove along towards Marbella through the resorts of Torremolinos, Benalmadena-Costa, and Fuengirola, Between built-up areas, the road took her past hoardings, building sites and, very occasionally, stretches of deserted beach.

Once in Marbella she booked into a featureless, high-rise hotel overlooking the marina. It was international, bland and comfortable and offered the various business services she might have need of. Her room had a small balcony which looked out over the gleaming waters of the Mediterranean, the yachts bobbing on their moorings, a glittering white in the early evening sunshine.

After showering and washing her hair Alexa felt almost human again and sat out on the balcony allowing her hair to dry naturally in a mass of becoming red-gold waves.

She dressed in a flame-red sleeveless silk top which clung to the contours of her perfect breasts, alluringly outlining the points of her pert nipples through the filmy fabric.

She wore it with an ivory cotton skirt which stopped halfway down her thighs leaving her lightly tanned legs bare. Picking up a matching jacket and her bag Alexa left her hotel room and set off towards the old town.

It was only a short walk uphill through some public gardens back to the busy coastal highway. Once she'd crossed that, Alexa strode confidently into the narrow alleyways which were part of the warren of Marbella old town.

Most of the little streets and alleys were too narrow to allow the passage of cars so it was a pleasant place to stroll, past shops, bars and restaurants all open and ready for another busy summer evening's trade.

The architecture had a strong Moorish influence and the twisting, turning streets were overlooked by tiny balconies embellished by intricate wrought-iron-work. Many of them held pots containing geraniums, bougainvillaea and other colourful summer flowers which trailed down the ancient stonework and brightened the shaded passageways.

It took Alexa a while to find the address she was looking for. Eventually, after asking several times, she found a narrow doorway flanked by two terracotta pots overflowing with lilies and hibiscus.

After ascending two flights of worn stone stairs she rang the old-fashioned bell beside a panelled door.

'Come in!' shouted a deep voice from within. Alexa opened the door and stepped inside, then stood with her hand on her hip smiling at the room's surprised occupant.

'Alexa!'

'Hello, Todd.'

Todd dropped the loaded paintbrush he was holding and crossed the cluttered room to embrace Alexa enthusiastically.

Of medium height, Todd had light brown hair and a slim supple body. He was wearing a tattered pair of jeans faded by innumerable washings and liberally spattered with dried paint. His chest and feet were bare and he smelt of foreign cigarettes and shampoo.

'What are you doing here?' he asked her, taking her hands and pulling her further into the room.

'I'm on holiday,' she returned lightly, 'so I thought I'd look you up.'

'I'm glad you did. How long has it been?'

Todd and Alexa had gone out together for a while at university and remained friends even after their brief affair was over. They'd both moved to London afterwards and had maintained a tenuous contact.

The last time she'd seen him had been several years previously, just before he'd tired of England and decided to try the expatriate lifestyle. She received the occasional postcard from him, the last one about a year ago, and fortunately he was still at the same address.

Todd was an artist who lived on what he earned from selling paintings of Marbella and the surrounding area to local galleries and, when he could, direct to tourists. The rest of the time he painted what he wanted to but was rarely able to sell any of this less commercial work.

Alexa had met Will Harper, the embezzler she was now in search of, through Todd, who was one of his closest friends.

'Glass of wine?' Todd asked her, then when she nodded, poured her some from a half-empty bottle of Rioja on the battered table.

Alexa looked around for somewhere to sit, but every surface seemed to be covered in clutter. The large room held only a table, a couple of chairs, an easel and a studio couch, but it was so untidy that it seemed full.

Seeing her hesitate, Todd swept an armful of things off the studio couch so she could sit down.

'What are you doing these days?' he asked her, clearing a corner of the table and sitting on it, his eyes wandering over her scantily clad body with interest.

'I'm happy to say that I'm a lady of leisure.'

'Yeah? How did that come about? I can't remember what you were doing when I last saw you.'

'I think I was working in publishing,' said Alexa, remembering her brief career as an assistant editor with a publishing house. It was just after that she'd commenced her equally brief career as a journalist. 'Now I don't need to work. A very wealthy aunt of mine died and left all her money to her favourite niece. So I go where I want and do what I want.'

'Nice,' he commented. 'If only I had an aunt as rich and obliging. How long are you in the area for?'

'Probably not long – I like to keep moving. Talking of which, have you eaten? I haven't and I'm hungry.' When she saw him glance at the handful of coins and notes beside him on the table she added, 'On me, or course.'

'Then I'll be delighted to accept. Can you give me ten minutes to clean up?'

The bathroom opened off the studio and he left the door open so they could continue a shouted conversation while he showered. She took the opportunity to prowl around the room, examining the various paintings stacked against the wall.

The room had several sets of floor-to-ceiling windows which opened onto little balconies overlooking the street. They were open and she could hear the sounds of the activity below and smell the faint appetising aroma of cooking drifting up from nearby restaurants.

She leant out and watched the people wandering around below for a couple of minutes. Todd's balconies, like those of his neighbours, held various potted plants, including a luxuriant vine which half obscured one of the windows, but they were all drooping from lack of water.

'Don't you ever water your plants?' called Alexa. 'Most of them don't look long for this world.'

Todd reappeared with a threadbare towel knotted around his waist.

'The landlady's always going on at me about them. She'll water them when she comes for the rent tomorrow.'

He proceeded to search through several overflowing plastic carriers of clothes, muttering, 'I know one of these is clean, I went to the launderette yesterday.' Eventually he unearthed a T-shirt and another pair of faded jeans, then he retired to the bathroom to dress.

They strolled through the teeming streets to the Square of the Orange Trees in the centre of the old town. Tables belonging to the numerous bars and restaurants were set up outside for those who preferred to drink and dine in the open air. In the centre of the square the leaves of the orange trees rustled in the warm evening breeze.

Todd steered her to a table belonging to one of the smarter restaurants.

'The food here is really good, but I can't often afford to eat it. Tapas bars are more my style.'

'Order whatever you like, it's on aunt Lily, after all,' Alexa urged him. 'Do you still eat as much?' For all his wiry frame she remembered Todd having a gargantuan appetite.

'When I can afford to.'

He was right about the food – it was delicious. As the sky darkened and a hazy dusk fell, they ate and drank companionably, discussing old times and the people they'd known.

'I seem to have lost touch with so many people,' said Alexa. 'You know someone for a while then you both move on and lose touch. It's sad really. Now I'm financially secure my plan is to travel the world, looking up old friends wherever I can find them.'

'And what will you do once you've found them?' asked Todd, his eyes straying from her face to where the skimpy silk top clung to the curves of her breasts.

'That depends.'

'On what?'

'On how the mood takes me.'

Alexa pushed her chair back from the table and crossed her legs so her skirt rode up over her bare, tanned thighs. Todd watched her through narrowed eyes, not troubling to hide his interest.

'You're looking absolutely gorgeous. Wealth obviously agrees with you,' he complimented her.

'You're looking good too.' It was true. Todd looked lean, tanned and more relaxed than she remembered him. His tight-fitting jeans emphasised his slim hips and hard thighs and she could see a few fronds of softly curling hair at the neck of his T-shirt.

'I like it here – the climate and the lifestyle suit me.'

'I can see that. Will you ever come back to England?'

'Not in the immediate future.'

They ordered brandy and coffee and sat enjoying the parade of passers-by, interrupted occasionally by traders selling everything from lace tablecloths to handmade jewellery.

Alexa paid the bill then said, 'How about strolling down to the marina for another drink?'

'Good idea. It's hot tonight, there'll be more of a breeze down there.'

They strolled hand in hand down to the sea front and had another drink at a little bar on the quay.

'Who else are you in touch with?' asked Alexa lazily. 'Do you ever see anything of Joanne?'

'Not for a while. The last I heard she was living in Houston and had just had a baby.'

'Do you have her address? I'll go and see her if I get that far.'

'I think I do somewhere. I'll have a look tomorrow.'

'How about Richard – what's he doing these days?'

'Teaching in Madrid. I don't know his address but I do know where he's working.'

'Yes, I must definitely stop off and see him. What about Will – do you ever hear from him?'

There was a pause, then Todd flashed a searching look at her.

'He was living in London until recently. Did you never bump into him?'

'Not for years. Where is he now?'

He lit a cigarette and exhaled before replying.

'North Africa somewhere, I think.'

This was what Alexa had come to find out. She knew if anyone was aware of Will's current whereabouts it would be Todd.

'When did you last see him?' she enquired casually.

Todd studied the end of the cigarette he held in his long-fingered hand.

'Fairly recently.'

'How was he?'

'The same old Will. Shall we have another drink?'

'Sure, but why don't we go back to my hotel and have it?'

Once in her room Alexa poured them both a drink, then sat in the one armchair while Todd sprawled on the bed. His eyes kept straying to her breasts while they chatted, particularly when she linked her hands behind her head.

'Alexa, there's something I have to say to you.'

'What's that?'

'Is there any chance of a fuck for old time's sake? Because if not, would you mind putting a jacket on? It's a long time since I've seen your breasts and I keep getting the urge to rip that flimsy little top off you and renew my acquaintance.'

Alexa laughed throatily, then rose languidly to her feet and crossed the room to join him on the bed.

'You were never one to beat about the bush, were you Todd? Since you ask, I'd say that there was a better-than-even chance.'

Slowly and seductively she pulled the silk top over her head.

'I want you to follow my wife.'

Tim Preece groaned silently to himself.

The managing director of an international electronics company was sitting opposite him in his office, and having made his unwelcome request, wouldn't meet Tim's eyes.

The electronics company had used the agency twice before. The first time was to discover who was stealing ideas in the development stage and selling them to rival companies. It had been a difficult case and one which took a while to solve.

The second had been an investigation into another

company which had suggested a merger. On the surface it had seemed as if it would be very advantageous to both companies, but Tim had managed to unearth some dubious skeletons from the other company's cupboard, with the result that the merger had not gone ahead.

When Kevin Bolton had requested this meeting, Tim had assumed he needed the agency's services for something similar. Instead the man had asked Tim to put his wife under surveillance.

'I'm sorry, Kevin,' said Tim at last, 'but the agency only takes corporate work – marital enquiries are a specialist field. But I can recommend an excellent agency which can handle it for you.'

Kevin Bolton still wouldn't meet Tim's eyes, he was evidently very embarrassed at having exposed some problem with his marriage to the other man. He cleared his throat.

'I'm going to ask you to handle this for me as a personal favour. You've worked for my company in the past and you'll certainly work for us again, but I need you to deal with this personal problem for me now. It'll be well worth your while.'

He named a figure.

It was very high, far too high to turn down. Especially when the agency's cash flow problems had just increased as a direct result of the large cheque he'd written Sherry.

Reluctantly Tim agreed.

He suspected that having got as far as telling Tim his problem, Kevin couldn't face doing it all over again with another private investigator, so he'd made him an offer he couldn't refuse.

Kevin, it transpired, suspected that his wife, Jenny, was seeing another man. He'd asked her outright if this was the case, but she'd laughed and denied it.

He'd tried to follow her himself for a couple of days but she'd spotted him three times and been very annoyed with him.

Now he wanted Tim to follow her and if she was seeing another man to obtain photos of the two of them together.

As he shook Tim's hand before leaving the office Kevin muttered, 'I'm sure it goes without saying that I'm relying on your total discretion about this.'

Tim nodded reassuringly.

'No one will ever hear about it from me.'

Tim really disliked this sort of case and was in a bad mood as he parked his car at a discreet distance from the house in St John's Wood.

He'd studied photos of Jenny Bolton but they didn't do justice to her shining chestnut hair, striking features or willowy figure.

And they certainly didn't do justice to her long-legged hip-swinging walk.

Five years ago, before her marriage to Kevin Bolton, she'd been a fashion model and still carried herself as if she were striding along the catwalk.

Tim watched her walk to the post box, a letter in her hand, then return to the house. There was something about the way her pelvis moved which made his mouth go dry. He had to admit to himself that if he had to follow someone, it made it less of a chore if it was an attractive woman.

But he was too busy working on other cases to give this one all his attention so he set Beth, the agency's newest recruit, on to it.

Surveillance was to be during the day only. Tim got the impression that Kevin Bolton took a dim view of his wife going anywhere without him in the evening.

In fact he'd come away from their conversation

strongly suspecting his client of being one of those pathologically jealous men, whether they had cause or not.

Jenny Bolton seemed to live a fairly blameless life. For the first couple of days Beth's reports showed that she shopped, met friends for coffee or lunch and did some voluntary charity work.

On the third day it got more interesting.

After going to view an exhibition at a private art gallery she took a taxi to a small but expensive hotel in Knightsbridge. Beth managed to follow her and entered the opulent foyer just in time to see her quarry vanish into the lift. Beth was able to ascertain that she got out on the third floor, but not the number of the room she went into.

After waiting around in the bar off the foyer for a couple of hours, Beth saw Jenny come out of the lift again and hand over her key. She just caught a glimpse of the number – room 314.

It didn't take Beth long to ascertain which side of the hotel room 314 was on, or to locate the room's window from outside.

Then she went back to the agency to write her daily report.

Sitting astride Todd's prone body on the bed in her hotel room, his cock buried deep within her, Alexa rather regretted that it was nearly time to be moving on.

She'd been in Marbella three days and a good part of that time had been spent with Todd's ramrod-hard shaft inside her.

Now she raised herself so that only a couple of inches of it remained in position, then bore down hard. Todd exhaled sharply, his hips moving upwards to meet her.

She was playing with him, he knew, moving on him in a way which gave her the maximum stimulation, while continuing to deny him the release he wanted.

Still pleasurably skewered on his member, Alexa commenced an erotic rocking motion, bending backwards and forwards while holding him tightly in place with her internal muscles.

Todd watched her through half-closed eyes, worked up to a fever pitch by the sight of her full, ripe breasts moving above him, her pointed nipples quivering deliciously.

She was naked, her silken red hair tumbling to her shoulders, a slick of sweat visible on her creamy cleavage. His eyes ran appreciatively down her body to where the base of his cock vanished into her, disappearing into the fuzz of her russet bush.

Reaching out he tickled her clit delicately with the tip of his forefinger, increasing the stimulation as she moaned softly.

She bore down on him again.

Unable to stand it any longer he seized her by the waist and rolled on top of her, then began to thrust forcibly in and out.

'Not yet,' she begged, but he ignored her, increasing the speed of his movements until at last with a loud and strangled groan, he erupted inside her.

They lay panting on the bed, damp limbs tangled, until Alexa reached out and stroked his hair.

'You cheated,' she accused him. 'You were supposed to wait for me to come first.'

'I didn't feel like waiting another couple of hours,' he told her amiably, easing some of his weight to one side. 'You were playing with me and you know it. You always were a tease, Alexa, but just to show there are no hard feelings . . .'

He rolled off her, his cock slipping out, then

reached between her parted thighs for the engorged bud of her clit and began to stroke it.

Alexa sighed with satisfaction, then lay back to await her third climax that afternoon.

There was a block of apartments opposite the side of the Knightsbridge hotel where room 314 was located. Several of them were to let and Tim made an appointment to view them.

Jenny Bolton had returned to the same room later that week for another couple of hours, leading Tim to hope it was a regular rendezvous.

An attractive female estate agent showed him around the flats and gave him a lot of unwanted information. He paid far more attention to the curve of her well-rounded buttocks under the skirt of her smart business suit than he did to what she was saying.

The second apartment she showed him was ideal for his purposes, it overlooked room 314 and was on the floor above it, giving him an excellent view of its interior.

The next time Beth reported that Jenny had again entered the marble portals of the hotel, Tim leapt into a cab and directed it to the block of flats.

It was the work of only a few moments to break in through the service door at the rear and take the back stairs to the fourth floor. The double locks on the door of the apartment itself presented no real problem and within a short time Tim was peering cautiously through the window.

What he saw made him drop the canvas bag he carried. It contained a set of tools, a camera and a collapsible tripod and it hit the floor with an ominous crashing sound.

Kevin Bolton was quite right in thinking that his wife was having an affair.

But it wasn't with a man.

It was with another woman.

The two women lay in each other's arms on the room's luxurious double bed. The other woman was petite and voluptuous with rich, honey-coloured hair. She was naked except for a peach-coloured suspender belt trimmed with black lace, a matching pair of frilly panties and a pair of black stockings.

He couldn't see her face, but from a distance her ripe body made an attractive contrast to Jenny's slender, long-legged form.

As Tim watched, Jenny Bolton kissed her way over her companion's luscious breasts. Tim was so mesmerised by the sight that it was a full minute before he remembered he had a camera with a telephoto lens which would give him a much better view.

Barely able to tear himself away he fell hastily to his knees and yanked the tripod out of the canvas bag. He struggled to fit it together, distracted by the throbbing in his own tripod, which was expressing a keen interest in the scenario across the road in its customary manner.

When he'd eventually got it assembled he mounted the camera on it and looked through the viewfinder. The telephoto lens was so powerful that he could see the faint dusting of freckles across Jenny Bolton's smooth-skinned back and the ivory globes of her buttocks.

She had her mouth closed on one of the other woman's caramel-coloured nipples and was sucking as eagerly as if they were in fact made of toffee.

When Jenny had sucked both puckered nipples into hard points, she turned her attention to her friend's gently curving stomach and licked and kissed her way down it until she reached the tiny panties.

She removed them with a deft grace, revealing the dark nest of wiry hair which nestled between the firm, milky thighs.

Tim held his breath as he saw the blonde woman part her legs invitingly. There was a pause and then he saw Jenny dip her chestnut head and bury the flickering tip of her pink tongue in her friend's honeypot.

The room began to swim and Tim hastily exhaled, then gulped in a lungful of air.

Shit. This was making him horny as hell.

His only regret was that he couldn't hear them as well as see them, but that was just being greedy.

Jenny licked and sucked away at the delicate folds of female flesh, slipping her hands under her companion's gorgeous backside to draw her closer. When he saw the blonde head on the hotel's snowy white pillowcase begin to twist from side to side, Tim knew she was approaching her climax.

It lasted a long time. He could see her full, pink lips forming a circle of pleasure, her eyes closed as she went with it.

The blonde woman reached down and drew Jenny up the bed into her arms. They kissed tenderly, then Jenny lay back while the other woman sat beside her and began to stroke her.

She took her time, stroking and caressing her way over the tall, willowy body, dropping kisses on her neck and delicate collarbone. She handled the small, pert breasts as if they were made of fine bone china, circling the tip of her finger around the rosy nipples.

Tim gulped when he saw Jenny's female lover stretch her own ripe, curvaceous body out on the bed next to her friend. They both turned on their sides to face each other, then began to rub their mounds together.

109

Tim gulped again and pressed his eye against the lens even harder.

The blonde moved away from Jenny then positioned her on her back with her knees bent and apart. Tim watched breathlessly as she slipped her hand between the parted thighs and began to stroke her.

He could see Jenny's taut bum rotating in response to the intimate caresses and then see her groaning and bearing down as two of the blonde's fingers vanished inside her.

The powerful telephoto lens revealed that her private parts were appealingly moist and getting moister by the minute. Soon her friend's fingers were glistening with creamy female secretions.

When Jenny finally shuddered into orgasm, her body quivering and shaking, Tim found that he was shaking too. Partly because what he'd just witnessed had been intensely arousing and partly because he'd been standing with his knees bent for so long, peering through the camera.

He straightened up to ease them, then bent down again just in time to see the two women doing a striptease in reverse and pulling on their clothes.

It was only after Jenny had left the hotel room, leaving her friend alone, that Tim realised he hadn't taken a single photo.

Chapter Eight

Jess decided to make her first contact with the head of the insurance company by phone – even so it was nerve-racking. Happily he was in a meeting so their conversation was brief. She merely told him what Tim told her to say and rang off after indicating she'd report in again soon.

Someone working within his company at quite a high level must be involved in the insurance fraud – that much was obvious. Jess continued to run checks on each of them by computer, in the hope of turning something up which would give her a lead.

As soon as each check was completed she wrote up a report and sent a copy to him. It was very absorbing but Tim wouldn't let her work for more than a few hours a day on it, insisting that she spend some of her holiday enjoying herself.

The morning after her evening out with Bob Beswick, Jess stood naked in front of Alexa's full-length bedroom mirror and examined herself carefully.

What had happened to dowdy, inhibited Jess?

She was still half in shock after the wildly exciting sex she'd enjoyed the night before, but she couldn't deny even to herself how pleasurable it had been.

Earlier that morning she'd managed to decipher

Alexa's handwriting to read what she'd put about Bob Beswick. The note said:

Thirty-one, attractive, amusing. Watch out – might pounce any time, any place. Nowhere's too public or uncomfortable for Bob.

She half wished she'd managed to decipher it yesterday, then she'd have been on her guard. But maybe she wouldn't have enjoyed herself so much.

It really did seem that since she was pretending to be Alexa, she could behave like her too, in a way she'd never have believed possible.

Examining her naked reflection in the mirror, Jess saw that for the first time in her life she actually looked sexy. Instead of stooping with her shoulders hunched and her head bent, she stood upright with her breasts jutting proudly out and one leg bent in an elegant pose which was pure Alexa.

Languidly she touched one of her own breasts, enjoying the feel of the firm, silken flesh under her fingers. Her nipples were still swollen after all the attention which had been paid to them the night before and she touched them too, then shivered as a frisson of sensation shot downwards to her groin.

She came to a decision.

From now on while she was pretending to be Alexa, she was going to treat sex the way Alexa did and get as much out of it as she could.

Tim was in his office preparing for a two o'clock meeting with a couple of his clients when Martha phoned through from the outer office.

'Mrs Preece is here to see you. She doesn't have an appointment and you are due to see Derek Wilder and Jean Hale from Senso in five minutes.'

Martha's tone was frosty in the extreme – she didn't like Sherry, who tended to treat her like the hired help. He knew there was nothing Martha would have liked better than to turn Sherry away saying he was too busy to see her.

'Send her in,' he said, wondering what his ex-wife wanted this time. There had to be something, she never just dropped by for the pleasure of seeing him.

Sherry undulated in through the door a few moments later. It spoke volumes that Martha didn't actually show her in but instead let her come in alone.

She was wearing a black leather trench coat tightly belted at the waist. The supple, shiny leather accentuated the thrust of her marvellous breasts and the seductive curve of her hips. Her dark hair fell around her shoulders in a soft cloud and her pouting lips were painted a vivid scarlet which matched her nail polish.

Tim groaned internally as his dick greeted her appearance in its customary manner.

'Hi, honey,' he said cautiously. 'What can I do for you?'

Her pout intensified at this rather unenthusiastic greeting.

'What – not, "Hello, Sherry, it's lovely to see you, I'm so glad you stopped by." Aren't you pleased to see me?'

'Sure, but I have a meeting in five minutes and I still have a couple of documents to run over.'

Sherry turned away, giving him the full benefit of her luscious back view. He noticed for the first time that she was wearing a pair of spike-heeled boots and that her black stockings were the old-fashioned type with seams down the back. She moved over to the door and locked it before turning to face him again.

'Sherry, honey, can this wait? I really need to ...'

Tim's voice trailed off as her hands went to her belt

and untied it, then she threw open the leather mac with a lascivious smile on her face.

Underneath she was wearing a tight black basque which barely contained her gorgeous, magnolia-skinned breasts. They spilled appealingly over the top above the tight lacing, tantalising him with their enticing fullness.

Her sheer seamed stockings were held up by black ribbon suspenders attached to the bottom of the basque, and the ripe fruit of her sex was hidden beneath a tiny pair of matching black panties.

Tim gulped audibly, all thoughts of his imminent meeting suddenly gone. His dick was straining against his trousers and he could feel the blood pounding uncontrollably through his veins as she let the mac drop to the floor and walked towards him.

With feline grace Sherry slid onto his desk and propped herself up on one elbow.

'Why don't you take my panties off, sugar?' she invited him in her husky Scarlett O' Hara drawl, running the tip of her pink tongue over her red lips.

Like a man in a trance Tim reached out and drew them down over her hips, then closed his eyes fleetingly as her shaven mound came into view and his dick threatened to spontaneously combust.

'Fuck me,' she invited him succinctly, laying back on the desk.

The phone went at that moment.

Tim couldn't tear his eyes from the moist promise of his ex-wife's succulent honeypot, but his hand reached out automatically to pick up the phone.

'Derek Wilder and Jean Hale are here for your two o'clock meeting,' Martha informed him crisply.

'Yeah,' he said dazedly, watching Sherry open her legs slightly so he could just see the tip of her clitoris protruding from between her outer lips. 'Hold my calls,' he managed to say, before dropping the phone in its cradle and unzipping his jeans.

He pushed Sherry's legs wide apart, the knees bent, then thrust himself into her, sliding her halfway along the desk with the force of the movement.

He began to shaft her vigorously, at the same time tearing at the laces of the constricting basque to release her full, ripe breasts. They tumbled free and he clasped his left hand over one and his mouth over the other as he continued to thrust away.

Tim tried to slow down and take his time, aware that he was going at it like a man possessed, but the sight of her writhing around beneath him with her breasts exposed was too much for him.

She wrapped her long legs around his waist, pulling him deeper into her and urging him on to greater efforts.

He didn't need much urging.

A few seconds later he ejaculated forcibly into her, pushing her so far along the desk that her head and shoulders hung off the end and he had to grab her by the waist and pull her back.

Tim lay on top of her breathing heavily, his jeans and briefs around his ankles. Sherry laughed softly beneath him and reached up to stroke his face. 'Now tell me you're not glad to see me,' she said huskily.

'I didn't say I wasn't,' he replied hoarsely. He eased his weight from her and stood up, reaching down to pull his jeans back up, then helped her down from the desk.

She wiped herself coolly on a handful of tissues and threw them into the wastepaper bin, then pulled her panties back on. Tim crossed the room to open a window, well aware that the room reeked of sex.

'By the way,' she said casually, tucking her gorgeous breasts out of sight and fastening up her basque, 'I stopped by to see if you'd take me to the awards dinner tomorrow.'

Here it was – the inevitable price.

Of all the things Tim had hated about being married to Sherry, escorting her to endless show business dinners had been high on the list.

He loathed it all. Having to dress up in a dinner jacket, make small talk with a lot of egotistical people he had nothing in common with and listen to a lot of boring speeches.

Worst of all was feeling as if he were one of Sherry's accessories – like the right dress and shoes. He could only assume that one of her current boyfriends must have let her down that she was asking him.

Reluctant though he was he found himself saying, 'Sure, Sherry honey – what time do you want me to pick you up?'

She pulled her leather mac on and tied the belt tightly around her narrow waist.

'Around seven. Oh and Tim, hire a limo for the evening, will you? And get a new dinner jacket – that old one's had it.'

With a gay little wave of her scarlet-nailed hand she left the room, leaving Tim to try to pull himself together for his delayed meeting.

Jess hummed to herself as she soaked in a deep bubble bath, her red-gold hair piled up on the top of her head.

One of Alexa's men friends had phoned to invite her round to his house for a meal and she was very much looking forward to it. Alexa's notebook said:

> Denson Blake, forty-five, head of a communi-
> cations consortium. Perfect gentleman,
> beautifully mannered – likes his women to
> dress up. Filthy rich, has a great chef who
> serves sumptuous, fattening meals.

Denson had phoned her yesterday and when she'd accepted his invitation had told her his driver would pick her up at seven forty-five. This afternoon a large bouquet of flowers had arrived from him.

She'd studied his photo and liked what she saw, a distinguished middle-aged man with light blue eyes, thick dark eyebrows and brown hair greying slightly at the temples.

She went through Alexa's wardrobe looking for something particularly smart to wear since he liked women to dress up. She eventually settled on a low cut emerald-green evening dress with a tight skirt split almost to the hip on one side.

Underneath she wore a set of Alexa's black silk underwear, with black stockings and black suede high-heeled shoes. As she waited for the car to arrive for her she did a little pirouette in front of the mirror.

She knew she looked pretty good in her borrowed clothes – she just hoped Denson Blake thought so too.

He lived in an imposing house in Belsize Park and came down the steps to greet her himself as his driver opened the car door for her.

'Alexa – you look stunning.' He kissed her hand with courtly grace then led her up the steps into the house. The drawing room bore all the hallmarks of an expensive interior designer's services and the walls were hung with what she suspected to be original impressionist paintings.

He poured her a glass of champagne without asking her what she'd like to drink. Alexa obviously expected her wishes to be anticipated by her male friends.

The dinner was superb and Jess thoroughly enjoyed herself. Denson was urbane and charming, paying her several compliments and solicitously plying her with food and drink.

There was an awkward moment after dinner when she decided she needed to visit the bathroom. Alexa would know where the bathroom was – she didn't.

There was probably a cloakroom downstairs, but she could hardly go around opening doors until she found one. She was just hesitating, wondering how best to handle the situation, when Denson said, 'I expect you'd like to tidy your hair?'

When she nodded bemusedly he took her hand and led her from the room and upstairs. Jess was baffled but followed him obediently. Had he read her mind? Or was he about to take her to bed and this was just a way of getting her into a bedroom?

He threw open a door at the top of the stairs saying, 'You'll find everything you need as usual. Come down when you're ready.'

She found herself in an opulently appointed bedroom with an en-suite bathroom opening off it. Somewhat to her surprise she saw there was a schoolgirl's uniform laid out on the bed. Was this his daughter's bedroom? It didn't look as if anyone used it regularly. There were no books, teddies or other teenage paraphernalia.

Approaching the bed she saw that the uniform consisted of a plain white shirt, a navy blue striped tie, a short pleated navy blue skirt, a matching blazer and a panama hat.

The wardrobe door was ajar and she pulled it open curiously. Her jaw dropped when she saw what was inside.

A dozen different costumes hung there including a nurse's uniform, a riding kit, a maid's outfit and a policewoman's uniform.

Jess could feel her head spinning and wondered if she'd had too much champagne.

What on earth was going on?

Belatedly it dawned on her.

Each of these costumes represented a different male fantasy.

That's what Alexa had meant when she said he liked his women to dress up.

Jess found that her legs were wobbly and she sat down suddenly on the bed. Why hadn't Alexa made it clearer what she meant? Was Denson sitting downstairs waiting for her to appear dressed as a schoolgirl?

Presumably he was.

She tottered into the bathroom and used it, her head spinning. Could she go through with this? Or should she just slip silently downstairs and leave? But that wouldn't be very fair to Alexa who must enjoy this sort of thing or she wouldn't do it.

Jess was beginning to suspect that Alexa's sex life encompassed things she herself had never even heard of and certainly never experienced.

Without making a conscious decision she found herself removing the emerald-green evening dress and pulling on the school uniform. As a finishing touch she tied her hair up in two bunches with ribbons she found on the dressing table.

She stared at her strange reflection in the mirror. She looked like one of the sixth formers at St Trinian's. The skirt was so short that her stocking tops and suspenders were clearly visible and she was sure that anyone looking would be able to catch glimpses of her frilly black knickers.

She walked slowly downstairs hoping she wouldn't bump into any of the staff. Dinner had been served by a housekeeper, but other than the driver she hadn't seen anyone else.

Denson was waiting in the drawing room and rose to his feet as she entered the room.

'More champagne, Alexa?'

Jess nodded shyly, then let him lead her over to the sofa and pull her onto his knee.

She sat there while he held the glass to her mouth, letting her take a sip at a time. His other arm was around her hip, the hand lying lightly on her thigh over the soft bare skin between her stocking top and the frilly black panties.

He tipped the glass he held to her lips too far and some of the foaming liquid spilt onto her tight white shirt. Placing the glass on the coffee table he loosened her tie then removed it before unbuttoning her blouse, saying, 'Don't worry – I'll get it.'

He leant forward and plunged his tongue between her breasts, licking at the damp patch on her cleavage. She wriggled on his lap then gasped as he picked up the glass and splashed some of the icy wine over the creamy mounds of flesh emerging from the black silk bra.

He began to lick and suck his way over the area, his tongue warm in contrast to the chilled champagne. It felt strange but very pleasant and Jess felt a tremor of erotic anticipation as he undid the clasp of her front-fastening bra.

She gasped again when he fitted the champagne glass as far as it would go over one of her perfect breasts and began to swill the sparkling wine around. It washed over her nipple, making the point harden and bringing the pale skin surrounding her aureola out in tiny goose bumps.

The glass was pressed against her firmly enough to make a seal, so none of the liquid was lost. When he withdrew it there was a faint mark where the rim had been and the circle of skin within it felt cold.

He bent his head and took the stiffened nipple in his mouth, sucking and tugging at it erotically with his lips. His tongue felt hot as it teased its way around the rosy pink peak of sensitive flesh.

Jess felt several threads of warm, expectant

pleasure snaking down towards her groin and her stomach gave an involuntary lurch. When the whole of her breast was warm and tingling he fitted the wine glass over the end of its twin and repeated the procedure.

It seemed like a very erotic and shameless way to behave – sitting on a strange man's lap letting him splash her breasts with champagne then lick and suck it off.

It was certainly a first for Jess. She couldn't imagine Ralph ever doing such a thing.

She felt the hand on her thigh sliding upwards, then it vanished beneath her short pleated skirt and he began to caress her bush through the slippery silk. His fingertips circled over the whole of her fluff-covered mound, detoured to stroke her hips, then vanished down the back of her frilly black knickers to explore the cleft between her buttocks.

Jess could feel how hard he was beneath her and shifted position so his erection was directly underneath her sex. As if of its own volition her backside commenced a slow circular movement, stimulating them both at the same time.

His hand ceased its exploration down the back of her knickers and slipped round to the front. She held her breath as he delved under the black silk and his probing fingers found her clit.

She whimpered with pleasure as he stroked the soft protruding flesh, then opened her legs wider so it was easier for him to reach. Two fingers slipped inside her while he continued to stimulate her clit. She bore down on him, gasping faintly as he moved in and out, then she let out a muted shriek as a convulsive wave of heat washed over her and she came.

A few seconds later she found herself flat on her back on the sofa with her legs over his shoulders as he plunged into her. Her skirt flipped up over her face and she felt as if she were choking in its serge folds, until she managed to grab the hem and pull it down.

He plunged in and out of her for a long time, setting a steady pace while Jess felt herself fast approaching another climax. She sensed he was holding back to let her finish first and moved her hips upwards to meet the next three thrusts.

He exploded into her with an inarticulate groan just as she was overtaken by another orgasm even more powerful and long lasting than the first.

Marrakech was hot, dusty and malodorous and it was a great relief to Alexa when she arrived at her air-conditioned hotel after a tiring journey.

The nearest she'd been able to get to establishing Will Harper's whereabouts was that he was in Marrakech. She'd have been happier if she'd been able to get an address from Todd, but if he had one he wasn't admitting to it.

Alexa had tracked down people in the past with as little information, but she knew it would make her task more difficult.

In the evening, after consulting the English-speaking desk clerk, she ventured out to a nightclub much frequented by expatriates.

Heads turned when she was led to a table in the smoke-filled, dimly lit room. She appeared to be the only unescorted woman in the place but it didn't bother her. Coolly she ordered a bottle of champagne then sat back to look around at leisure.

The club had a wide expanse of marble floor and its high ceiling was supported by a series of stone pillars. The walls were hung with faded crimson velvet curtains, lavishly embellished with gold tassels.

Each table had its own red-shaded lamp and a matching plastic flower in a vase. A small stage at one end of the room was currently unoccupied, but off to the side a pianist played a selection of melodies from another era.

The overall atmosphere was one of subdued, affluent decadence and Alexa detected a faint but unmistakable whiff of hashish beneath the stronger mingled smells of cigarettes and cigars.

Casually, she studied the other occupants of the room as well as she could in the dim light. There were a few couples dancing on a tiny dance floor in front of the stage, holding each other closely and barely moving from the spot they occupied.

Men outnumbered women by about two to one and Alexa guessed that many of the women present were paid escorts working in the upper echelons of prostitution.

She could feel about a dozen pairs of eyes boring into her and knew it wouldn't be long before someone approached her.

She was right.

A slim, dark-haired man with a silky moustache strolled nonchalantly over and bowed from the waist. In faintly accented English he asked her, 'May I buy you a drink?'

Alexa waved a casual hand in the direction of the bottle of champagne cooling in its ice bucket. He studied it with disdain then said dismissively, 'House champagne is not good enough for a woman of your beauty. Waiter!'

He ordered a bottle of Moet & Chandon then stood poised with one hand on the back of a chair.

'May I?' he asked.

She nodded and he joined her at the small table.

'Allow me to introduce myself. I'm Philippe Dinon.'

'Alexa Carlisle.' He took her hand and kissed it lingeringly.

'You haven't been here before – I would have noticed you,' he told her. 'Are you on holiday?'

'Not really. I'm just travelling around. And you?'

'I live in Marrakech – at least at the moment.'

He took out a packet of Gauloises and after offering one to her, lit it and regarded her inscrutably through a wreath of blue smoke.

'And do your travels have any particular purpose?' he asked her.

'Looking up old friends.'

'And making new ones?'

'That too.'

His dark eyes roamed over her body. He was obviously mentally undressing her and not troubling to hide it.

'My beautiful Alexa, you were made to be made love to,' he observed at last.

Alexa raised her eyebrows sceptically at the corniness of the line. He seized her hand and lifted it to his lips again, planting several hot kisses on the back, then on the palm. 'Will you accord me that privilege?' he asked. 'Will you allow me to make love to you?'

Alexa glanced around the crowded room.

'Here?' she enquired sweetly. 'Isn't it a bit public?'

He nipped at the soft flesh on the palm of her hand with his white teeth.

'Not here,' he admonished her playfully, 'but in your hotel room. I will show you pleasures you have never experienced before.'

Alexa doubted it – still, it might be interesting to try.

Chapter Nine

Tim and Beth continued to take it in turns keeping Jenny Bolton under surveillance. It was almost a labour of love for Tim, who couldn't see her without remembering the steamy scenario in room 314 and getting hot under the waistband all over again.

Unfortunately he was dealing with too many cases to follow her all the time, so he split the shift with Beth, who was under strict instructions to contact him immediately if Jenny went back to the Knightsbridge hotel.

Tim was still kicking himself for getting so immersed in watching the two women make love that he hadn't taken any photos. He could only hope he'd get another opportunity.

He was kicking himself for another reason too – letting Sherry manoeuvre him into taking her to the awards dinner.

He'd known from the moment Martha announced her presence in the outer office that she wanted something – she always wanted something.

If she'd just phoned him up and asked him to escort her, he'd have been quick enough off the mark to invent a good reason why he couldn't. But by turning up unexpectedly and letting him screw her, she'd thrown him off guard and then taken advantage of him.

Would he never learn? Sherry had his measure so well that she could manipulate him at will.

He brooded about it on his way to pick her up. The limousine cost so much that he'd baulked at the expense of buying a new dinner jacket and hired one instead. He'd only kept the old one because he occasionally had to wear it when he was working – he hated dressing up.

The agency was snowed under with work, but it didn't seem possible to get the money in quickly enough to stay in the black in a business so heavy on expenses.

He was dealing with so many cases himself that he was permanently dog tired, but there was never time to find new staff and train them up.

Beth was the latest recruit and she'd been with the agency for eighteen months. Jess was doing great on the computer but she was only covering for Alexa for a few weeks. That being the case there was no point in wasting his time training her, so he couldn't send her out on field work.

And he was worried about Alexa. North Africa was no place for a woman on her own, even one as competent as her. She hadn't phoned in today at the usual time and although there could be any number of reasons for that, he couldn't help but worry. He'd phone the office later and play back the messages on the answering machine.

First, he had to endure the boredom of some Brit awards dinner, instead of doing what he should be doing and working. He must have a spine of pure jello to allow Sherry to do this to him.

Tim yawned as the limo pulled up outside the house in Fulham. Telling the driver to wait, he climbed out and pressed the bell. It must have been a full two minutes before she opened the door – Sherry didn't hurry for anyone.

She was wearing a gorgeous, and obviously expensive, evening dress in a smoky steel blue which matched her eyes. It was also slightly too tight.

'My zip's stuck – can you free it?' she demanded by way of greeting. She turned her back on him and Tim bent down to be immediately enveloped in a cloud of her seductive perfume. The skin of her bare back was warm and smooth beneath his fingers as he struggled with the recalcitrant zipper.

She was patently not wearing anything under the dress – or at least not above the waist. Below the waist she might be wearing a suspender belt or ...

'Hurry up,' she urged him impatiently, 'we're going to be late.'

He managed to free it at last and fastened it for her, his hands lingering on her back when he'd done so. He just about fought an urge to slip them round to the front and cup her breasts, then pull her back against him so she could feel the size of his hard-on.

Sherry picked up her bag and after one last glance in the mirror was ready to go. She spent the journey fussing with her hair and applying more lipstick, leaving Tim to his own thoughts.

Once at the dinner, it didn't take him long to size up the situation. Among the other people sharing their table was the producer of a soap in which Sherry had recently had a small part. He was with his wife – a dumpy, pie-faced woman whose glassy-eyed demeanour indicated she'd already made considerable inroads into the wine.

It was soon evident that there was something going on between the producer and Sherry – a fact which was also apparently obvious to the producer's wife.

Resigned to the inevitable, Tim ordered a double scotch and sat back to mull over one of his cases and hope that if he drank enough whisky, the evening might pass in a bearable haze.

He'd reckoned without the producer's wife.

He could just about stand to sit there and watch Sherry and her latest boyfriend put on a show of being barely acquainted, when they'd probably only got out of bed a couple of hours before. But what he hadn't bargained for was the wronged wife deciding to give her straying husband a taste of his own medicine.

She began a drunkenly flirtatious conversation with Tim which lasted all through dinner. Feeling sorry for her he struggled gamely to respond, but as she got drunker and drunker she became more and more embarrassingly amorous until beads of perspiration started to stand out on his brow.

Unfortunately, the one person she wanted to notice – her husband – was too busy staring down the front of Sherry's dress to pay any attention. Everyone else at the table was watching them and Tim got the definite impression that they were all blaming him for the situation.

There was a respite during the awards – for once in his life Tim wished the interminable speeches would go on even longer than they did – then the dancing began.

Sherry and the producer vanished onto the dance floor, along with most of the people from their table. Tim looked desperately around to see if there was any hope of rescue from his predicament, but there was none.

By this time his companion was hanging onto his sleeve and saying in a loud slurred voice, 'He thinks I don't know whash goin' on but I do. And do you know wha'? Well, I'm going to tell you. Your dirty little bitch of a wife is having an affair with my husband. Wha' d'you think of that?'

Tim thought that he wished he was any place on the planet other than where he actually was.

It got worse.

'I want to dansh. Dansh with me,' she exhorted him, stumbling to her feet and knocking over her chair in the process. She grabbed him by the arm and tried to haul him to his feet. Tim looked frantically over to the dance floor where Sherry and the producer were dancing so close together that they might have been Siamese twins.

There was obviously going to be no help forth-coming from them. His drunken companion meanwhile was still trying to force him to his feet by dragging determinedly at his arm.

He considered simply bolting, getting a taxi home and leaving Sherry the limo, but reluctantly rejected the idea.

Heads all over the room were turning in his direction as the woman's voice rose to an ear-splitting pitch.

'Dansh with me! I want to dansh!'

Tim ran a hand through his crisp fair hair, then seeing no alternative rose gloomily to his feet and allowed her to lead him onto the dance floor. She clung around his neck, rubbing her pelvis against his in what was clearly a desperate attempt to excite his interest.

He attempted to steer her around the floor in a grotesque parody of a recognisable dance, while she stumbled and staggered in his arms. He soon gave up the attempt and instead settled for keeping to the same spot and swaying to a rhythm dictated more by her drunken lurching than any tempo set by the band.

Thankfully, after two dances she wanted another drink and insisted they return to the table. She downed another glass of wine, then launched into a monologue about her husband's shortcomings.

Tim glanced furtively at his watch – would the evening never end?

They were alone at their table. Tim noticed that their fellow diners were either dancing or had moved to sit at other tables. He didn't blame them. He became aware that she was staring at him owlishly, and realised she'd just asked him something.

'Sorry – what was that?' he asked, glancing around to see if he could spot a waiter.

'I said, would you like to have shex with me?' she repeated.

A waiter materialised at that moment giving Tim the opportunity to order another double scotch. When he turned back his inebriated companion was just vanishing under the tablecloth. Tim assumed she'd dropped her bag or an earring and hoped rather ungallantly that she'd pass out under there.

He was completely unprepared to feel a hand groping at his crotch, then his zip being undone. Before he could react, his recumbent dick was unearthed from his briefs and he felt a wet mouth close over it.

For the first time in his life Tim wasn't delighted to feel a pair of female lips close over his member. His dick, unfortunately, wasn't quite as discriminating and was already exhibiting a tentative interest in the proceedings.

The producer's wife continued with her enthusiastic, if inexpert, attentions while Tim tried miserably to pretend this wasn't happening. She sucked away determinedly as he drank his scotch, glancing huntedly around to see if anyone had noticed.

In the heady few seconds before ejaculation becomes inevitable, the mouth was suddenly withdrawn and he felt a heavy body slump across his feet. Peering cautiously under the tablecloth he saw that his earlier wish had indeed been granted – the producer's wife had passed out and was now snoring gently.

130

He could only wish she'd had the consideration to stay conscious for another few seconds.

His dick strained frantically upwards, quivering like a water diviner's rod as it searched for somewhere warm and wet to bury itself. In its current tumescent state he had some difficulty in stuffing it furtively back into his trousers without anyone noticing.

At that moment Sherry and the producer returned to the table. The producer glanced at his watch.

'Have you seen my wife?' he asked Tim. 'We need to get back – the babysitter's only booked till midnight.'

'Try under the table,' suggested Tim sourly. 'Are you ready to go, Sherry? Because if you're not I'll get myself a taxi and leave you the limo.'

The producer lifted the tablecloth at that moment, revealing the somnolent figure of his comatose wife.

Sherry took one look, giggled and slipped her hand under Tim's arm. 'I'm ready to go if you are.'

He steered her hastily towards the door before the producer could ask for their help in getting his wife upright and out of there.

'Did you see that?' asked Sherry, giggling again. 'She'd passed out under the table. Were you plying her with drink in the hope of humping her?'

Tim wasn't in the mood for his ex-wife's witticisms.

'She didn't need any plying,' he growled. 'She was drinking to blot out the sight of you winding yourself around her husband. Is he fucking you? I hope you get more than a walk-on part this time, or you'll have sold yourself too cheap.'

They reached their limousine and Tim held open the door for her while she climbed elegantly in.

'Jealous?' she enquired sweetly.

Tim didn't reply. He stared moodily out of the window until they reached Fulham, then when the car pulled up outside Sherry's door he said to the driver, 'Just hang on, will you? I'll only be a minute.'

He waited until she'd unlocked the door then said, 'I need to use your phone.'

'Would you like a nightcap?' she asked as he dialled the office number. He glanced at her. She was leaning sinuously against the newel post, her arms behind her back, her luscious bosom pushed forwards.

'No thanks,' he said shortly.

He activated the playback mechanism on the office answering machine and listened to the various messages. Alexa had called in so that was one less thing to worry about. Thankfully there was nothing which needed dealing with tonight.

Sherry looked put out by his terse rejection of her invitation. Too damn bad – he'd had more than enough of her games for the moment.

'Good night,' he said abruptly, turning towards the door.

'Tim . . .'

'What?'

'Will you just unzip my dress before you go? It might get stuck again.'

She moved seductively towards him and turned her back. He yanked impatiently at her zip, getting another heady whiff of her exotic perfume. It slid smoothly down exposing her naked back to where the cleft of her buttocks began. The dress fell to the floor with a faint rustle, leaving her standing there naked except for a wisp of a steel-grey suspender belt and a pair of sheer black stockings.

'Damn it, Sherry – don't you ever wear panties?' he demanded, transfixed by the sight of the pale globes of her ass, each one beautifully bisected by one of the back suspenders.

She turned slowly round so he could see her knock-out breasts, each of which he knew from experience would fit nicely into the palm of his hand.

She stood with her hands on her hips, smiling at him provocatively. His gaze dropped to her shaven mound. He could smell the musky scent of her sex beneath the perfume she wore and knew she was in a state of arousal.

Tim glanced undecidedly towards the door, willing himself to have the strength to leave.

'What's the matter, sugar?' she asked softly, 'don't you want to screw me?'

Hips swaying, she walked over to the stairs with feline grace and sat down, her knees bent and her feet in their high-heeled shoes wide apart. He could see the moist folds of her pussy glistening invitingly and swallowed hard.

She stretched out a hand and reached delicately between her legs.

'No?' she enquired silkily.

With a groan Tim unzipped his trousers and strode over to her. Yanking her to her feet he led her into the sitting room and pushed her so she was half lying, half bent forwards over the back of the sofa.

He slipped his hand between her legs and felt how wet she was. She squirmed with excitement, raising one long leg to lay along the back of the sofa, the other still on the floor. He stood over her, feeling the waves of heat breaking over him at the sight of her widely parted legs and the slippery juices dripping from her dark pink sex.

He slid two fingers inside her and she moved so she was astride the back of the sofa, gripping it tightly between her knees, but bent well forward. She writhed against his hand, bearing down on it and jamming it further into her.

With his other hand he stroked her ivory-skinned

backside, running his fingers along the darker shadow of her cleft, circling the puckered pink bud of her anus. He could see that she was grinding her clit against the sofa, making little mewing noises as she did so.

He bent over her and entered her from behind, thrusting his iron-hard dick all the way in. He plunged in and out of her in the grip of the sheer animal lust she always managed to arouse in him, his hand moving under her to cup her shaven mound and touch her clit.

She panted and writhed beneath him, coming twice in the short space of time it took Tim to reach his own urgent climax.

He lay along the back of the sofa, half on top of her and half behind her, his breathing laboured. Within a minute he felt her thrusting her mound against his hand again, demanding more attention.

She was insatiable.

He stimulated her again, taking an almost savage delight in making her moan with pleasure. When she shuddered into another long-drawn-out climax, her internal muscles rippled over his cock, still held tightly inside her, and amazingly he felt himself grow hard again.

Withdrawing from her he lay down on the sofa and pulled her down to sit on top of him. She raised herself, positioned his member at the entrance to her honeypot, then sat smoothly down. Tim inhaled sharply as he glided into the overflowing, velvet-lined core of her sexuality and she began to move above him.

This time it took much longer with Sherry controlling his movements, squeezing him between her thighs if he showed an inclination to hurry.

He fondled her magnificent breasts with both hands, enjoying their weight and toying with the prominent nipples as she satisfied herself one more time.

At last, he reached the crescendo of another lengthy orgasm and cried out as he pumped the last remnants of his sperm into her, helped by the soft pressure of her fingers as she stroked his trembling balls.

The doorbell went at that moment.

Tim had completely forgotten that the limousine he'd hired was still waiting outside.

Jess had lunch with Daniel Moult, the head of the insurance company whose case she was working on.

She was very nervous, although Tim had coached her carefully in advance. A glance in the mirror went some way towards reassuring her. With every day that passed she seemed to fit more comfortably in Alexa's skin.

Who would have thought it would be so exciting to dress up as a schoolgirl, then have her breasts splashed with champagne? She felt a warm tingling between her legs whenever she thought about it. She couldn't wait for her next date with one of Alexa's men friends.

Alexa had phoned her a couple of times and she'd told her about her evenings with Bob Beswick and Denson Blake. Alexa had laughed out loud when Jess related how she'd dressed in a particularly stunning evening dress for her dinner with Denson, thinking that was what Alexa had meant by her note about dressing up.

Daniel Moult was pleasant and avuncular and Jess felt she acquitted herself reasonably well in her account of her investigation of the insurance fraud to date.

He was obviously a worried man.

'One of the senior management team must be in on it,' he said gloomily. 'I just wish we could find out who it is.'

'Something's bound to come up,' Jess reassured him. 'I'll just keep on digging until I find it.'

'Meanwhile the company's losing vast sums of money,' he pointed out. 'We're holding off paying out wherever we can, but that's not good for our reputation. Maybe you ought to be working on it from within the company.'

'What do you mean?' asked Jess in alarm.

'What we discussed before. That you should pretend to be a new employee and keep your eyes and ears open until you find out who's involved in this.'

Jess took a nervous gulp of her drink. Alexa might be able to carry off such a deception, but Jess knew quite well that she herself couldn't.

'It's probably a little soon to think about that,' she said. 'Let me carry on digging for a while and hold that plan in reserve.'

'You're the investigator, but I hope you come up with something soon – this is keeping me awake at nights.'

Jess returned to the office to find Tim frantically trying to decide who to send out on a surveillance job. Two partners in an antiques import-export business who were supposed to be spending the day closeted with their accountant had changed their plans at the last minute.

Their informant, a temporary secretary often planted by the agency within companies under investigation, had just phoned in to say that one partner was going to have lunch in the city and the other was driving to an auction in Surrey.

Tim had already despatched Adam to follow the first partner but no one else was available to follow the second. This situation seemed to be arising with increasing frequency – he was going to have to force himself to make time to recruit and train some more staff.

'I can't go because I've got a meeting in half an hour,' he told Jess, 'and there isn't anyone else.'

'Could I go?' offered Jess helpfully.

'You'd lose him in ten minutes,' returned Tim absently.

'I might, but then again I might not,' she argued. 'What do I have to do other than follow him?'

'See what he does, where he goes and who he talks to. Take photos of anyone he has contact with and if possible get the number of the car they're driving. Make a note of anywhere he stops off and anything else he does, whether it seems significant or not.'

'If there isn't anyone else to go, surely it's better for me to give it a shot than nothing?' suggested Jess.

He looked at her blankly, then jumped to his feet saying tersely, 'Come on.'

He grabbed a set of car keys from Martha and led her outside to where one of the agency cars, an unobtrusive Ford Escort, was parked. Throwing her the keys he swung his tall body into the passenger seat saying, 'First right, then first left.'

On the way there he gave her rapid instructions about the most effective methods of tailing both cars and people. Jess found it hard to take it all in, particularly as she was having to concentrate on the heavy traffic.

They eventually pulled up near a discreetly elegant antiques shop.

'I'll point him out as soon as he emerges – he's called Paul Sears, incidentally. After that you're on your own,' he told her. 'I'll get a taxi back to the office. Phone in every hour or so if you can . . .'

137

He suddenly smote his forehead with the palm of his hand. 'Shit. I forgot to give you a phone – or a camera, for that matter. What the hell – you'll probably lose him anyway. If you don't and you're near a phone, call in. If you do lose him just come on back to the office.'

He turned to look at her, his hazel eyes touched by concern.

'Are you sure about this, Jess? Working on the computer's one thing, being out in the field is another altogether.'

'I'll be fine, don't worry. As you say, I probably won't be able to follow him for long, but if I can't there's nothing lost.'

A man came out of the antiques shop at that moment and paused long enough to don a pair of sunglasses. He had blond hair worn brushed back and a long face dominated by a strong jaw. He was casually dressed in a light-coloured linen jacket, a T-shirt and a pair of khaki cotton trousers.

'That's him,' said Tim briefly. 'Good luck.'

He swung out of the car, then bent down to say, 'Cover your hair if you can. It's just so damn noticeable.'

He vanished into the crowds of shoppers milling along the street. Jess rummaged in her bag. She knew she didn't have a scarf with her but she did have a piece of ribbon – tying her hair back was the best she could do.

Tim's instructions about tailing cars went straight out of her head. The traffic was so heavy that she considered it a major achievement just to keep him in sight, and if that meant that sometimes she was directly behind him it was too bad.

It was a warm, sunny afternoon and Jess was in high spirits. Who would have thought a month ago when she was dreading the prospect of the summer

stretching endlessly ahead, that she'd be having such
an exciting time?

She woke up every morning with a sense of pleasant
anticipation. She enjoyed being in the agency working
with Alexa's colleagues, it made such a contrast to
being a college lecturer which was her only other
work experience. She also enjoyed being in London –
shopping, visiting exhibitions and generally exploring.
Now here she was tailing someone to an antiques
auction. It was all very exciting.

The traffic thinned out a little as they left London
and Jess tried to keep a couple of cars behind Paul
Sears. Happily he was driving an E-type Jaguar in
British racing green, so he was fairly conspicuous.

Eventually he turned off the main road onto a winding country lane and Jess dropped back. There was
very little other traffic now and she didn't want him
to notice her.

The road twisted and turned until inevitably she
came to a junction and had no idea which way he'd
gone. She mentally flipped a coin and turned right.
After following the lane for about a mile it widened
and eventually joined up with a busy A road.

That was it – she'd lost him.

On the point of pulling into the road and joining
the traffic heading back to London, Jess suddenly did
a U-turn. If he'd turned left at the junction instead of
right and the antiques auction was anywhere near
there, she might still just catch him. She retraced her
route to the junction, keeping a look out for posters
advertising an antiques auction.

She was in luck.

She was driving past a small pub when she spotted
his car in the car park. Stamping on the brake she
reversed and turned in, then sat behind the wheel in
an agony of indecision.

Should she go into the pub and see if he was

meeting anyone? Or should she wait in the car and follow him when he emerged?

But it was only a very small car park and he'd probably notice her when he came out. Jess bit her lip anxiously. She was sure Alexa would know what to do, but she certainly didn't.

After a couple of minutes' hesitation she got out of the car and went nervously into the pub. There were two rooms and she chose one at random. He was in the other but she could see him across the bar, sitting in the corner and tucking into a late lunch.

There were only a few people in the pub at that time and he'd obviously come in to get something to eat rather than meet anyone. Jess ordered an orange juice then sat in a corner where she could keep an eye on the door. As long as they were both sitting down they couldn't see each other, but she'd be able to spot him as he left.

He wasn't long. Within ten minutes he was back in his car and roaring off down the quiet country lane. Fortunately the auction was only a couple of miles away and Jess was easily able to follow him there.

It was being held in a small stately home and there were crowds of people milling around, inspecting the various pieces and job lots which would go under the hammer later that afternoon. Jess congratulated herself on doing a good job as she followed Paul Sears unobtrusively.

She pretended to be interested in a rosewood table as he inspected a set of chairs further down the room, then followed him as he moved on into the dining room.

He worked his way slowly through the house, making notes in his catalogue and pausing occasionally to exchange words with other dealers. Upstairs, he toured the bedrooms while she lurked at the far end of the gallery, pretending to study a rather blood-thirsty oil painting of a battle.

When he suddenly headed off down a narrow passageway she followed him, half running along the gallery to keep up.

Hurrying round a corner in hot pursuit she was startled to find him waiting for her and, unable to stop in time, ran straight into him with considerable force.

She would have fallen if he hadn't grabbed her by the arm and held her upright.

'Sorry,' she gasped, trying to pull free.

The grip on her arm tightened. 'Who are you?' he asked, 'and why are you following me?'

Chapter Ten

Jess's immediate reaction was to turn tail and flee. She tried to pull away but he tightened his grip on her arm. In a complete panic she struggled with him and managed to wrench free, but before she could run away he grabbed her round the waist and dragged her back against him.

She thought about screaming for help, but the whole situation was too embarrassing for words. They struggled silently in the narrow corridor, but he was much stronger than she was and within a few seconds he had her pinned back against the wall.

How could she have allowed such a ridiculous situation to arise? Trying to run away had been a really stupid reflex reaction. Why hadn't she said she was looking for the toilets or something similar?

Now Paul Sears had her trapped against the wall in a deserted corridor and was staring down at her as she glared back up at him.

'Let go of me,' she demanded crossly.

'Not until you tell me why you're following me.'

Jess found herself speechless. Actually, come to think about it, she didn't really know why she was following him – all she knew was that agency had him under surveillance.

But she could hardly say, 'I'm pretending to be my sister at the moment and she works for an investigation agency, so I've been told to follow you but I haven't a clue why.'

Instead she found herself blurting out, 'Because I find you devastatingly attractive.'

He stared at her blankly, then stepped away from her, still keeping hold of her waist. She was wearing a primrose yellow linen dress with a V-neck and buttons down the front. It was a new purchase and she knew it suited her and showed off her figure to advantage.

He took a good look at her, taking in the curves of her breasts where they thrust against the tight-fitting material. Her top button had come undone in the struggle, revealing the deep valley between her breasts and the lacy edge of the beige silk camisole she was wearing underneath.

She was flushed and slightly dishevelled after their struggle and her red-gold hair had come loose from its ribbon and tumbled down around her shoulders.

He looked sceptical, amused and then interested all at the same time.

'Do you now?' he asked, loosening his grip on her. 'Then why did you act like you'd accidentally run into Jack the Ripper?'

'I was embarrassed,' she retorted, with more than a degree of truth. 'I didn't expect to bump into you like that. Will you let me go, please?'

He released her and she hastily did up her top button, then ran her hands over her untidy hair.

Actually, now she could see him close up she did find him very attractive. His blond hair was clean and silky and a lock of it had flopped forward over his forehead. His strong-jawed face wasn't particularly handsome, but he looked intelligent and as if he had a sense of humour.

'I noticed you in the pub,' he told her. 'How long have you been following me?'

'Since then,' she replied, praying he hadn't spotted her on his tail before that moment.

'Let me get this straight. A beautiful woman stops at a country pub for a drink, sees me across the bar and is so smitten that she followed me to an antiques auction and trails me around every room?'

Jess flushed. And she'd thought she was being unobtrusive.

'More or less,' she muttered.

'And what were you hoping to do?'

'Get into conversation with you.'

'Come on,' he said, taking her hand.

'Where are we going?' she asked as he led her down the corridor.

'Somewhere we can have the conversation you were hoping for,' he replied blandly.

Pulled along reluctantly behind him, Jess considered her options. She had to convince him that her story was true. She didn't know why he was under investigation, but she was pretty sure it would blow the whole thing sky high if he suspected she wasn't telling him the truth.

The main gallery was deserted and she guessed the auction had just started. He opened one of the doors then drew her into an opulent, faded bedroom.

It was magnificently, if sparsely, furnished. Against one wall there was a four-poster bed hung with ancient royal blue velvet curtains, flanked by a massive chest of drawers. The sun shone brightly in through the leaded windows, highlighting the dust, the peeling wallpaper and the threadbare carpet. Nevertheless it had obviously once been a beautiful, luxurious room.

Jess was alarmed when he locked the door behind them.

'Wh ... what are you doing?' she asked nervously.

'Making sure our conversation isn't interrupted.'

He strolled across the room and sat on the window seat, stretching out his long legs in front of him.

'Tell me about yourself,' he invited.

'What would you like to know?' she asked, cursing herself for having handled the situation so badly. Now she had to convince him that she genuinely fancied him.

She was still standing nervously by the door. Getting a grip on herself she crossed the room and tidied her hair in the spotted, cloudy old mirror hanging above the empty fireplace.

'What do you do?'

She could see in the mirror that his eyes were roaming over her body.

'I'm a college lecturer,' she said, turning to face him.

'You don't work for the Customs and Excise, then?'

'No I don't. Why do you ask?'

'Never mind. Do you live around here?'

Jess had a vague memory of reading in a detective novel that to convince someone you were telling the truth, you had to keep what you were saying as near to the truth as possible, so she said, 'No, Altrincham. I'm on holiday. I'm staying with my sister in London.'

She moved across the room towards him. Without taking his eyes off her face he reached out and pulled her to stand between his outstretched legs.

'Do you often go around picking up strange men?' he asked her.

'No, this is a first,' she replied honestly.

'That's very flattering. I wonder if it's true.'

With one hand he traced the curve of her hip over her yellow linen dress. She moved a little closer and felt him slide his hand behind her to smooth over the rounded contours of her backside.

It suddenly seemed hot in the room and Jess felt

a faint prickle of perspiration between her shoulder blades. He placed both hands on her hips, the thumbs stroking her hip bones, then slid them downwards to the hem of her dress.

His eyes never left her face as he stroked her bare thighs beneath her skirt. She felt a slow flush creeping over her body and knew that her throat and cheeks had turned pink. Slowly he undid her dress a button at a time until it hung open, revealing her beige silk camisole and camiknickers.

His eyes dropped from her face to take in the creamy tops of her breasts, then moved slowly downwards. Her mound was level with his face and only a few inches away, with just a flimsy layer of silk concealing it from his gaze.

Jess's pulse was racing and the sound of her own breathing seemed to fill the sunlit room. She guessed that their struggle a few minutes previously had aroused him and her assertion that she found him attractive had fanned the flames.

Glancing downwards she saw the unmistakable contour of an enormous erection beneath his cotton trousers.

She was pretty aroused herself. She could smell the scent of his light cologne and had enjoyed his touch when he had caressed her. The gleam of humour was still in his eyes, but not as strong as the glint of pure lust.

He placed his hands on her buttocks and pulled her forward, then delicately touched the thin strip of silk between her legs with the tip of his tongue.

Instantly she was on fire and any doubts she might have had about this vanished. She parted her legs for him and he probed at her gently with his tongue, then kissed and nibbled his way over her silk-covered mound.

Hooking his thumbs in the waistband of her cami-knickers he eased them down her thighs and steadied her while she stepped out of them. The fuzz of her red-gold bush was already damp at the edges where it covered the outer folds of her labia.

It was soon much damper as his tongue flickered and licked erotically between her legs. Jess closed her eyes and threw her head back as he worked her to a level of arousal where the rush of heat over her body was so intense, she thought she might explode.

She stood in front of him naked from the waist down, while he took his time about bringing her to a climax. At last it swept over her and she buried her hands in his silky blond hair as convulsive shudders of sheer erotic pleasure swept over her.

He stood up and efficiently stripped off his own clothes while she sat weakly on the edge of the four-poster bed. His erection was huge, the head of his cock a deep marbled purple, and she could already see a drop of liquid gathering on the swollen tip as he approached her.

They climbed onto the bed and sank down onto the faded brocade cover. Jess knelt beside him and grasped his shaft firmly before bending her head and taking it in her mouth. He freed her full breasts from the silk camisole and stroked them as she sucked away at his rock-hard cock.

He groaned when she swirled her tongue over the tip, then ran it along the underside of the ridge surrounding it. She slid as much of it into her mouth as she could, then eased it out slowly, sucking hard as she did so.

His hands left her breasts to cup her buttocks then he slid a finger inside her. She intensified the pressure of her mouth, pushing her backside against his hand as he slid the finger in and out of her well lubricated honeypot.

He pulled her down beside him on the bed and parted her legs. She felt the ecstatic sensation of him filling her up with his huge cock, then they began to move against each other in the hot, still afternoon.

Jess woke up feeling dazed and disoriented. She was hot, her mouth was dry and for a few moments she couldn't remember where she was. She was lying on her side with her knees drawn up under her chin and she realised that she'd been woken up by a feather-light touch on her private parts.

She lay with her eyes closed as it all came back to her. She was lying on the dusty coverlet of a four-poster bed with a man she was supposed to be trailing unobtrusively.

She must have dozed off as they collapsed in each other's arms after a bout of sex as protracted as it was erotic.

The touch between her legs was light enough to be almost frustrating. It brushed over the damp fronds of her pubic hair and grazed delicately over her clit, circling it and then dabbling in the creamy moisture surrounding it.

She made a little murmur of pleasure and heard him chuckle softly as he realised she was awake. The head of his cock nudged up against the soft folds of her pussy and she jammed her backside demandingly down to meet it. His cock forged swiftly inside her causing her to gasp as she felt herself penetrated with satisfying ease.

He moved in and out of her, slowly at first then faster as she wriggled her bottom hard against his groin. He played with her breasts with one hand and her clit with the other while she moaned aloud as her excitement mounted again.

She came in a gratifying welter of sensation, as his iron-hard shaft continued to plunge in and out of her.

149

It was a while before he came himself, but Jess enjoyed every moment of their hot, breathless coupling.

When at last they separated she asked, 'What time is it?'

He glanced at his watch.

'Five o'clock.' He looked at her wryly. 'Do you realise that I've completely missed the auction? My partner will kill me when I go back without a single one of the items I was meant to be bidding for. All I can say is that it was well worth it.'

Jess climbed reluctantly off the bed and began to dress.

'How long are you staying in London?' he asked her, reaching for his trousers.

'I'm not sure,' she replied vaguely.

'May I see you again? How about dinner tomorrow night?'

Jess wondered fleetingly what Tim would say if she told him she was having dinner with someone she was supposed to be keeping under unobtrusive surveillance. Or that she'd just spent the afternoon enjoying hot, sweaty sex with him on the dusty brocade cover of an antique four-poster bed.

Somehow she didn't think Tim would be very happy about it. But at least she must have convinced Paul Sears that she was following him because she fancied him and not for any other reason.

'Dinner would be lovely,' she said in reply to his question. 'But my sister may have made plans for us. May I call you?'

He took out a card, scribbled something on the back and handed it to her.

'I'll be at the shop most of tomorrow or you can reach me at home this evening – that's the number on the back.'

He took her in his arms and kissed her lengthily before saying, 'I've got to go. Call me soon.'

Jess found a bathroom and did her best to repair her appearance, but she still looked dishevelled. She was convinced that everyone she passed on her way out could tell what she'd just been doing.

The journey back into London in rush-hour traffic seemed interminable, but at least it gave her plenty of time to consider what she was going to say to Tim. She didn't want to go into the office in her current rumpled state so she drove directly to Alexa's flat and phoned from there.

'Jess – are you okay?' he asked when she got through.

'Yes, I'm fine thanks, Tim. Sorry I wasn't able to phone before.'

'What happened? How long did you manage to stay with him? I've been worried.'

'Till about five,' she said truthfully. 'Tim, I made a terrible mess of it. I managed to follow him all the way to the auction but he spotted me – he'd noticed me in a pub he stopped at on the way there.'

'Did he speak to you?'

'Yes. He asked me why I was following him.'

'What did you say?'

'I . . . I said it was because I found him devastatingly attractive,' wailed Jess. 'I know it was a stupid thing to say, but I just couldn't think of anything better.'

She was taken aback when Tim burst out laughing. She'd expected him to be angry with her and to tell her not to bother going into the agency again.

'How did he react to that? I'll bet you made his day.'

'We went for a cup of coffee, then for a walk,' Jess told him mendaciously. She didn't want to lie to Tim but she could hardly tell him what had really happened. 'He wants to see me again tomorrow evening.'

151

'What did you tell him about yourself?'

'That I'm a college lecturer, live in Altrincham and I'm staying with my sister for a few weeks.'

'Do you think he bought it?' asked Tim thoughtfully.

'I think so. Tim, why is he under investigation? He asked me if I worked for the Customs and Excise.'

'Did he, now? He and his partner import and export antiques, which involves a lot of hassle with the Customs and Excise about licences and so forth. The reason we're watching him is because his company is part of a group operating throughout Europe and North America.

'The French company was tipped off that he and his partner are passing off reproductions as the real thing. If that is the case, the reputation of all the affiliated companies will be in jeopardy, so the head of the group is retaining us to investigate.'

'What should I do?'

'Let me think about it. Will you be in tomorrow?'

'Yes, if you still want me to.'

'Sure I do. You're doing great work on the computer. Don't worry about today – I should never have let you follow him but you did real good for someone with no experience.'

'I'll see you tomorrow then, Tim.'

'Bye, honey.'

Alexa found Philippe an amusing and attentive companion. It didn't take her long to discover that he made his living from gambling. At the moment he was renting a plush apartment on the outskirts of the city, but she suspected that his standard of living fluctuated with his luck.

He set himself out to charm her, probably as much in the hope of getting his hands on some of her non-existent money as to get her into bed, Alexa thought cheerfully.

She allowed herself to be seduced with only enough of a show of reluctance to whet his appetite. He turned out to be an accomplished lover, with an ever ready hard-on and an a seemingly insatiable appetite for sex.

If she hadn't been on an assignment Alexa would probably have spent even longer in bed with him than she did. It was often with some reluctance that she got dressed. He was happy to accompany her around the city while she played at being a tourist, when in reality she was searching for Will Harper.

She knew if she went out enough she was certain to run into him. The expatriate European community tended to eat, drink and socialise in the same places.

It suited her to have Philippe as her escort. It meant she could move around the city relatively freely without being pestered by other men too much.

On her third day in the city she woke up in her hotel room to find Philippe straddling her, an impressive erection rearing up from between his thighs.

The grey light of dawn was filtering in through the gauzy curtains, indicating, as far as Alexa was concerned, that it was too early to wake up.

'Philippe, no – I'm too tired,' she said weakly.

They'd only fallen asleep about four hours previously. After visiting several nightclubs yesterday evening they'd returned to her hotel and enjoyed a protracted bout of sexual activity.

Alexa's limbs were still aching from some of the unusual positions Philippe had suggested and she wanted more sleep. But already the sight of his long, thick rod was stirring her.

'Poor *bébé*,' he murmured soothingly. 'Don't worry – I will do all the work.'

Alexa closed her eyes and felt his hands on her breasts. He petted and stroked them until her nipples were hard and swollen, then bent his head and sucked gently until she felt threads of pure carnal desire shooting down to her groin.

He caressed her hips and thighs lingeringly, grazing the palm of his hand over her flat belly and red-gold bush. Alexa was soon lost in an erotic trance, enjoying the dream-like quality of his lovemaking.

He parted her outer lips and slipped his finger between them, searching for the bud of her clit. When he found it he began to slide it lightly backwards and forwards between his finger and thumb. Alexa's whole body was suffused with languid pleasure as he worked her skilfully towards a climax.

It was almost like an erotic dream. Philippe became her phantom lover, as in the dim light of dawn he manipulated the hard little point of flesh. Her velvety tunnel ran with moisture which trickled slowly between her thighs and onto the starched, snowy sheet. She could feel it gathering and overflowing as she lay there.

His ramrod-hard shaft was poised at the entrance to her honeypot and when he felt the first shuddering wave of her orgasm he plunged it in. He felt her flesh pulsating around his cock, gripping it tightly as the waves washed over her and he began to move rapidly in and out.

Alexa's hips rose to meet each thrust as he screwed her tirelessly. It went on a long time and the hot morning sun was shining through the gauzy curtains, filling the room with hazy golden light, before Alexa at last fell into a deep sleep.

She awoke to the sound of the shower going and a few minutes later Philippe emerged from the bathroom with his dark hair damp and beads of moisture clinging to his chest hair.

'I regret I have to leave you for a time,' he told her. 'Business, you understand.'

Alexa knew that this meant he was planning to spend the afternoon at cards.

When he'd gone she showered, dressed and went out to get some lunch.

The restaurant she chose was off the Avenue Mohammed V. It was cool and shady with large overhead fans stirring the air to create the illusion of a breeze. Banks of lush plants around the walls and between the tables were welcome to the eye after the heat, glaring sunshine, and exhaust fumes in the street outside. The tables were covered in starched linen cloths in mint green and the walls were painted a toning shade of eau-de-nil.

After she'd been shown to her table, Alexa nodded to a couple of people Philippe had introduced her to.

The expatriate crowd had the sort of decadent lifestyle which appealed to a part of her. Some of them had chosen to live away from the country of their birth, some were no longer welcome there.

Usually they had too much time on their hands which they tended to fill by indulging themselves in pleasure of any kind – but particularly the pleasures of the flesh.

Alexa had been greeted with enthusiasm by everyone Philippe had introduced her to. A beautiful, independently wealthy woman was a more than welcome addition to their crowd. She'd already received several invitations to parties and judging by the expressions on the faces of the men, she would have received invitations of a different kind if Philippe hadn't been standing with his arm possessively around her.

She ordered vegetable couscous, a mixed salad and half a bottle of rough, Moroccan red wine. She sipped her wine contentedly as she waited for her food. Alexa loved travelling – as long as she could do it in comfort. She was enjoying her stay in North Africa. She loved the atmosphere in the Médina, the louche nightclubs and most of all the food.

They'd dined last night on an exotic lamb casserole, cooked for hours in red wine and served with an array of Mediterranean vegetables. Philippe was dismissive about Moroccan cuisine, saying it was much inferior to French, but Alexa loved it.

Philippe was also adding to her pleasure in her stay. He had proved to be a more than satisfactory lover – her languidly aching limbs were a testament to that. She knew she'd have to say goodbye to him as soon as she located Will, but for now she intended to enjoy him as much as possible.

Alexa lingered over her lunch, finishing off with two tiny cups of powerful black coffee. She was just lingering over the second, when a tall figure loomed up over her.

'Hello, Alexa. You're looking even more beautiful than I remember.'

'Hello, Will,' she returned calmly. 'How are you?'

Chapter Eleven

Jenny Bolton ate a light lunch of chicken salad, washed down by a glass of apple juice.

Tim, who never seemed to have time to eat proper meals and was hungry, ordered a sirloin steak and french fries. When he saw the meagre size of the steak and the small portion of fries, he wished he was back in the good old USA. He wished it even more when he bit into his first chunk of steak and found it stringy and tasteless.

What was it with the Brits? They wouldn't know a decent steak if it bit them on the ass. Any chef in North Carolina serving this crud would be lynched by the diners. And rightly so. Sometimes Tim craved a pound of home-reared, prime American beef so badly it gave him a pain in the gut.

He took a morose swallow of beer and forked down a mouthful of french fries. The waitress came over at that moment.

'Is everything alright for you, sir?' she asked, smiling shyly at him from above her saucy waitress's black uniform with its cute starched apron.

'Fine, thanks,' he managed to say through a mouthful of half-masticated sirloin. She was very pretty and if appearances were anything to go by, definite jailbait. So pretty, in fact, that he couldn't bring himself to favour her with his pithy opinion of his unappetising lunch.

He'd been tailing Jenny Bolton since she'd arrived in Knightsbridge at around eleven. Beth had been watching the house since eight-thirty and she'd called him when a cab had picked Jenny up in the late morning.

Tim had immediately arranged to take over surveillance. He wasn't about to miss a possible opportunity to watch Jenny and her female friend make love again.

He'd trailed her around Harrods, then various other shops, before she'd entered this busy restaurant for lunch. Tim was ravenous and didn't feel like hanging around outside, so he took a chance and followed her in. She was, after all, unlikely to notice him among all the other people lunching.

Unfortunately for him it was a shoppers' restaurant frequented primarily by women and most of the food on offer was geared towards its female clientele. He'd studied the menu with disgust.

Salads, quiche, wholemeal sandwiches – he wanted a real meal.

Luckily, as an afterthought, there were a few hot dishes including steak and french fries. What a pisser that they were barely edible.

Tim had enjoyed trailing Jenny Bolton around Harrods. He'd had plenty of time to admire the sway of her taut, shapely butt and her long-legged walk.

He watched her carefully from behind racks of frocks with price tags which made him blanch – why any woman in possession of her faculties would pay so much for a frock, particularly when usually there was so little of it, he really couldn't begin to imagine.

When she selected a couple of diaphanous nightgowns from the lingerie department and vanished into the changing rooms, his imagination was working overtime. He only wished there was some way he could get in there and watch her try them on unobserved.

The worst thing about trailing her was that he was approached several times by saleswomen asking if they could help him. It was particularly embarrassing in the lingerie department.

He guessed that the woman wondered if he was the sort of pervert who got off on women's underwear. Well as a matter of fact he did – but only if there was an attractive woman wearing it at the time.

He felt forced to buy an expensive pair of silk stockings as an alibi. What the hell – he'd give them to Sherry sometime if she needed sweetening.

Tim was very skilled at trailing people. He had the ability to blend in with the background by subtle changes in his demeanour.

In Harrods he projected the image of a well-off, but rather hapless Yank.

The Brits always liked that one.

The saleswoman was charm itself when he diffidently requested she show him some stockings, then admitted engagingly to not knowing what size the lady he was buying them for took.

Whenever the opportunity presented itself he stood near a woman shopping alone, so if Jenny glanced round he appeared to be with someone and she was more likely to notice the woman than him. Women always looked to see what other women were wearing.

Tim could see her now on the other side of the restaurant, reflectively sipping the last of her apple juice. She was sitting sideways on to him and he could see the firm thrust of her breasts in profile.

She was wearing a crisp, short-sleeved white blouse made from some sort of flimsy cotton. Beneath the blouse he could make out the outline of a lacy white bra and the darker shadow of her cleavage.

He wondered how Kevin Bolton would react when he saw the photos Tim hoped to take of the lovely

159

lady in the arms of her equally lovely companion.

Kevin suspected his wife of having an affair – how would he feel about it being with another woman?

Tim knew that he'd have felt a whole lot better about Sherry's infidelities if they'd been with other women. Particularly if they were anything like as gorgeous as Jenny's voluptuous blonde friend.

He wouldn't have made any particular objection – especially not if they'd let him watch.

Or even better, join in.

He felt his dick hardening at the idea – it had been up and down all morning while he was following Jenny. Images of the erotic scenario he'd spied on last week kept imprinting themselves on his overheated brain and the way she walked with her pelvis thrust forward in that sexy way, drove him wild.

He could quite see why women were attracted to each other. They smelt so damn good and they were so soft and warm ...

'Excuse me – but are you following me?'

Lost in his erotic reverie Tim hadn't registered that Jenny Bolton had left her table and was now standing in front of him.

His heart sank and so did his dick.

Shit! How come she'd noticed him? He must be losing his touch.

'Er, excuse me?' he said, playing for time.

'I said, are you following me?' she repeated patiently.

Tim wished the ground would open up and swallow him whole – he'd been one of the most effective agents in the CIA, now it seemed he couldn't follow a woman around a department store without her spotting him.

He'd been philosophical about it when Jess had told him that Paul Sears, the antiques dealer, had noticed her, and blamed himself for letting someone with absolutely no experience try to tail someone.

Now here he was in the exact same situation – but there was no excuse for him. Mesmerised by Jenny's alluring body he must have been careless and let himself get too close. Beautiful women were always his downfall.

She was standing gazing thoughtfully down at him waiting for his reply.

'I'm not really following you,' he found himself saying. 'The truth is that I noticed you in Harrods because you're so beautiful, then we just happened to be walking the same way. I saw you coming in here and thought it looked like a good place for lunch.'

He plastered his most engaging and ingenuous smile on his face and hoped he didn't come across like a serial killer. He didn't want to frighten her into calling the police.

Close up, he could smell her intoxicating perfume. It was light and floral and it did things for him. He could also see how incredibly beautiful she was with her striking features and large dark eyes.

She looked at him sceptically while his engaging and ingenuous smile started to feel like the grimace of a particularly ugly gargoyle.

'So my husband isn't paying you to follow me?'

Hell, this was getting worse and worse. He looked desperately round trying to think of what to say. The best he could come up with was, 'Hell no, honey, but I'll follow you for free if you ask me nicely.'

What an asshole he sounded.

He grinned at her cheesily, hoping he was coming across like some hick from the corn belt. Amiable but harmless.

He must have convinced her because she smiled suddenly and murmured, 'I'm sorry – I must be getting paranoid.' Turning on her heel she left the restaurant leaving Tim mopping his sweating brow and wishing fervently he'd let Beth stay tailing her.

He didn't dare follow her again, but acting on a hunch he waited about ten minutes, then went straight to the block of apartments opposite the hotel.

He was in luck.

Jenny's blonde friend was stretched out on the bed wearing a set of forties-style satin underwear in soft, dusky pink satin.

Even better, she had her hand between her legs and was stroking herself languorously over the shiny strip of satin which covered her pussy.

Working fast, Tim soon had the camera mounted on the tripod. How he wished the lady he was watching was mounted on his own tripod.

He clicked away, taking photo after photo while the movement of her hand became faster and faster until she suddenly stiffened, arched her back and enjoyed what was obviously a satisfying climax.

A few minutes later she went to open the door and Jenny stepped into the room. The two women embraced, then the blonde woman reached down and began to unbutton her friend's blouse.

Jenny was wearing a lacy white bra, a matching pair of tiny briefs and a dainty little suspender belt holding up a pair of pale, sheer stockings.

They sank onto the bed together and embraced again, then the blonde woman removed Jenny's bra and kissed the two pert, upward-pointing breasts which sprang eagerly free.

Through the telephoto lens Tim could see how prominent Jenny's rose-pink nipples already were. When he'd been watching her in the restaurant, had she been fantasising about and anticipating her female friend's soft hands and mouth on them? Was that why they were so hard and swollen?

The two women moved together on the bed intent on their mutual pleasure, completely unaware that Tim was capturing every erotic embrace on celluloid.

When at last it was over, the blonde woman left first after bidding a Jenny a fond farewell. Jenny vanished into the bathroom and emerged dressed in her underwear again, then poured herself a drink and sat back on the bed to watch TV.

Tim stashed the camera and tripod away in the canvas bag then went over to the window to take one last look at Jenny's slim, scantily clad form. Unfortunately she chose that moment to wander over to the window of the hotel room, drink in hand, and saw him.

Their eyes met across the distance that separated them, then she backed hastily into the room and closed the curtains, but not before he'd seen how scared she looked. What was worse, he was certain she recognised him as the man who'd been following her earlier.

Tim left the apartment building, crossed the road and went round the corner to the main entrance of the hotel. He took the lift up to the third floor and tapped on the door of room 314.

She opened it on the chain and he saw that she'd pulled on one of the hotel's snowy towelling dressing gowns over her underwear. She tried to slam the door shut but he put his foot in it and said urgently, 'Please don't be frightened, Mrs Bolton. I'm Tim Preece, a private investigator, and you were right the first time – your husband is paying me to follow you.'

He held out his identification for her to look at. She took it and studied it for a moment before saying, 'What do you want?'

'I'd like to talk to you if that's possible – downstairs in the bar if that would make you more comfortable.'

She looked at him long and hard then pushed the door shut, removed the chain and opened it again.

'You'd better come in.'

She sat on the edge of one of the chairs and indicated that he should take the other. She had her hands in the pockets of the dressing gown. It was much too big for her and made her look young and vulnerable.

'How long have you been following me?' she asked calmly.

'Just over a week – but it hasn't always been me.'

'I take it you saw what went on in here. I imagine you've even taken photos.' She glanced meaningfully at his canvas bag.

Tim nodded. 'Your husband thinks you're seeing another man – he asked me to follow you and get photos of you both together. How's he going to feel about the fact it's a woman?'

Jenny Bolton rose to her feet and went over to the window.

'My husband's a very possessive and jealous man. He doesn't like me to have friends of any description because he wants me all to himself. He's also very strait-laced – when you show him the photos you've taken, our marriage will be over. He'll probably consider that this is even worse than another man – he'll think it's perverted.'

There was a gleam of humour on her face as she spoke.

'In fact Kevin thinks any form of sex which doesn't involve a married couple in the missionary position is perverted.'

The towelling dressing-gown had parted over her stocking-clad thighs giving Tim a close-up of just how slender and shapely they were. He could also smell her light floral perfume, mingling with the provocative scent of female arousal.

Tim swallowed and shifted on the chair. A woman of Jenny Bolton's obvious sexuality deserved more imaginative sex than the missionary position every time. No wonder she'd sought excitement in the arms of another woman.

Who could blame her?

Certainly not him.

'Why are you here?' she asked him suddenly.

She had him there. He wasn't altogether certain what had prompted him to come up to the hotel room and see her, rather than just reporting back to her husband. Except that he didn't want to scare her and make her think she was being stalked by a psycho.

'You spotted me following you earlier,' he told her truthfully, 'then saw me in the window across the street. I couldn't let you think there was some crazy guy trailing you and let you be scared half out of your wits.'

She smiled at him.

'Well, thank you for that at least.' She finished her drink and went over to the mini-bar, her chestnut hair swinging out in a bell shape over her collar. 'Would you like a drink?'

'Sure. Scotch please.'

She went to sit on the bottom of the bed and crossed her legs.

'I do love my husband, you know,' she told him reflectively. 'It's just that we're not very sexually compatible. That and the fact that if it were up to him I'd never see anyone else at all. Veronica's an old friend of mine from college. We used to share a room in the hall of residence.'

She leant across to put her drink down and the

towelling dressing gown slipped from one smooth, tanned shoulder, taking her bra strap with it. She didn't seem to notice as she continued, 'We weren't lovers at college – we both had lots of boyfriends, but Veronica discovered she preferred women a while ago and after that it seemed the natural thing to do.'

Tim's eyes were riveted to her exposed shoulder. he wanted to press his lips to it, then trail them down over her collar bone until he reached the swelling of one small, pert breast. Then he'd take the hard little point of her nipple into his mouth and . . .

'Do you share my husband's views about sex?' she asked him suddenly, bringing him back to reality with a jerk.

Tim coughed and cleared his throat. 'Er . . . not exactly.'

She leant back on the bed, 'Did you enjoy watching us?' she enquired huskily.

Enjoyed it? He'd had a hard-on bigger than a guided missile.

Still had, come to that.

When he didn't reply she appraised him speculatively.

'I think you did. I think you enjoyed it a lot.' Her gaze flickered over his groin knowingly.

'Do you prefer women too?' he found himself saying.

'Not generally. Veronica's the only other woman I've ever been to bed with. It's special with her, but generally I like men.'

She leant forward and took his hand, her robe falling open at the front as she did so.

'Tim, do you have to show my husband those photos? If you do it'll be the end of my marriage. After all, where's the harm in what we're doing?' She fixed her large, dark eyes appealingly on his face .

Tim felt himself melting. Her hand felt so small and fragile in his and he could see the tops of her breasts where they emerged from the lacy cradle of her flimsy white bra.

He could always tell Kevin Bolton that he'd trailed Jenny for days and submit a detailed report of her movements – but omit any mention of her afternoon rendezvous.

But he had his professional ethics to consider. How could he falsify a report and deliberately mislead a client about his wife's extra-marital activities? If he betrayed his client's trust he wouldn't deserve to call himself a private investigator.

Jenny took his hand and placed it on one of her breasts.

On the other hand if he passed up an opportunity like this he wouldn't deserve to call himself a man.

'I'm sure we can come to some arrangement,' he said hoarsely.

She pulled him gently down onto the bed next to her.

'Just promise me one thing,' she murmured, undoing the buttons on his shirt.

'What's that?'

'We don't have to do it in the missionary position.'

Tim was unable to reply because she wound her arms around his neck and kissed him, her tongue sliding in between his lips.

While they were kissing he managed to shrug himself out of his leather jacket, then turned his attention to the much more interesting task of undressing her. He opened her enveloping towelling dressing gown revealing the stirring sight of her slim, luscious body.

Her small, pert breasts strained upwards, pushing hard against the triangles of white lace which struggled to contain them. He could see the darker

167

circles of her rose-pink aureoles under the flimsy fabric and the round, hard points of her nipples, which were sharply erect.

His eyes travelled downwards to where the narrow strip of her suspender belt encircled her slender waist. The two front suspenders ran down to the tops of her pale stockings, snaking under the tiny triangle of her flimsy briefs. A few stray wisps of her chestnut bush were just visible at the edges.

Tim had seen her body before, but only through the powerful telephoto lens of the camera. Only now he was close to her could he see how satiny the texture of her skin was, with its light dusting of freckles.

The earlier erotic scenario he'd witnessed between Jenny and her friend Veronica had left her with the sharp, musky scent of female arousal rising faintly from between her thighs. It mingled with her perfume and the smell of her freshly washed hair to add fuel to the fire of Tim's excitement.

He removed her dressing gown and threw it on the floor then unfastened her bra, bent his head and took one of her swollen nipples into his mouth.

He sucked for a long time, flickering his tongue over it and nibbling gently with his lips. Jenny wound her hand into his fair hair and made little moans of pleasure as he stimulated one of her primary erogenous zones.

When both her nipples were so swollen they looked like small ripe raspberries he began to kiss his way down over her flat stomach to her mound. The strip of white lace between her legs was already damp and there was a trickle of clear moisture on her inner thigh.

He felt between her legs, the panties weren't just damp – they were sodden.

She squirmed when he touched her there and

murmured, 'Take them off.' Tim obeyed with alacrity. He peeled the tiny scrap of fabric down her thighs revealing the secret delta of her chestnut-covered mound, nestling between her slim tanned thighs. He was about to plunge his face into it when she stopped him.

'Let me undress you first.' She removed his shirt and jeans, running her hands over the firm muscles in his arms and chest and tangling her fingers in his chest hair.

When she came to his briefs, she paused to caress the straining contour of his dick through its cotton covering before taking it out. It had been ready for lift-off for several hours and was more than eager for some action.

'Mmm,' she said teasingly, dropping a kiss on the swollen purple end, 'this is going to be quite an afternoon.'

Tim certainly hoped so.

She pushed him down onto the bed then climbed astride with her back to him. Bending forward, she licked up the drop of moisture which had gathered on the end of his dick with the tip of her tongue.

Pursing her full lips she took his cock into her mouth a couple of inches. Sucking hard she grasped it tightly in her hand and moved it in and out, with an erotic rocking motion.

Tim had a close-up view of the taut cheeks of her backside and further down, the soft, swollen folds of her labia. Clear moisture glistened over the deep pink tissue and her clit looked swollen and engorged.

Grasping her by the hips he pulled her backwards until her pussy was over his face. Like a man who has finally come home after a long journey, he plunged his tongue into her dripping honeypot.

She knelt over him on all fours for a long time,

with her heated private parts against his face and her mouth around his cock, while they both licked, sucked and nibbled feverishly.

Tim drew her clit between his lips but he had difficulty keeping it there because she had a way of rotating her pelvis which drove him wild.

He lost all sense of time as he started the count-down to ecstasy. She was moving his dick in and out of her mouth, sucking hard all the time, as he roared towards his climax at dizzying speed.

When he came it was with all the force of a nuclear explosion, leaving him spent and wasted.

He was brought back down to earth when she wiggled her pussy in his face, reminding him that he might have finished – at least for a short while – but she hadn't.

She wasn't far behind him. Her cry of satisfaction was loud and long-drawn-out, then she rolled side-ways and lay weakly panting next to him.

Chapter Twelve

Alexa felt it immediately.

A jolt of dark sexuality so strong that she felt everyone in the room must be aware of it.

Memories she'd kept repressed for over five years suddenly came clamouring to the surface, half arousing, half frightening her.

Nothing of this showed on her face except for a faint flush over her high cheekbones. She appeared cool and composed as Will joined her at her table and lit a cigarette.

'I understand you're now a lady of independent means,' he commented, his eyes lingering briefly on her breasts.

'That's right,' Alexa confirmed. 'Dear old aunt Lily.'

'I spoke to Todd a couple of days ago. He said you were heading this way and looking up old friends – I've been hoping to bump into you.'

'I asked him for your address, but he didn't have it; so I just had to hope our paths would cross,' she told him, sitting casually back in her chair and nodding at the waiter to pour her some more coffee.

'I've just rented a house – I was staying in a hotel until last week. I was surprised to hear that you were thinking of looking me up, considering how determinedly you ditched me a few years ago.'

Alexa took a sip of her coffee.

'Situations change – so do ways of perceiving them.'

Will blew smoke lazily to one side, his heavy-lidded eyes half closed. He'd changed more than Alexa had expected. When she'd last seen him he'd been very slim, now his shoulders looked broader and he'd put weight on. His dark hair was receding slightly but he was still a good looking man.

His eyes were the same cold, compelling grey. She'd forgotten how watchful they were – he often looked as if he was hoping to catch someone out. But Will had always had his dark side, it was one of the reasons she'd stopped seeing him.

He hadn't accepted it easily and if it wasn't for this job she would certainly never have got in touch with him again.

'So what brings you to Marrakech?' she asked him lightly, when he didn't reply to her last observation.

'Business.'

'Will you be here long?'

'That depends on how the business goes. How about you? Are you thinking of making a long stay?'

'My plans are completely flexible. I intend to travel around, but other than that I'll just do whatever I feel like doing.'

'That's an enviable position to be in.'

Alexa gave him the full benefit of her most seductive cat-like smile. 'You bet.'

They chatted for a while, mainly about mutual acquaintances, then he reached across the table and took her hand, his eyes flickering over her body.

In the past, Will had only had to look at her in a certain way and she was immediately ready for sex, her private parts moist and open in readiness for him. It was a power he'd had over her which she'd always found disconcerting and which he'd used ruthlessly to manipulate her.

Alexa had convinced herself it was a power he would no longer possess. Now, sitting here with him touching her, she wasn't so sure. She felt it would be a wise move to leave and pull herself together.

'It's good to see you again, Alexa.'

'And it's good to see you too, Will. But now I'm afraid I've got to go.'

'Can we get together again later?'

'Certainly we can. Why don't you call me at my hotel? I should be back about five.'

'I'll look forward to it.'

Kneeling up on the bed, naked except for her stockings and suspender belt, Jenny Bolton clutched the headboard and said through clenched teeth, 'Don't stop . . . not yet.'

Tim had no intention of stopping.

Kneeling behind Jenny with his cock buried up to the hilt in her dripping honeypot, he withdrew slightly, then made another of the corkscrew thrusts which were driving her wild.

Her pelvis was jammed against the headboard and she rotated it rhythmically, pulling him further in. Tim had been fantasising for several days what it would feel like to have his dick clutched high up in her fanny while she moved her pelvis around him.

Now he knew.

It felt fantastic.

So fantastic that he never wanted it to stop.

His hands cupped her apple-hard little breasts and he withdrew again until just the tip of his cock was held by her pulsating pussy.

She cried out as he thrust upwards and forwards in a taut spiral, then she ground her buttocks into his groin. Leaning back against him away from the headboard, she panted, 'I'm nearly there.'

Tim dropped one of his hands downwards to find her clit and began a soft, insistent stroking movement which he already knew would have her climaxing again within a very short time. His fingers slipped around in her plentiful female lubrications and from behind he rocked his cock in and out of her.

A few seconds later she cried out and arched her spine, her head falling back onto her shoulders.

Tim enjoyed every last one of the muscle spasms which racked her slim body and squeezed his dick so pleasurably.

'Let's lie down,' she murmured when the last spasm of pleasure had finished washing over her. Carefully, they edged down the bed and lay together like spoons, with Tim's cock still embedded deep within her.

As far as he was concerned, this had been practically a record hard-on. He'd kept it up through a seemingly endless series of positions and it still showed no sign of waning.

Jenny appeared determined to make the most of the situation – she wanted him to do all the things which her husband wouldn't do.

And there were a lot of them.

Cradled in his arms she said regretfully, 'I'm going to have to leave soon.'

He nuzzled her neck and tightened his hold on her, 'Not just yet, honey – there are still a couple of ways we haven't done it.'

She laughed throatily. 'There can't be.'

'Sure there are.'

He withdrew from her slowly, ignoring her little whimper of protest, then rolled her onto her back. Taking two of the hotel's downy pillows he placed them under her hips then pushed her legs back over her head, thighs wide apart, until her toes almost touched the wall above the headboard.

He paused for a moment to admire the aesthetic effect. The taut globes of her ass looked firm and luscious, each one bisected by a lacy white suspender. Her soft, swollen little pussy glistened invitingly, showing what a deep state of arousal she was in.

He slipped a couple of fingers into her and moved them around – she was virtually molten inside, bubbling with hot moisture. He took his dick in his hand and moved the tip over her clit, then slid it in about an inch. When she lifted herself and tried to get more of it inside her he withdrew it teasingly.

He did the same thing again.

And again.

'Fuck me!' she gasped pleadingly. 'Don't torment me – fuck me!'

Tim was more than happy to oblige.

Jess had done what work she could on the computer and was looking around for something else to do.

'Is there anything else I can help with, do you think, Martha?' she asked Tim's secretary.

Martha thought for a moment, pushing her spectacles on top of her head and massaging the bridge of her nose.

'There are some tapes which need transcribing,' she said at last, 'but it's a purely clerical job – I just haven't had time to do it yet.'

'I'll make a start on those then, shall I?' said Jess cheerfully.

She sat with the headphones on and her hands poised over the keyboard and activated 'play' with the foot control. The tape was one from a phone line Tim had put a tap on a few days ago.

The first couple of calls dealt with routine domestic matters and Jess transcribed them on screen so she could run off a print-out later.

The third call took her by surprise.

It was from the man under surveillance to an unknown woman. Jess knew that the man was in his fifties but she didn't know anything about the girl, but judging by her voice she was quite young, perhaps in her early twenties.

'Hello, Melly – it's me.' The man's voice was cultivated and held a note of authority.

'Hello, you. I was hoping you'd ring.' There was a rustling sound, as if she were making herself more comfortable to take the call.

'Where are you at the moment?'

'In the hallway.' There was a pause, as if he were picturing the scene.

'What are you wearing?'

'The red dress. The very short one that you like so much.'

'What do you have on underneath it?'

'The black satin underwear with the scarlet lace. But I'm only wearing the suspender belt and French knickers – I didn't feel like wearing a bra.'

'Are you sitting or standing?'

'I'm sitting on the wooden chair in the hallway – the uncomfortable one with the carved seat.'

'I want you to stand up, take your knickers off, then sit down again astride the chair. Pull your dress up right around your waist.'

Again, Jess could hear a rustling noise, then when the girl spoke there was a hint of breathlessness in her voice.

'I'm doing it.'

'What does it feel like?'

'It's hard under my bum and if I sit here long enough the pattern carved on the seat will be on my bum too. But it does feel nice and cool, though – it's such a warm day.'

'Now undo the front of your dress and let your

176

breasts show.' There was more rustling and then she giggled.

'It's to be hoped no one comes to the door. There's a frosted glass panel in the middle you can see right through if you stand close enough.'

'Now I'm going to tell you what's going to happen next time we meet and while I do that I want you to touch yourself.'

The man began to describe a sexual encounter in such graphic detail that a slow flush crept up over Jess's throat and her cheeks went pink.

She'd never in her life heard anyone talk like that.

She could hear the faint sound of what she assumed to be the chair creaking in the background together with little female gasping noises and could only think that the girl was doing as bidden.

The man's voice continued, 'Then I'm going to sit you on the edge of my desk and stroke your little clitty until you come again. But you won't be able to make a sound because right outside the door is my secretary's office where there'll be several people waiting to see me.'

Jess undid a couple of buttons on her shirt. The office suddenly felt hot and airless even though there were two windows open. She was the only one in there. She could hear the sound of Martha moving around next door, but everyone else was out.

Breathing hard she continued to play the tape. As if of its own volition her hand crept down between her legs and unable to help herself she traced a path between her thighs.

She rubbed the centre of her own pleasure through the soft material of her dress, then glancing round to make certain she wasn't observed, pulled it up out of the way and stroked herself over her pair of flimsy cotton panties.

Within a very short time her panties were damp

and she could feel the outline of her clit beneath the thin material. She just couldn't help it.

The deep, cultured voice spoke on, describing a sexual encounter which made her feel red-hot.

The gasps coming from the girl on the other end of the phone were getting louder and the chair beneath her was creaking away audibly in the background.

'What are you doing now?' asked the man suddenly, 'tell me about it.'

'I'm rubbing myself,' said the girl breathlessly. 'And I'm pushing down against the seat of the chair. I've made it all wet and slippery and my clit keeps rubbing against a bit of the carving. It's making me so hot . . .'

It was making Jess hot too.

She pushed her fingers beneath the elastic on her panties and touched the slick little point of flesh, then rubbed her index finger backwards and forwards.

The girl on the tape moaned loudly, then said, 'I'm nearly there . . . nearly there . . . Aah!'

Her long-drawn-out cry sent Jess over the edge and she gritted her teeth so no sound escaped as she was overtaken by the rush of her own climax.

When Martha came in a few minutes later she said, 'Are you alright, Alexa? Sorry, I mean Jess. You look a bit flushed.'

'I'm fine thanks, Martha,' she managed to say. 'It's just a little warm in here.'

'Oh, I forgot to mention that Tim said there was some sexy talk on one of the tapes – if you don't want to transcribe that one just leave it for me.'

Philippe took it philosophically when Alexa told him she wouldn't be able to see him again. They had a last drink together in the bar of her hotel in the early evening.

It helped that he'd lost heavily at cards that afternoon and it was obviously on his mind. She knew that to a compulsive gambler like him, losing a lover was much less important than losing lady luck.

It didn't, however, stop him from suggesting that they retire to her room to say goodbye properly. But Alexa felt she needed a clear head for her evening out with Will and didn't want to be in a post-coital daze after being expertly and lengthily screwed by Philippe.

She dressed seductively for the evening in a low cut, sage-green silk dress. She didn't actually intend to have sex with Will that night, but she wanted him to want her. If one of them was to be in the sexual thrall of the other, she'd rather it was Will in hers. However unlikely that seemed when she remembered the nature of their past relationship.

They met in a small bar near the Médina, then moved on to the restaurant of a private club for dinner.

Alexa could see immediately why Will had chosen this place. The waitresses wore traditional North African harem costumes, but with one difference. The short bodices which left their midriffs exposed were completely transparent so their breasts were clearly visible.

Will had always been obsessed by the naked or partially clothed female form. When they were having their affair he regularly frequented the strip clubs and revue bars in Soho. He often asked her to go with him and sometimes she did so – even if she didn't particularly feel like it. She'd always found it hard to say no to him.

Her own low cut dress obviously met with his approval – his eyes kept flickering to her cleavage. Alexa knew that if Will carried a mental picture of her, or any other woman for that matter, it wouldn't be one of just her face.

He was a man who undressed all the women who came within his range with his eyes. It used to make some of her friends uncomfortable.

She knew quite well that for a good part of the meal he was imagining screwing her and although she knew that embarking on a renewed sexual relationship with Will was potentially dangerous, she couldn't help but feel hot with reluctant anticipation.

Over dinner she asked him what sort of business had brought him to Marrakech. His expression immediately became watchful – even suspicious – before he said, 'Why do you ask?'

'I'm just interested,' she replied innocently.

There was a long pause while he helped himself to more salad, then he said, 'I'm setting up a deal here.'

'Will you be going back to England when you've done that?' she asked, keeping her tone casual.

'Unlikely. I'm *persona non grata* in some circles there at the moment.'

'Really? Why is that?'

He smiled without humour.

'Let's just say I found a way to make a lot of money quickly and certain people resented it.'

'People do, don't they?' she agreed ingenuously. 'I found that when I came into money myself.'

'Did you come into a lot?'

'Enough to change my life,' she told him untruthfully.

Will poured the last of the wine into her glass.

'Shall I order another bottle?'

'Why don't you do that? The first one didn't go very far.'

After the meal there was a floorshow. The first act was a belly dancer who shimmied and gyrated her way gracefully among the tables. She was a beautiful, exotic looking girl with large dark eyes heavily outlined with kohl. A veil covered the lower part of her face and she was wearing a costume similar to that of the waitresses, except that her chiffon bodice was covered by a short embroidered waistcoat.

After she'd removed the waistcoat the murmur of conversation ceased altogether as the audience watched her full breasts move around erotically under the transparent bodice.

Alexa could see that Will was mesmerised. He lit one cigarette from another without his eyes leaving the swaying orbs. After weaving her way among the tables the dancer stood in the centre of the room, her hips continuing with their rhythmic movements, while slowly and seductively she removed her top.

She tossed it carelessly aside and threw herself into a faster version of the dance, so her breasts jiggled and wobbled, causing more than one male member of the audience to break out in a sweat.

After touring the tables again she returned to the small dance floor in the centre for her *pièce de résistance*. Again her hips kept up the rhythm while she reached slowly inside her turquoise chiffon harem pants.

With a sudden tug she released the pair of silk panties she was wearing under the harem pants and pulled them free. Alexa thought they must have been held in position by tiny strips of velcro for her to be able to remove them so easily.

Her prettily trimmed bush was clearly visible through the see-through material and she embarked on another brief tour of the room, dancing frenetically without once missing a beat.

At the conclusion of her dance the girl bent over backwards with her legs wide apart and her arms extended behind her, her body forming a perfect bow and her breasts jutting proudly upwards.

Alexa joined in with the applause and wondered what a woman on her first date with Will would think if he took her to such a place. She could imagine that some women would be shocked, or even insulted. She'd been half expecting something like this and took it in her stride. She was even a little aroused – the dance had been very erotic, after all.

Will ordered two cognacs, then sat back in his chair and studied her through half-closed eyes.

'Do you know what I remember most vividly about you, Alexa?'

'My sense of humour? My sweet nature?'

'I remember how much you liked sex. A lot of women pretend to like it, but you really did. I can still remember how you looked when you came – I always used to watch your face at that moment – it was a turn-on in itself.'

Alexa smiled and raised her eyebrows slightly. Inside she felt her stomach muscles lurch and her honeypot began to itch and throb in response to his words.

He leant forward and touched the lowest part of her cleavage with the tip of his forefinger.

'A deep pink flush used to start just here, work its way over your breasts and up to your cheeks. Are your breasts still as beautiful? Do those coral-pink nipples still tilt upwards?'

'I certainly hope so,' returned Alexa mildly, keeping her excitement hidden with difficulty. 'It's only been five or six years – I don't think gravity has begun to take its toll yet.'

'No, I can see that it hasn't,' he observed, looking at them hard.

'For goodness' sake, Will,' Alexa protested, 'stop staring – you're embarrassing me.'

'I mean it as a compliment. Are you ready to leave,

Alexa? I thought we'd go back to my house.'

'Think again,' she said. 'You seem to be assuming we're going to take up where we left off.'

'Well, aren't we?'

'I'll let you know when I've decided.'

Alexa beckoned a waiter and asked him to call for a taxi. Will tried to insist on taking her back to her hotel, but she was determined to return alone and he reluctantly acquiesced.

It took a lot of willpower to leave him sitting there, instead of going home with him and letting events take their natural course.

But she needed to keep the whip hand if she was going to achieve her aim and she mustn't allow herself to be sidetracked by her own demanding sexual needs.

And that was going to be difficult.

Jess was dressing for an evening at the opera.

When Jess had confessed to him that she quite liked Paul Sears, Tim had decided that it might be a good idea for her to see him again. In a social situation it was possible he'd let something slip which could be useful information.

'Just stick to your original story that you're a college lecturer staying with her sister,' he advised her. 'Tell the truth wherever you can and get him to do most of the talking. Try and remember everything he says, however unimportant it seems. Slip off to the ladies and make notes if you get the chance.'

Accordingly she'd phoned the number on the card Paul had given her. He was delighted to hear from her and told her that when he'd suggested having dinner that evening, he'd forgotten that he was taking a party of people to the opera. But he'd very much like to see her again, so would she like to come too? – they could have a late supper after the performance.

Jess didn't know much about opera, but she was quite prepared to learn more. As she dressed she found herself in a highly charged state of sexual anticipation.

The sex she'd enjoyed with Paul in the bedroom of the stately home had left her wanting more. The phone call she'd transcribed from the tape that afternoon had aroused her to such an extent that even bringing about her own climax had only satisfied her temporarily.

She was glad she had the whole of Alexa's wardrobe to choose from – she needed something very special to wear to the opera.

In the end she chose a black silk taffeta skirt which was split up to mid-thigh, then fastened up to the waist with a series of small black pearl buttons. It had a matching off-the-shoulder black bodice with a ruffle around the top, which made an exotic frame for her creamy bare arms and shoulders.

In the bar before the performance Jess met Paul's partner in the antiques business. She'd been expecting a man but his partner was an elegant blonde in her mid-thirties called Marcia. She was cool and poised with a lovely sensual face and a stunning figure.

Jess saw several men appraising Marcia, their eyes travelling over her curves, set off to great advantage by the pale pink evening dress she was wearing. Marcia seemed appreciative of the male attention she was attracting and Jess saw her exchange glances with more than one admirer.

She was with a much older man called John, who was pleasant enough but whose eyes rarely left his blonde companion. The other two members of the party had cancelled only an hour before, due to a sudden death in the family.

Jess found to her delight that Paul had booked a

box and shortly before the performance was due to start they made their way there.

Seated at the front of the box next to Paul, Jess felt a tremor of lust at his close proximity. She was looking forward to the opera, but she was looking forward to what she felt sure would happen later even more.

She could feel his arm pressed against hers and squeezed her thighs together, trying to suppress a tingle of heat between her legs. She told herself sternly to concentrate on the story unfolding, but it was difficult when she remembered the weight of his body on hers and the feeling of his bone-hard cock moving inside her.

After about half an hour Marcia suddenly stood up, looking pale and drawn, and left the box, supported by her escort. Paul followed them out and returned a few moments later to whisper that she'd been taken ill, but John would get her home safely.

Glancing around the shadowy confines of the darkened box Jess realised that they were alone now – it made her hot just to think about it.

The thought had obviously crossed Paul's mind at the same time. She felt his hand on her stocking-clad knee and he began to stroke it softly, sending shivers of excitement darting up to her groin.

He stroked his way up her thigh as far as the split in the tight skirt would allow him, then continued upwards over the stiff taffeta to stroke her hip. Below them on the stage the characters enacted their own drama, but to Jess it was nowhere near as exciting as the one taking place in their box.

He obviously found the layer of stiff fabric less attractive than that of her sheer stocking, because he soon returned his hand to her thigh and resumed its erotic caress.

By undoing a couple of the pearl buttons he was

able to reach the soft skin above her stocking top and trailed his fingers around it in a way which made Jess gulp and catch her breath. Another couple of buttons were soon undone, giving him access to the skin of her inner thigh.

The tips of his fingers were only a couple of inches from the tiny throbbing sliver of flesh she'd been driven to stimulate herself that afternoon. The throbbing was like a hot itch which she wanted scratching.

His hand became entangled in her skirt and obviously impatient with the restrictions it placed on his movements he undid the last few buttons.

Without taking her eyes off the stage Jess pulled it apart and let it settle on either side of her, revealing her high-waisted black satin panties, suspender belt and sheer black stockings.

'That's better,' he murmured in her ear, while his hand roamed freely over her thighs and stomach. He eased her legs apart and she groaned audibly when she felt him touch her satin-covered mound with the tip of one finger. She parted her thighs even further, then inhaled sharply as he began to stroke her directly between the legs.

It felt so good to have him touch her like that. Hot moisture began to gather in the overheated recesses of her private parts and it wasn't long before he felt it too, as it drenched the thin layer of material.

'You're soaking wet,' he muttered softly, feeling the dampness spreading swiftly outwards. He tried to slip his fingers under the elastic of her panties, but they were the tight-fitting type designed to show off the curves of the female form to advantage and he couldn't manage it.

'Take them off,' he ordered her in a whisper.

Raising her bottom from the padded seat of the chair Jess peeled them swiftly down, praying that no one noticed, and wondered what on earth she was doing.

She stuffed them down the side of the seat then sat back with her legs apart, naked from the waist down except for her flimsy suspender belt.

It was the most erotic thing Jess had ever experienced, to be sitting in the opera house in full view of thousands of people, apparently fully dressed, but in reality with her sex exposed and a man's hand between her thighs.

She heard him groan when he felt the full extent of her arousal. Her clit was hard and swollen and his fingers slipped around in her female lubrications as he explored the soft, moist folds of her pussy.

Although her eyes were fixed on the stage Jess had completely lost track of what was going on. All she was aware of was Paul pushing two fingers inside her and moving them in and out. He did it for a long time while she tried hard not to draw attention to them both by squirming and bearing down on the hand which was giving her so much pleasure.

He withdrew it and she felt it slipping down behind her to explore the cleft between her buttocks.

'Lift yourself up,' he whispered. Jess obeyed him, then gasped when he pushed three fingers inside her from behind. She contracted her internal muscles as he explored her velvety interior, stroking and stimulating her so that waves of heat washed over her trembling body.

When she felt as if she were about to explode, he withdrew his hand and took her clit between his finger and thumb. He squeezed and rubbed it gently while Jess gripped the chair with trembling hands. The music soared up around them, higher and higher, filling the vast space, but Jess didn't hear it. There was only one thing she was focusing on.

She was about to reach her own crescendo in front of an audience of thousands of opera lovers.

Chapter Thirteen

Ideally Alexa would have liked to have left it a couple of weeks at least before resuming a sexual relationship with Will, but there were two reasons why that wasn't practical.

The first was that time was running out – she only had a few brief weeks to convince him to return the money. If she couldn't persuade him, then the company flotation wouldn't take place and she would have failed in her mission.

The second was that she didn't feel she could wait much longer herself – Will only had to look at her for her to feel hot and her permanent state of frustration was eating her up inside.

She spent several sleepless nights tossing and turning, her body drenched with perspiration as she mentally relived some of their past sexual encounters.

The memories were so potent that she knew she'd been wise to suppress them all these years – it was the only way she could cope with them. She masturbated herself to orgasm again and again but no sooner had the waves of one died down, than she wanted another.

Her only consolation was that she successfully managed to hide her agitation from Will. Or at least she hoped she had – sometimes his cold grey eyes looked as if they could see right into her soul.

A few days after their first meeting she went to see

the house he was renting. Set amid the luxuriant, well-watered greenery of one of Marrakech's garden suburbs, the house was the last word in elegant, understated luxury.

Painted a dazzling white, it was built in the Moorish style with a wide shaded terrace running round two sides. In the well-tended garden, palm trees taller than the house cast flimsy shadows over the profusion of colourful shrubs and flowers. A small aquamarine swimming pool shimmered in the heat haze, making Alexa long to tear off her clothes and plunge in.

Inside, the floors were of pale, cool marble and in the heat of the day the shutters were closed to keep out the blinding sun. It was expensively and tastefully furnished and the marble floors were strewn with richly textured, hand-woven rugs.

Lunch was served on the terrace by two demure and attractive Moroccan girls wearing the traditional costume. It was a hot August day and Alexa was grateful for the overhead fan stirring the still air. Sprinklers played on the garden, making a pleasantly musical background sound.

'I'm staying at one of the plushest hotels in Marrakech,' she told Will, sipping her iced tea, 'but it isn't anything like as luxurious as this. It must be costing you a fortune.'

He smiled enigmatically.

'It is.'

'Your money-making scheme must have been very clever.'

'It was. And it was only the first of many.'

'Are you going to tell me about it?' she invited him.

There was a pause before he said, 'I don't think so.'

'Why not? I'd love to hear about it.'

'Some other time. Tell me something, Alexa – why have you just decided to look me up? You could have done that any time these last five years – we've both been living in London, after all. Did you hear that I'd just become a rich man?'

'I haven't heard anything about you in ages. Does anyone know? Todd certainly didn't mention it.'

'These things have a habit of getting around. And you haven't answered my question.'

Alexa took a sip of her tea.

'When I realised that thanks to aunt Lily I never needed to work again, I sat back and took stock of my life. Sometimes people make decisions which seem right at the time but which they subsequently regret.'

She paused, then added lightly, 'But let's not make a big thing out of this, Will – let's just see what happens. As I was saying – I love your house.'

'You can move in any time you want – I'd like you to be my guest here,' he told her.

One of the maids padded out onto the terrace at that moment to deposit a large bowl of salad and a dish of olives.

When she'd returned inside Alexa said teasingly, 'You don't seem to lack for company.'

He grinned at her.

'They don't speak very good English.'

'You must have changed, Will – I don't remember conversation being high on your list of leisure pursuits,' she returned sweetly.

He took an olive from the dish and chewed it thoughtfully. 'Maybe when I was with you I just found you too damn sexy to have much room in my head for anything other than the purely physical. Or maybe we did do a lot of talking, but looking back we can both only remember the highlights of our time together – and those were undoubtedly when I was fucking you.'

Alexa shifted slightly on her seat. It was true that

her memories of Will were exclusively sexual. Screwing was all they'd seemed to do together, in fact, but although some of the memories were fairly dark, they still intruded remorselessly into her consciousness, making her velvet cavern run with hot, prickly moisture.

She'd been young – only in her early twenties – and Will was older, more worldly and more sophisticated. She was fairly sexually experienced when they met – she'd always loved sex from her very first time – but he'd introduced her to pleasures she hadn't met either before or since.

The way he was looking at her now made her feel as if ants were crawling down her spine. The whole of her groin felt so hot and tingly that she doubted if even sitting in a bath of icy water would cool her down.

Of all the men she'd known he was the last one she'd have chosen to take up with again – his power over her had been too great.

For a long time she'd been in his sexual thrall and it hadn't been a comfortable experience. She'd only torn herself away with great difficulty and now here she was about to start it all up again.

But this time she needed to be the one in control.

Throughout lunch she was aware that Will had only one thing on his mind.

So did she.

Why delay the inevitable any longer?

When they'd finished eating she decided it was time to take the initiative. She was no longer the malleable young girl Will had known five years ago – she was a cool, poised woman with a job to do.

She'd seduce him now but stay well in control of the situation.

Rising to her feet she moved sinuously around to where he was sitting and perched on the edge of the table opposite him.

She was wearing a khaki-coloured, short-sleeved silk shirt tucked into a matching skirt. Her long bare legs were tanned and she crossed them casually.

'It's been a long time,' she said softly.

'Much too long,' he asserted.

Leaning forward he placed his hand on her bare thigh. It was cool and dry but his touch was so electric that she felt as if he'd burnt her. He slid it slowly up under her skirt, watching her face all the time. Alexa felt herself tremble and knew that he felt it too.

'Are your maids likely to come outside again?' she asked him, trying to keep her voice even.

'Not unless I ring for them,' he replied, grazing the palm of his hand over one silk-covered breast.

Her nipples hardened and thrust forward through the fine fabric of her shirt. Will undid the buttons down the front, revealing a lace-edged cream silk bra. He could see the darker shadows of her coral-pink aureolae through the transparent fabric and bending forward took one jutting nipple between his lips and sucked it sensually through the silk.

Alexa's head jerked backwards and in the still, silent afternoon she heard herself panting like a bitch on heat.

A few seconds later she pulled him down on top of her on the table and dragged his zip down, feverishly grabbing his cock. Plates and dishes crashed to the ground as the frustration which had kept Alexa in a state of barely controllable tension throughout the last few days at last became too much for her.

Will obviously felt exactly the same way. His mouth came down hard on hers as he reached beneath her skirt and dragged her silk panties around her thighs. He didn't take the time to remove them completely, just left them there as he plunged the full length of his huge, stiff cock all the way into her.

Alexa writhed beneath him on the hard, tiled table

top like a woman possessed. She wound her arms around his neck and pushed her hips against him to meet each one of his hard, fast thrusts.

She wanted to wrap her legs around his waist and pull him closer into her, but her thighs were effectively hobbled by her own rolled-down silk panties.

The table's tiled top sent a welcome chill striking up through her back. Her skirt was bunched up around her waist and she could feel the cold, smooth surface below her backside as she slid up and down it in response to Will's frenetic, rhythmic movements.

He dragged her bra up and burrowed his face between her full, firm breasts, licking and nuzzling them until the whole area felt as if it were on fire.

Suddenly he stopped moving.

Instead of thrusting in and out of her like an engine-driven piston, he remained immobile while she jammed her hips against him and tried vainly to start his motor again.

When he still didn't move, she tried to wrench her panties off, so she could roll on top of him and ride him until she achieved the satisfaction she wanted so desperately.

He pinned her to the table top with his hips and, grabbing her wrists with one hand, held them down above her head. She struggled with him, hating him for stopping so suddenly.

Reaching down, he raised himself enough to get his hand between them and found her clit. She was in such an overheated, aroused state, that it only took him a few seconds to bring her to a gasping, choking climax.

Her eyes fluttered briefly open as she felt it sweeping over her and she saw that he was watching her face intently.

With a sudden jerk he tore her panties off, thrust

his knee between her thighs to push them wider apart and began to drive in and out of her again.

She wrapped her legs around his waist and her pelvis rose and fell eagerly to meet each thrust.

She became aware that her lower half was lying in a puddle of icy water – they must have knocked over the earthenware jug of mineral water at some stage. It felt good in contrast to the molten heat inside her.

She came again, just before Will boiled over into his own long-drawn-out climax and pumped his hot juices into her in a series of vigorous, convulsive spurts.

He withdrew from her and collapsed into a chair, wiping himself on one of the linen table napkins before zipping his trousers up again.

Alexa lay on her back on the table, panting weakly. After a few minutes she recovered enough to sit up slowly and swing her legs off the side.

Will lit a cigarette and watched her through half-closed eyes as she tried to rearrange her clothing. She pulled down her bra and fastened her shirt but her panties were ripped in two and completely un-wearable. Her short silk skirt was soaked through with spilt mineral water and she looked at him ruefully as she tried to wring it out.

He rang a little brass bell on the table.

'One of the girls will dry it out and press it for you,' he told her. When the maid appeared he spoke to her in French. Alexa expected the girl to conduct her to a bedroom and find her something else to wear before taking the skirt away.

Instead, before Alexa realised what was happening, the maid reached out and undid the skirt, so it fell to the floor, leaving her naked from the waist down.

Alexa flushed furiously as the girl picked it up and went off with it.

195

'Will,' she protested, sinking onto a chair, 'I can't sit here like this in front of your household staff. Ask her to bring me something else to wear.'

Unperturbed Will gazed at her closely clipped, red-gold bush.

'Yours is the most beautiful bush I've ever seen. I want to admire it for a while.'

If there had been a tablecloth Alexa would have wound it around herself, but there was nothing and she had to sit in a state of undress until her skirt was dry.

As well as her affair with Veronica, Jenny Bolton had another secret she kept from her husband. She modelled in charity fashion shows.

'When we got married Kevin insisted I gave up modelling,' she told Tim, as they lay among a tangle of damp sheets one afternoon. 'He wanted me to be his wife and nothing else. Any modelling career is short-lived and I knew that at best I probably only had a couple of years left.'

'I don't see that,' protested Tim. 'You're absolutely gorgeous.'

'Well, thank you for that very nice compliment, but it's true – it just isn't a long-term career. So when Kevin issued his ultimatum I gave in. But after we'd been married a few years I started to find the life I was leading ... restricting. I love Kevin but he's obsessively jealous. Every evening over dinner we have a debriefing session where I have to account for all my movements throughout the day.'

'Don't you find that annoying?' asked Tim, lazily stroking her breast.

'Yes, very. But if I'm evasive or reluctant to discuss it he interrogates me relentlessly.' She shifted position to fit herself comfortably into the crook of his arm. 'So it's simpler just to tell him everything – except what I don't want him to know.'

She told him she'd been invited to take part in a charity fashion show a few months ago and enjoyed it so much that she'd begun to appear in such shows regularly.

It occurred to Tim that if he revealed this to her husband, it would in all probability allay his suspicions – far more so than if there was nothing to tell.

Accordingly they decided that when he sent in his report it would include details of two shows she'd been in recently. That way Kevin would put any lingering traces of the excitement he thought he'd seen on her face down to a performance on the catwalk rather than in some other man's bed.

'And I can continue with my rendezvous with Veronica,' said Jenny wickedly. 'The ridiculous thing is that I don't honestly think he'll mind about the charity shows – it's the sort of thing which will go down well with his clients. The real reason I didn't tell him was because I feel the need for privacy in some aspects of my life and I do resent his possessiveness. Anyway – it's a great idea, thanks Tim.'

'Glad to be of service, ma'am,' drawled Tim, rolling onto his back and pulling her on top of him. 'Talking of which, is there anything else I can do for you before I have to be on my way?'

She sat astride him and reached for his dick, which in the last few minutes had awoken from its post-coital slumber and begun to sit up and take notice again.

'I think there just might be,' she said.

Alexa expected the countryside around Marrakech to be dry and arid, but on the way to the Ourika Valley the car wound its way through fertile farmlands and orchards as lush and green as anywhere in northern Europe.

The snow-capped peaks of the High Atlas dominated

the horizon, half obscured by cloud but still an impressive sight in the late morning sunshine.

Seated beside Will, Alexa was in a state of stomach-churning excitement. He'd suggested a lunch time picnic in the foothills at the base of the mountains, but knowing Will she was sure that more than food and drink was going to be on offer.

He'd picked her up at her hotel earlier that morning and assured her that his staff had packed a feast for them in the large coolbag in the boot of the car.

He sat silently beside her as he drove, staring impassively ahead. When he'd picked her up he'd repeated his invitation to move into his house with him. He asked her every time they met and he was obviously finding her continued refusal annoying.

But Alexa knew she needed to spend some of her time away from him, otherwise most of their waking hours would be spent in one form of sexual activity or another.

And being in a permanent sexual daze might make her lose sight of her mission.

Alexa was quite happy to make the journey without conversation. She was wondering how soon she could get him to admit that he'd embezzled a considerable sum of money from his ex-employers.

The sooner the better. Then she could offer to share aunt Lily's mythical millions with him and try to persuade him to return the stolen funds.

In the meanwhile she had to work on gaining his total confidence, and what better way was there than going along with whatever sexual scenarios he dreamt up?

She knew she wouldn't have to pretend to find them exciting – her problem was going to be not getting so caught up in them that she forgot the object of her stay here.

Will parked the car in the shade of a tree, then led the way along a rocky path into a flower-strewn orchard. On the outskirts they passed a couple of villagers who greeted them civilly before continuing on their way.

Eventually he chose a small clearing among the trees as the ideal picnic spot and threw down a rough woven cotton rug for them to sit on. Alexa sank gracefully onto it as he opened the bag and pulled out a couple of bottles of chilled beer.

She was wearing a fuchsia-pink sleeveless sundress which showed off her smooth, lightly tanned shoulders and long shapely legs.

Will had complimented her on her appearance earlier. She knew that to please him all she needed to do was show the maximum amount of flesh.

He had always got off on escorting her somewhere and seeing the envious looks on the faces of other men. There was no outfit she could wear which he considered too revealing and he had often urged her to wear even shorter skirts or lower cut dresses.

He sat with his back against the trunk of a tree smoking a cigarette, while she sipped her beer and admired their peaceful surroundings.

'Are you hungry?' he asked her.

'I am, as a matter of fact. I've only had coffee so far today and even half a bottle of beer has made me feel light-headed.'

'Let's eat, then. But first of all take your dress off.'

'I don't think that's a very good idea,' protested Alexa. 'Anyone might come along.'

'It's doubtful. Most people will be starting their siesta around now and we'd hear them before they saw us.'

'I'd still rather keep it on.'

'Take it off.' His cold grey eyes locked with her

green ones and somehow she found herself reaching behind her to unfasten the buttons. Underneath she was wearing a short ivory silk slip over a matching bra and panties.

He studied her admiringly and said, 'We must go shopping sometime soon – I owe you a pair of panties to replace the ones I tore. Now let's see what we have for lunch.'

Lunch turned out to be a selection of Moroccan delicacies including hummus, falafel, ful, stuffed aubergine, vine leaves and tiny savoury pastries. There were various salads and a stack of pitta bread to accompany the meal.

Alexa made a little moan of greed and reached out to take a pastry but he caught her hand and stopped her.

'Just a minute – there's something I need to do first.' He flipped the shoulder straps of her slip down her arms, then deftly undid her bra and removed it. Alexa hastily pulled the slip back up over her breasts, saying, 'Will – I'm definitely not going to sit here nude to please you and risk being ogled by a party of passing locals.'

He took no notice, merely pulled her wrists behind her and tied them swiftly together with her bra. She strained futilely at the makeshift bonds but couldn't free herself.

'And just how am I supposed to eat like this?' she demanded crossly.

'I'm going to feed you,' he replied unperturbed. 'Relax, Alexa – we're at least half a mile from the nearest path.'

He took one of the little pastries she'd been reaching for and popped it into her mouth. Alexa munched it hungrily while he ate a stuffed vine leaf, his eyes never leaving her scantily clad form.

There was something very erotic about sitting in the open air wearing only her diaphanous slip and panties with her hands tied behind her back with her own bra. The position made her breasts thrust forward and drew attention to the twin points of her stiffened nipples.

Will alternated between feeding her and caressing her. Alexa was starving but even so she found it difficult to eat while he traced sensual arabesques on her bare thigh.

She moaned when he cupped one full breast over its flimsy silk covering, then ran his thumb backwards and forwards over her bullet-hard nipple. He pulled her shoulder strap down and fondled her bare breast with one hand while with the other he selected another delicacy for her to eat.

He left her with one breast bare while he helped himself to some aubergine, ignoring her half-hearted protest. She wasn't particularly surprised when he slid his hands up her thighs under her slip and began to draw her panties down her legs.

She was in such a state of arousal by this time that she was past caring and, leaning back on her tied hands, raised her bottom awkwardly to help him. He arranged her with her legs apart and returned to feeding her.

She could feel the hot throbbing of her private parts and wished he'd touch her there. Or even better, unzip his trousers and slide the full, satisfying length of his swollen cock inside her.

She glanced at his groin and saw that he had an impressive erection straining against his trousers. He saw her looking and smiled, then slowly pulled down the zip. He took out his cock and came to kneel up in front of her.

Bending forward, she opened her full lips and took

it between them, letting it slide in as far as it would go. Sucking hard, she slowly withdrew her mouth until only the plum-shaped end remained inside.

She heard him inhale sharply as she ran her tongue lasciviously around the glans, probing the underside then flicking backwards and forwards over the ridge running around the head.

She planted a series of light kisses all the way down the rearing shaft then again took it into her mouth, exerting an erotic suction with her full lips.

She sucked at it like a greedy child with a stick of rock, then abruptly removed her mouth and sat back.

'I'll try some of the hummus now, I think,' she told him, smiling sweetly.

He leant down and scooped some onto a piece of pitta bread.

'Open your legs,' he ordered her. She obeyed and felt his hand gliding between them as he offered her the food with the other. She immediately lost interest in eating as he manipulated her swollen clit. He delved into her yielding interior, grunting under his breath when he felt how wet she was.

'I wasn't planning to screw you until we'd finished eating,' he muttered in her ear, 'but I've just changed my mind.'

'You'd better untie me, then,' Alexa suggested breathlessly.

'I don't think so,' he returned, pulling her to her feet, then standing her with her back to the tree trunk. She leant against it and pushed her pelvis forward invitingly as he caressed her mound then the swollen folds of her labia.

Alexa could barely catch her breath as slowly – too slowly – he slid the full length of his granite-hard shaft into her. Her internal muscles squeezed it welcomingly then he commenced a slow, steady pace.

She could feel the smooth bark of the tree on her bare back and pressed the palms of her bound hands against it to help balance herself. He had her firmly by the waist as he shafted her with long, slow strokes.

It felt wild and wanton to be screwing up against a tree in the middle of a Moroccan orchard. Alexa could smell the mingled scents of the wild flowers around them overlaid by the more pungent smell of hot, dirty sex.

In the heat of the early afternoon they were soon both covered in a fine film of perspiration. Alexa could feel it trickling down her cleavage as she was overtaken by the rush of heat which preceded her climax.

She gasped and gasped again as she came, then she felt the abundant hot spurting inside her as Will joined her only a few seconds later.

Chapter Fourteen

Ralph continued to phone Jess regularly. He stopped asking her when she was coming home because she simply terminated the phone call whenever he did.

Instead, he asked her how she was spending her time and listened with apparent interest as she described exhibitions she'd seen or art galleries she'd visited.

She omitted any mention of working for Tim or her sexual escapades.

It was not unpleasant to have him listening to her for a change. In recent years his business had taken up so much of his attention that he'd never seemed to have time for her. Now he tried to keep her on the phone for as long as possible.

Jess wouldn't allow herself to think about the future. It was only August, after all, and she didn't need to be back at college for pre-term meetings until mid-September.

She still couldn't quite believe it when she caught sight of herself in the mirror. The woman she saw there glowed with sexy vitality, from her gleaming red-gold hair right down to her elegant high-heeled shoes.

She knew a lot of it was down to the transformation Alexa had overseen at the health farm. But some of it she knew was a direct result of all the sexual attention she'd been receiving recently. There was nothing like anticipating an exciting sexual encounter, or dreamily reliving one, to make her whole body feel wonderful.

Except sex itself.

She'd worry about the future when the time came.

Jemaa el Fna in the heart of old Marrakech was a bustling square with constant open-air entertainment in the form of dancers, fire-eaters, mystics, musicians, snake-charmers and fortune-tellers.

Alexa and Will strolled among the crowds for a while, examining the goods on offer and watching the various spectacles being performed for their amusement.

But Will soon grew tired of the hubbub and the demands of the begging children and determined vendors. They retreated to one of the roof-top cafés overlooking the square to rest and refresh themselves with mint tea.

'It's ridiculous for you to keep going back to your hotel to bathe, change and sleep, when we're spending so much time together,' he expostulated, returning to a subject he'd been mentioning with increasing frequency. 'I really don't understand why you won't move in with me.'

'And I've told you it's because I don't want to rush things. And anyway I like to have some privacy,' she returned patiently.

'It's a big house – you can have as much privacy as you want. Even your own bedroom and bathroom if you like.'

'Will, you know quite well that I'd never be able to as much as take a bath without you wanting to watch me,' Alexa pointed out.

Will had always been a voyeur. She was aware of how much he'd like to watch while she prepared herself for their evenings together.

She knew the scenario.

He'd sit silently in the room while she acted as if she were alone. Disrobing, bathing, perfuming and powdering would all take place under his unwavering gaze. All the while she was applying her make-up, drawing her stockings up her shapely legs then slipping into a set of sumptuous silk lingerie, his eyes would linger on her hungrily.

It could be very erotic, particularly as she could never be certain that a few moments later she wouldn't find herself bent over the washbasin being shafted vigorously from behind.

Or on her back on the bedside rug while he straddled her.

Or pulled onto his knee with his cock embedded deep within her.

But it could also be embarrassing. As far as Alexa was concerned the less a lover knew about removing superfluous hair or any of the other less attractive aspects of personal grooming, the better.

Besides, she just liked to be alone sometimes.

She had an uneasy suspicion that if she moved in with Will she'd get drawn into an existence where only pleasure had any meaning. Suddenly, six months would have passed and she'd have completely forgotten why she'd engineered their reunion in the first place.

But he wasn't easily diverted from something he'd set his mind on. Already he was showing signs of the possessiveness she'd always found a problem. He didn't want her out of his sight and she was finding it increasingly difficult to get away from him for even a couple of hours.

It was late afternoon now and she wanted to be alone so she could make her daily phone call to the office and talk to both Tim and Jess. Rising to her feet she said decisively, 'I have some things to do now, Will. Where would you like to go tonight?'

'What things? I'll come with you.'

'I have some calls to make and I want to take a nap. If you're with me I know damn well it won't be sleep which will be on the agenda.'

He smiled wryly but she knew he was annoyed with her.

'I know what,' she suggested. 'I'll let you choose how we spend the evening – make it a surprise. I'll be ready about eight.'

She kissed him and hurried off. She was going to have to work fast to persuade him to return the money – her resolve was already weakening.

A car picked Alexa up at her hotel at eight and took her to Will's house. She was already regretting her suggestion that he decide how they spend the evening – it meant she'd lost any power of veto.

Will was nowhere in sight, but one of the shy Moroccan girls greeted her and led her up the wide marble staircase to the first floor.

When she was conducted to a sumptuous bathroom she guessed what was in store.

She'd already bathed and performed the various other aspects of her grooming routine, but now it looked like she was going to have to go through it all again.

Will was obviously making the point that she might as well have done it here anyway.

The room was dominated by a huge, sunken marble bath and Will was stretched out on a chaise longue to one side of it with a drink in his hand. He didn't speak or greet her and she knew he wanted her to act as if he wasn't there.

One of the girls gave her a glass of chilled white wine and she drank it gratefully. There were three of the maids in the room and they looked so alike that she wondered if they were sisters.

Alexa had dressed carefully for the evening in a midnight blue evening dress which left her shoulders bare. Underneath she was wearing only a pair of pale blue camiknickers and a matching suspender belt holding up a pair of pale stockings.

The three girls began fussing around her. One of them undid her dress and helped her step out of it, leaving her naked from the waist up. She sat on a chair while another pinned her lustrous red-gold hair on top of her head and the third ran a deep bath into which she poured a small bottle of carnation-scented oil.

Alexa allowed them to undress her completely, carefully rolling her stockings down her legs, then removing her suspender belt and camiknickers.

She could see herself reflected in one of the mirrored walls, her breasts voluptuous above her narrow waist, her hips curving down to her long, slender legs.

The water was pleasantly warm and she sank into it gracefully. The girls arranged themselves around the bath and one of them picked up a small natural sponge and rubbed it against a tablet of pink scented soap until she'd worked up a rich lather.

She took one of Alexa's hands and washed her way up to the shoulder, soaping her skin an inch at a time while one of the other girls began on her legs. Alexa leant dreamily back with her head on a small cushion and relaxed.

She couldn't deny that it was pleasant to be pampered this way – particularly when her breasts were thoroughly lathered and rinsed, leaving her coral-tinged nipples eager for more of the same sensual treatment.

When her whole body had been bathed, one of the

girls rinsed her with a hand-held shower spray to remove the last traces of soap.

Alexa stood naked on the marble floor while each girl dried a different part of her with a thick fluffy white towel. Even her bush was patted gently dry.

She glanced at Will while that was happening and saw that his eyes were riveted on her. She wondered idly if the maids had performed the same service for him earlier that evening.

She was led to a towel-covered massage bench and rubbed with carnation-scented oil, recalling memories of a similar scenario with Sam. Only this time instead of one pair of large masculine hands moving over her body, there were three pairs of small feminine ones.

The end result was the same.

By the time they'd finished she was horny as hell.

She wished the girls would go away and leave her alone with Will, but instead they began to dress her again. She couldn't believe the costume. Will had really excelled himself this time.

There was a tight-fitting gauze bodice in a deep pink which only just contained her breasts. It finished just beneath them and was so transparent she might as well have been naked from the waist up.

The matching harem pants were actually open at the crotch, revealing the whole of her private parts to anyone who cared to look. A heavy belt of gold coins was hung around her bare waist and matching bracelets placed on her arms.

The maids left the room taking the damp towels with them while Alexa regarded herself quizzically in the mirror.

'What's this – slave girl for the night?' she asked Will, 'or favourite concubine, perhaps?'

When she was standing with her feet together the

folds of gauze hid her floss-covered delta. Experimentally she opened her legs: the thin material parted to reveal her silken bush and the very tip of her quivering pink clit where it protruded from between the moist folds of her outer lips.

Will swung his long legs to the ground and came to stand behind her, his hands on her waist over the heavy gold coin belt. 'I always thought you had the makings of the perfect concubine,' he murmured in her ear. 'You're like me – you live for pleasure. Imagine what a life together could be like. We've both been freed from the need to grub around earning money. Think how we could live – where we could go.'

His hands travelled caressingly down over her stomach until they came to her exposed bush, exotically framed by the deep pink chiffon. She leant back against him as he slid his index finger through the furry nest until it touched her clitoris.

They both watched in the mirror as she parted her legs further, pushing her pelvis forward so the whole of her glistening, pink pussy was in clear view.

He stroked the shaft of her clit, then the hood, making her tremble with lust. With his other hand he fondled her full breasts over their filmy covering.

Taking the initiative, Alexa moved over to the massage table, hips swaying invitingly. She climbed up and knelt on it, then bent forward placing part of her weight on her hands so she was on all fours.

She could see her reflection from all sides in the slightly angled mirrors. The creamy globes of her buttocks were half veiled by the chiffon of the harem trousers, leaving the cleft which bisected them completely exposed. Her full pink labia lay half unfurled like peony petals, a slick of clear moisture covering the whole area.

Will followed her to the table and she watched him

run his hands over the smooth skin of her bottom, gliding beneath the gauze, then dipping between her legs to push two fingers inside her.

Alexa gasped and pushed her backside against his hand. There was a fiery heat burning in her groin and she wanted his cock inside her more than she wanted anything in the world.

'Fuck me!' she demanded breathlessly.

He needed no urging. Unzipping his trousers he came up behind her and positioned his cock at the entrance to her overheated honeypot. She felt the swollen glans moving over her clit a couple of times, then in one long, smooth thrust he entered her.

She moaned and moved her hips back to meet him. With every thrust she could feel his balls slapping against her backside and his hairy thighs rubbing against the back of her chiffon-covered ones.

With one arm around her waist he bent forward over her and ripped the thin covering of gauze from her full breasts, so they swung free and he could caress them in their naked splendour.

The tempo of their movements quickened, the silence broken only by her moans and his half-audible grunts. As Alexa approached her climax she felt as if the friction of his swollen member was about to make her ignite internally.

When she came, it was like a white-hot explosion which rocked her entire body and prompted Will to discharge himself into her with the force of a geyser erupting.

In the last throes of his orgasm he panted, 'Say you'll move in with me.'

Alexa pushed her rump hard against his groin.

'Shut up, Will and fuck me again.'

'What do you mean – you're leaving?' demanded Tim disbelievingly.

'I'm sorry, Tim, but Geoff and I are moving to Wales to start a smallholding,' explained Beth apologetically.

'A smallholding!' ejaculated Tim in astonishment. 'Isn't that some sort of farm?'

She nodded nervously. Taking a deep breath Tim said, 'Beth, you were born in Battersea. You've lived in London all your life. What on earth do you know about living in the sticks and getting back to nature?'

'Not a lot,' admitted Beth, 'but it's what Geoff wants to do.'

Tim suppressed an urge to put his head in his hands in despair. The agency was operating to capacity, he'd told all his employees not to even think about taking a holiday in the foreseeable future and his best operative was still running up huge expenses in the fleshpots of Marrakech.

When Alexa had phoned in earlier today he'd urged her to bring matters with Will Harper to their conclusion, whatever she had to do.

'I need you here, honey,' he'd told her. 'I'm juggling four different cases, most of the others are handling three and even Jess is dealing with two.'

Alexa had assured him she was working as fast as she could. Tim had seen her in action and knew how she operated where men were concerned, but even he recognised what a delicate case it was and that it wouldn't do to rush it.

Jess was still working on the insurance fraud but was under increasing pressure from Daniel Moult to join the company and work from within.

She was also spending a lot of time with Paul Sears, but Tim knew that she liked the antique dealer a lot and he was concerned that her personal involvement with the man would blind her to anything which pointed to his dishonesty.

At least Jess's open involvement with Paul had

meant that Tim could transfer the temporary secretary he'd placed with the antiques business to another case, but he was still drastically under-staffed.

Now here was Beth giving notice and about to leave him in the lurch.

'When were you thinking of working till?' he asked her.

'The end of the week,' she confessed.

'Your terms of employment require a month's notice,' he reminded her. 'I was hoping you'd make it two.'

She looked down at her feet.

'I'm sorry, Tim, but Geoff wants us to go on Saturday. He gave notice on our flat without telling me and we have to be out by the weekend.'

Tim sighed heavily. Beth was obviously determined to go whether he liked it or not – and he didn't like it. His only consolation was that she'd probably be wanting her job back within a few weeks, having tried the simple life and not liked it.

Which was absolutely no help to him at the moment.

'Okay, Beth – ask Martha to sort the paperwork out tomorrow, will you? I'm real sorry you're going, you've done some good work in the time you've been here.'

As soon as she'd left the room Tim poured himself a shot of Bourbon and considered the situation. There was nothing else for it – he'd have to work a double shift. He was getting little enough sleep now, but he'd have to manage on even less. He glanced at his watch. Ten-thirty. He was beat but there was too much to do to go home yet.

Beth had been keeping Paul Sears' partner, Marcia, under surveillance. From Saturday he'd have to get Jess to cover them both whenever possible and he'd have to follow Marcia the rest of the time.

Life was a bitch sometimes.

After they'd eaten, Will suggested they go into the city and visit a couple of clubs. Alexa changed back into her midnight blue dress and Will's driver dropped them at one of the city's most popular nightclubs.

After a couple of hours they moved on to another club, but from the moment they walked through the door Alexa realised that this place was a long way from the glamorous, cosmopolitan nightspot they'd just left.

Dimly lit and seedy, it was only half full and it didn't take Alexa long to deduce that she was probably the only woman in there not being paid for her favours.

They'd arrived during a break in the entertainment, but a few minutes after they'd settled at a table with their drinks, a spotlight lit up the small, dusty stage.

When a plump, blonde woman appeared carrying a depressed-looking snake, Alexa groaned and hissed, 'Will – do we really have to sit through this? We both know what she's going to do with the snake, and it doesn't look too happy about it.'

Will's only reply was to place his hand on her stocking-clad knee without taking his eyes off the stage. Alexa sighed and settled back resignedly.

When it was over she yawned and said, 'I think it's time for me to go back to my hotel.'

'Not just yet,' he insisted, 'there's something else we've got to see.'

He took her hand and led her to a door in a dark corner where an old woman sat at a table. He spoke to the woman briefly, handed her some money, then opened the door and went through it taking Alexa with him.

A narrow, ill-lit corridor led off into the darkness

215

with several doors opening off it. Will stopped at the third then turned the handle and went in, pulling Alexa behind him.

The only light in the room came through what Alexa, well versed in such matters because of her job, recognised as a one-way mirror. Through it she could see into a bedroom with a circular bed in the centre covered with a nylon magenta spread.

'Will – this is a peepshow,' Alexa accused him.

'That's right,' he agreed, sitting in the one chair and pulling her onto his lap. She could see that there were several identical mirrors overlooking the bedroom, each doubtless with a small room behind it like the one they were in.

There was a stale musty smell and she suspected she was the only woman to have visited this room in recent memory.

After a short wait, an exotic-looking dark-haired girl entered the room and glided over to the bed, where she arranged herself in a seductive reclining position. She was wearing a black mini-skirt with black stockings and stiletto-heeled shoes. Her large breasts were crammed into a low cut, tight-fitting, gold lurex top which gave her a cleavage with dimensions which approached those of the grand canyon.

The bed began to revolve slowly while the girl stroked her own breasts and kept changing position so that all the hidden watchers caught frequent glimpses of her stocking tops and the lacy edges of her black panties above them.

Her caresses became more lascivious as she stroked her own hips and thighs. Alexa felt Will's cock, already hard, swell even more beneath her as the girl drew her scarlet-nailed finger over her black panties, her skirt hitched up around her hips.

Alexa felt Will's hand slip up her thigh under her

216

skirt. He smoothed over the bare skin above her stockings then probed delicately between her legs with his fingertips. She knew he was checking to see if her own camiknickers were damp.

They were.

The woman on the bed removed her mini-skirt just as Will slipped his fingers underneath the loose edge of the pale blue satin and explored the slippery wetness he found there.

The dark woman had plump hips and thighs with well-rounded buttocks and a luxuriant bush, both barely covered by her brief panties. She rubbed her mound with a seductive smile, then knelt up and squeezed and fondled her ample bottom.

Alexa wriggled her own backside further into Will's lap then parted her legs encouragingly so he could get two fingers inside her. While he moved them in and out of her the woman slowly removed her gold lurex top revealing a stunning pair of large breasts which she proceeded to massage, rolling the large dark brown nipples between her finger and thumb.

Will's fingers moving in and out of her dripping tunnel were making Alexa want more.

She lifted her weight from him, swiftly undid his zip and released his cock from his briefs, while he impatiently pushed her skirt up around her waist out of the way and pulled her camiknickers down around her thighs.

Positioning herself carefully so the bulbous head of his rock-hard cock was nudging against the entrance to her velvety chamber, she sat slowly down onto it, feeling him filling her up completely.

The woman they were watching slowly removed her panties, revealing the thick thatch of her pubic hair covering the hidden delta between her legs.

As the woman stroked her bush, Alexa rode Will's

cock, rising and falling on it, helped by the pressure of his hands on her hips as he lifted her and pulled her down in time to their movements.

He felt so big and hot inside her that Alexa was driven into a frenzy. The chair had no arms and there was nothing to brace herself on and she was finding it frustrating.

'Stand up,' she urged Will.

Holding her around the waist he stood up so she could lean forward against the one-way mirror between them and the woman they were watching. Alexa stood with her legs wide apart and the palms of her hands flat against the glass as Will shafted her forcefully from behind.

By now the woman had her own legs wide apart and was masturbating, while the bed continued to revolve slowly to give all the watchers a chance to see her rubbing her deep pink vulva and dark red clit.

Alexa's own private parts were hot, swollen and dripping and she could feel moisture trickling into her stocking tops as she jammed her hips backwards to meet each thrust.

Will was plunging into her like a man possessed. She felt herself hovering on the brink of an earth-shattering climax and held her breath. Will's last three, piston-driven thrusts flattened her against the glass, her head falling back as the first of several waves of hot, shuddering pleasure swept over her.

She registered the hot jets of Will's sperm erupting inside her, just as the woman on the bed reached her own very public orgasm.

Alexa wondered how many of the woman's hidden audience were enjoying a private, self-induced climax at the same time.

Probably all of them.

Chapter Fifteen

Jess liked both Paul Sears and his partner Marcia and was quite happy to spend as much of her time as she could spare from working on the insurance fraud keeping tabs on the two antique dealers.

It hadn't taken her long to discover that Marcia had an enormous number of male admirers and appeared to have a social life which rivalled Alexa's. She was constantly receiving phone calls from different men and rarely a day went by without one or more of them appearing in the shop.

While Marcia was on the phone late one afternoon, Paul was showing Jess a particularly beautiful chest of drawers he'd recently bought at an auction.

They were standing towards the back of the shop, behind the chest of drawers, while Jess examined the fine craftsmanship. Over by the window an elderly couple were looking at a set of bone china and exclaiming over its delicacy.

Jess was trying hard to hear what Marcia was saying so she could report back to Tim, but it was difficult to concentrate because she could feel Paul's hand gliding up her leg under her skirt. He particularly liked to touch her intimately in public, but covertly so no one else could see.

Jess had been horribly embarrassed the day before to have Marcia suddenly come out of the office and see Paul fondling one of her bare breasts. There were a couple of people in the shop but Jess had her back to them. Paul had undone the top two buttons of her blouse, pulled her camisole to one side and was caressing her while appearing to show her something in a catalogue.

It had been very exciting but she hadn't been expecting Marcia to appear – she'd thought the blonde woman was upstairs. Jess had blushed scarlet and hastily refastened her dress, while Marcia had continued on her way with an amused smile on her face.

Now, as Paul's hand stroked the lower cheeks of her bottom, Jess strained to hear Marcia's side of the conversation. Whatever she was saying it had a conspiratorial tone to it.

She heard her say, 'Yes, I know it – the one just outside Windsor? Mmm, yes, I love their way of doing duck. Eight o'clock tomorrow, then? Bye. Yes – you too.'

Marcia hung up, scribbled something in her diary and started towards them. Paul's hand left Jess's bottom and when Marcia came round the side of the chest of drawers they weren't touching.

'It's nearly closing time,' said Marcia, glancing at her watch. 'Could you possibly lock up, Paul? I've got to dash.'

'Hot date?' he teased her.

'Red-hot,' she agreed. 'I'll lock the safe before I go.' She vanished into the office just as Paul's attention was attracted by the elderly couple looking at the china.

Left alone at the back of the shop, Jess wandered over to where Marcia's diary was lying open next to her bag. A quick glance showed her that Marcia had scrawled 'Henry. Red Barn. 8 p.m.'

It shouldn't be too difficult for Tim to keep tabs on

Marcia if he knew where she was spending the evening.

Will was being difficult.

He and Alexa had spent the afternoon together relaxing by his swimming pool and now she was preparing to take her leave.

'Why do you have to go?' he persisted.

'Will! It's only going to be for a couple of hours. I want to make some calls and then get showered and changed,' she explained patiently.

'You can do that here.'

'Not in private, I can't.'

'Who are you calling that you don't want me to know about?' he demanded.

Alexa sighed and rose to her feet, pulling her sundress on as she did so.

'You're being tiresome, Will. Keep it up and I may decide not to see you at all tonight.'

Will stood up and pulled her against him, winding a hand in her thick red-gold hair. She could feel the hardness of his erection against her despite the fact they'd only finished screwing about half an hour ago.

'You will see me tonight, Alexa, because I've arranged a surprise for you.' Despite her annoyance Alexa immediately felt herself becoming excited again.

'What is it?' she asked reluctantly.

Will's hand traced a path down her back then caressed her backside with an arousing circular movement.

'It's something you're going to love,' he breathed in her ear. 'Something that's going to make you so hot you'll keep me awake all night begging me to fuck you over and over again.'

Alexa felt a faint bubbling sensation between the

221

folds of her labia and knew that hot moisture was gathering there in eager anticipation.

'Tell me,' she urged him huskily. He released her and lay back down on his sunbed, looking faintly triumphant because he knew he had her interest.

'I'll pick you up at your hotel at around eight-thirty.' He put on his dark glasses and picked up a newspaper.

Tim pulled tiredly into the car park of the Red Barn and looked for a space. After following Marcia from London he'd waited down the road for a few minutes to allow her time to get inside the restaurant. He was now resigned to a wait of at least a couple of hours.

It was a beautiful summer evening and the country lanes around Windsor were like dim green tunnels overhung with trees in full leaf. The sun was sinking slowly to the horizon, bathing the fields and meadows in golden light. But the lovely rural surroundings were wasted on Tim, who could barely keep his eyes open.

He just wanted to know who Marcia was meeting so he could have whoever it was checked out. All he needed was to see which car her escort drove off in and he could trace him through the number plate. After that he could go home, do a couple of hours' paperwork and go to bed.

Following Marcia while she pursued her hectic social life was tiring Tim out, but there just wasn't anyone else to do it. To date he'd checked out six of her male friends in the hope of finding one with some sort of criminal connections, however tenuous, but so far to no avail.

In a paper bag on the passenger seat he had a cheese sandwich and an apple – an evening meal which didn't exactly make him salivate with anticipation. He considered driving into Windsor and seeing if he could get a takeway burger and fries, but reluctantly rejected the idea. He couldn't take the risk that they'd leave before he got back.

He'd brought a pile of paperwork to do – no point in wasting any time. He was just reaching for his briefcase when he was startled by a tap on his window.

Turning his head sharply to the right he was taken aback to see the woman he was supposed to be keeping under surreptitious surveillance smiling at him and indicating he should roll down his window.

Where the hell had she sprung from? The car park had appeared to be deserted when he'd arrived and she certainly hadn't just come out of the restaurant, the entrance was in full view.

Groaning to himself he opened the window.

'I'm sorry to bother you,' she said sweetly, 'but do you have any tools in your car?'

She was bending down to look in through the window and Tim caught a waft of her perfume as she spoke to him. He could also see close up that she was even more stunningly lovely than when viewed from a distance.

She had the full, sensual lips of a woman who enjoyed the pleasures of the flesh and they were curved in the sort of provocative smile which made his dick sit up and take notice, despite his state of near exhaustion. They were the sort of lips a man couldn't look at without imagining them sliding up and down his member; wet, warm and welcoming.

She was wearing a dark green jacket over a scooped neck white silk top. The way she was bending forward meant that Tim could see right down the front of it. The upper curves of her full, firm breasts were displayed for his delectation only a few inches from his face.

Resisting the impulse to pull her close and bury his

face between them Tim managed to say, 'Excuse me?'

'Do you have any tools with you? I've dropped one of my earrings and I think it's rolled under a car and I can't reach it.'

Resigning himself to the inevitable, Tim opened the door and swung his long legs out. He towered over her even in her high-heeled shoes.

'Where?' he asked laconically.

'Over here.' She led the way to the far side of her car and indicated the one next to it. That's why he hadn't spotted her – she must have been bending down out of his line of vision and he'd assumed she'd gone into the restaurant.

'It fell off as I got out of my car. I've searched the whole area and there's no sign of it, so I think it must have rolled under there.'

She smiled at him beguilingly and bent forward to try to see under the car. Her skirt tightened over the glorious rounded curves of her backside and rode up her thighs, making Tim gulp and rooting him firmly to the spot.

'Can you see it?' she asked him.

He squatted down and peered into the shadows under the vehicle. He could see something twinkling on the tarmac and straightened up.

'I think so.' He went back to his own car and opened the boot. Taking out a crowbar he returned to her side and bent down again. She gave the crowbar a quizzical look but didn't comment and Tim mentally kicked himself for not producing something more innocuous – a spanner, for example.

Hopefully, she was more interested in the return of her earring than why he was carrying such an implement in his car.

After a couple of attempts he managed to hook the tiny piece of jewellery and pull it out. He picked it up and handed it to her.

'Thank you so much,' she said with a dazzling smile, clipping it back in place. 'I would have hated to disturb someone's meal by asking them to come and move their car.'

'My pleasure, ma'am.'

'You're American,' she exclaimed delightedly. 'Which part of the States are you from?'

'North Carolina.'

'Really? I visited Charleston once – it's a beautiful place. Do you live over here or are you just visiting?'

'I live in London.'

'Really? So do I.'

Tim knew. In fact he knew exactly where.

She glanced at her watch.

'I'd better not keep Henry waiting any longer – I must have been out here for about fifteen minutes. I hope I haven't made you late for your own meal.'

She began to stroll towards the restaurant entrance, pausing by Tim's car as he stowed the crowbar away. He realised that she was waiting for him so they could enter the restaurant together.

He couldn't see any way out of it. Why would he have been in the Red Barn's car park if not about to dine there? No plausible reason sprang into his tired mind.

What the hell – at least he'd get a decent meal.

Just before they reached the canopied doorway, Marcia caught one of her high heels in a cracked paving stone and would have fallen if Tim hadn't caught her. In a reflex reaction his arms closed around her and he held her tightly to his chest.

He could feel her soft, feminine curves pressing against him and was immediately swamped by a wave of pure lust. He knew that his hard-on was digging into her stomach and tried to ease it away as soon as he was sure she'd regained her balance.

To his surprise she didn't seem in any hurry to leave

the circle of his arms and if he hadn't been so tired he would have sworn she was pushing her hips against him slightly harder than was necessary.

She smiled up at him apologetically, her hands holding lightly onto his shoulders.

'I'm sorry – high heels may look good but they aren't very practical.'

She tried to free her heel but it seemed to be wedged in the crack and she lost her balance again. Tim kept her enfolded to his chest while the blood pounded against his temples and he tried to block out the several erotic scenarios which presented themselves to his heated imagination.

'It seems to be stuck,' she murmured ruefully.

'Let's take a look.'

Regretfully he released her and bent down while she held onto his shoulder to keep from overbalancing. The heel was firmly lodged in the crack and in an attempt to free it he fastened one large hand around her slender ankle and the other around the back of the shoe.

Her ankle felt delicate and fine-boned and from up her skirt he caught another whiff of her seductive perfume, suggesting that she'd sprayed it all over her gorgeous body.

He had a mental image of her, naked except for her stiletto-heeled shoes, lavishly spraying first her high, firm breasts so the nipples hardened, then . . .

'Won't it come out?'

Tim was jerked back to reality by her question and with a firm tug he managed to free her. He stood up again and asked, 'Is your shoe badly damaged?'

Marcia stood on one leg and leant against him while she examined it.

'Ruined, I'm sorry to say,' she said cheerfully. 'Not to worry – I've got more shoes than I ever wear.'

She replaced it on her foot, then to his astonishment wound her arms around his neck and kissed him with parted lips, her tongue sliding into his mouth. After a moment's hesitation Tim pulled her hard against him and kissed her back, his hands travelling over the fine fabric of her dark green jacket.

When she released him she said, 'That's just to say thank you.'

'You're welcome,' he responded automatically.

'Now I think we'd better go in – Henry must have given me up.'

He followed her dazedly through the door and watched her follow a waiter to her table where a supercilious looking middle-aged man was waiting. He himself acceded to the waiter's suggestion that he take a seat at the bar.

Tim took one look at the menu and blanched at the prices. What was this place? The starters alone were more than his weekly food bill. Rather belatedly he realised he was also seriously under-dressed. All the other men were wearing collars and ties while he was in his usual casual garb of jeans, shirt and leather jacket. He'd thought the waiter seemed a bit sniffy.

Too damned bad.

He decided to throw caution to the winds and enjoy his meal, even if it did cost a fortune. After taking his order the waiter led him to a small table by the wood-panelled wall, directly opposite Marcia and her supercilious companion.

The restaurant was broken up into a series of small rooms each with only a few tables, giving it an intimate atmosphere.

Marcia acknowledged his arrival with a smile and a faint enigmatic lift of her perfectly arched eyebrows. He watched her surreptitiously while she chatted to her companion, enjoying the sight of her stocking-clad legs sexily crossed under the table.

It didn't take Tim long to deduce Henry was a first-class prick: he had a loud voice and an arrogant manner and Tim took an instant dislike to him.

Marcia was listening politely but Tim saw a faint expression of annoyance flit across her face when Henry interrupted her as she began to say something.

A minute later her first course arrived – it looked like mushrooms in some exotic sauce – and as she raised her fork she looked Tim straight in the eye.

The way she took the mushroom into her delectable mouth was one of the sexiest things Tim had ever seen. He caught a glimpse of the pink tongue which had been flickering between his own lips a short while ago and felt sweat forming on his brow.

His starter was placed before him and he began to eat it without really tasting it as he watched Marcia transform eating into a form of sexual foreplay.

He tried not to watch her too obviously, but fortunately the other diners were all too intent on their meals and Henry on the sound of his own loud voice to notice.

The waiter had just removed his plate when Tim's attention was attracted by a flash of white below the table opposite him. Glancing across the room he saw that Marcia's skirt had ridden up her thighs so far that as she uncrossed her legs he could see the frilly edges of her white panties, her stocking tops and her suspenders.

Tim gulped and took a mouthful from his unbelievably over-priced glass of wine.

He looked furtively from side to side but quickly realised that the only person in the room able to see this stirring sight was him. She wasn't in anyone else's line of vision.

Was she doing it deliberately?

In answer, she did it again, taking even longer about it this time.

Tim was transfixed.

His imagination wasn't the only thing running riot and he pulled his napkin further up his lap to conceal his straining erection.

While she ate her main course, Marcia continued crossing and uncrossing her legs, sometimes giving him a glimpse of a palish fuzz around the frilly white underwear before her knees crossed again.

Tim paid so little attention to his own beautifully cooked meal that it might as well have been the cheese sandwich and apple.

When she'd finished eating, she picked up her bag and undulated across the room to the ladies. She was gone a while and when she slid gracefully into her seat again Tim looked across at her and found himself staring directly at her delectable pussy.

He closed his eyes briefly, thinking that exhaustion had got the better of him and he was hallucinating.

He looked again.

He could definitely see her fluffy, blonde bush.

She must have taken off her panties in the ladies.

When her hand slipped between her legs and she began to stroke her clit, he moaned aloud, then hastily turned it into a cough as a couple of heads turned at a neighbouring table.

Above the table she was sipping coffee and apparently listening politely to Henry, below the table she was delicately masturbating.

If Tim hadn't been so aroused he'd have laughed at the idea of the hapless Henry completely unaware of what was going on under his nose.

It was more than he could stand. He was almost overpowered by a desire to walk over, take her by the hand and lead her outside.

Then fuck her in the first private spot he could find.

He'd noticed her attracting admiring glances from other men in the room, their eyes lingering on the curves of her breasts under the skimpy, scooped neck top.

He was getting a lot more than that – his own private X-rated show.

She suddenly rose to her feet while Henry was in mid-flow said something to him, picked up her bag and jacket and left the room, shooting a provocative glance over her shoulder at Tim.

Henry was thrown into consternation by her sudden departure and indicated to the waiter that he wanted the bill – evidently with the intention of following her.

Tim was quicker.

He also carried a large amount of cash – in his business you never knew when you might need it. He already knew roughly what his exorbitantly priced meal had cost and threw down enough cash to cover it, together with a generous tip.

Hurrying outside, he was just in time to see Marcia's tail lights disappearing as she pulled out of the car park in her sleek white Mercedes.

He raced to his own car, leapt in and set off in hot pursuit. He was a good and fast driver and experienced in chase manoeuvres from his years in the CIA, but even so he had difficulty keeping up as she raced along the dark country lanes. He was used to driving in the city and found the winding, unlit road difficult to read.

She stayed a tantalising distance ahead of him, but he stuck grimly to her tail. She turned into an even narrower country lane and vanished from sight.

He roared along it as it wound steeply upwards, then he suddenly stamped on the brakes and came to a screaming, skidding halt. She'd pulled off the road and onto the verge.

Tim was pretty much on the verge himself when he saw that she was lying across the bonnet of her car stretched out on one elbow, her sensual lips curved in a provocative smile.

'What took you so long?' she purred.

'I'm not used to chasing fast women,' he replied, his eyes devouring her body.

'Then your education's been sadly neglected,' she teased him. 'Tell me, do you like your women fast? I think I'd better warn you – I like my men slow, very slow. And I don't mean slow on the uptake. I mean I like them to take their time.'

She leant back on the car bonnet, arching her back and drawing one leg up beneath her. They were parked on the brow of a hill and although it wasn't quite dark a full moon had already risen and was bathing everything in pale, silvery light.

Tim caught another glimpse of her shadowy crotch and moved towards her. He slipped one hand inside her white top and closed it on her firm, naked breast. The nipple was already hard and felt like a small marble against the palm of his hand.

She leant forward and unzipped his trousers, releasing his dick and closing her luscious wet mouth over the swollen head. Her hand cradled his balls as she sucked hard, drawing more of it into her mouth.

It felt wonderful.

Tim caressed her full breasts as she flicked her tongue along the full throbbing length of his shaft, his exhaustion forgotten.

He was already so worked up after her impromptu exhibitionism, that he suspected he was going to erupt like a volcano within a very short time.

And there was a lot he wanted to do first.

Reluctantly withdrawing his ecstatically happy dick from the hot wetness of her mouth, he pushed her skirt up around her hips to get a close-up of her lovely pussy. The silken blonde fuzz of her bush only partially concealed her daintily spread private parts.

He parted her outer lips with his hands and pushed his tongue into her, licking and probing her velvety tunnel. She wriggled her bare bottom closer to him across the cold, slippery surface of the car so he could bury his face in the heated liquid of her honeypot.

He took his time about it and didn't stop until he'd brought her to a shivering, throbbing climax. When he withdrew his mouth and stood up she was lying back across the car bonnet, her back arched, her head thrown back and her legs spread in a position of complete abandon.

He rubbed his dick against the wet, swollen entrance to her pussy, then slid it slowly into her. The walls of her honeypot gripped it tightly as he commenced a steady seductive rhythm.

She pulled him down on top of her, wrapping her legs around his waist. Her buttocks made a faint slapping noise against the paintwork as they rose and fell to meet each controlled thrust.

The silence of the warm summer evening was broken only by the sounds of hot, dirty sex as they screwed frantically away on the bonnet of the Mercedes.

At last, when Tim couldn't hold back any longer, he pumped his sperm into her in a series of powerful gasping thrusts, holding her tightly against him with his hands beneath her backside.

He rolled off her and they lay side by side across the bonnet.

'Well now,' she said, 'that really wasn't bad as an appetiser.'

An appetiser?

Tim was well and truly knackered and only regretted that they weren't lying in his bed so he could now close his eyes and get some much-needed sleep.

His exhaustion had caught up with him and he felt as if someone had given him a good kicking. He ached in every limb and had about as much strength left as a three-day-old kitten.

Playing for time he said, 'That was quite a show you put on in the restaurant.'

'I know,' she agreed, 'I just couldn't resist it.'

'Do you make a habit of it?'

She snuggled up against him and he put his arm around her. His left hand came to rest a tantalising couple of inches from her breast and he couldn't resist slipping it inside her clothing to fondle the full roundness he found there. She sighed with pleasure as he rubbed his thumb over her nipple.

'Not really. I succumbed to a sudden impulse.'

Succumbing to a sudden impulse himself, Tim pushed her skirt back up above her thighs and exposed her glistening honeypot. The memory of her sitting there in the expensive restaurant, showing herself to him without anyone else knowing, made his dick stir again.

He traced the edges of her bush with his forefinger.

'I'm glad you did – you made my day.'

'Only your day?' she teased him. 'Not your week? Or your month?'

'Probably my year,' he admitted. Or at least it felt like that at the time.

His forefinger slid between the soft, glistening grooves of her labia and encountered the throbbing little point of her clit.

She squirmed against him, her breathing immediately ragged. He took her clit between his finger and thumb and rubbed it gently, making her moan faintly and move closer.

Amazingly, his dick rose from its recumbent

233

position and reared hesitantly skywards.

Marcia was making little gasping, mewing noises as she got nearer and nearer to her climax and, unable to believe he was doing this in his current state of collapse, Tim scooped her up and laid her face down with her legs wide apart.

The sight of the smooth white cheeks of her backside framed by the frilly little suspender belt she was wearing made him catch his breath.

Overworked and tired out as he was, he somehow found the strength for one last bout over the car bonnet.

Chapter Sixteen

The lights in the room seemed dazzling and a sour smell rose from the nylon magenta coverlet on the circular bed. Kneeling there with her legs wide apart, the woman caressed her own breasts, paying particular attention to her coral-tinged nipples, and wondered exactly how many men were watching her.

It was a strange feeling knowing that on the other side of the four walls, total strangers were able to see her pleasuring herself and presumably finding it exciting. As the bed slowly revolved, Alexa found herself wondering which of the mirrors concealed Will.

She wasn't even sure why she was doing this. When Will had told her what he'd arranged her initial reaction had been an outright refusal.

But then somehow she'd looked into his cold grey eyes and found herself agreeing.

He'd dressed her for the occasion in a black basque trimmed with purple lace, matching briefs, a suspender belt and a pair of fishnet stockings. The upper part of her face was hidden behind a mask to preserve her anonymity, but she'd unlaced the basque so her full breasts were exposed for all to see.

And soon she'd have to remove her panties and expose her private parts to the unseen eyes.

Her hands moved slowly up her thighs, stroking

and caressing them over the fishnet stockings, then glided upwards to hook in the elastic of her panties and slowly, oh so slowly, draw them down over her legs.

Tim watched the lights go out in Marcia's flat before starting his car and driving back towards the shop. She'd been working late there until around eleven when she'd at last emerged and driven straight home.

Tim had decided it was time to do a little breaking and entering to see what he could find both lying around and locked in the safe. Jess had done her best but she couldn't go snooping round too overtly and risk being caught by either Paul or Marcia.

He'd phoned her earlier on his car phone to ask if she knew why Marcia was working so late, but as far as Jess knew Marcia was planning to leave as soon as the shop shut.

The shop had a very sophisticated security system but Jess had ingenuously questioned Paul about it and passed on enough information for Tim to be confident of immobilising it.

Once inside he began a methodical search. The safe contained nothing of any real interest. Certificates of authentication, insurance documents, cash and cheques.

Upstairs in one of the storerooms, however, he found two large packing cases. It took him a while to get them open so it would be undetectable, but when he eventually did examine the contents by the light of his powerful torch he let out a silent whistle.

The contents of each case were identical. Both contained what appeared to be the same four pieces, but as they couldn't all be the real McCoy, one case obviously contained reproductions.

So, was it Paul, Marcia or both of them shipping

out forgeries as genuine antiques? And where were the real ones headed?

A sound just behind him made him turn his head. Standing in the doorway was Marcia and what she was holding in her hand made his blood run cold.

An old but perfectly serviceable World War Two Luger.

Tim had been around guns often enough to be terrified of them. He'd seen at first hand too many times just what an horrific effect a bullet could have on flesh and bone.

One of the advantages of working in England was that the people he was investigating rarely had access to firearms, so the risk of getting shot at was minimal. He owned a gun himself but usually it stayed locked in his safe at home.

He didn't dare move a muscle.

'Well now,' said Marcia softly, 'if it isn't my American friend. May I ask who you are – other than a damn good fuck, that is?'

She advanced into the dark room, which was lit only by Tim's torch and the light shining in from the street lamps outside. He watched her warily, noting that she kept a safe distance from him.

When he didn't reply she continued, 'Are you from the Customs and Excise? It seems unlikely since you're American, but our meeting in the car park can't be the chance encounter I assumed it was. You must have been following me. I want you to take out your wallet, very slowly, and toss it onto that packing case.'

Tim obeyed. He was no fool. He had no idea whether she knew how to use a gun or would be prepared to do so – but he wasn't about to find out the hard way.

She picked up his wallet and rifled through it

without taking her eyes off him, then glanced swiftly at his Private Investigator's identification card.

'Who hired you?' she demanded.

'The head of the group.'

'Why?'

'He was tipped off that reproduction antiques were being passed off as the genuine article by either you or your partner.' He nodded towards the packing cases. 'Looks to me like his information was right. Is your partner in on this or is it just you?'

'Just me. Paul's far too straight to get involved in anything shady – more's the pity. It would have been much easier for me if he was in on it. Anyway, at the risk of sounding like a cliché – I'll ask the questions.'

She silently considered the situation for a while.

'This has suddenly become very complicated,' she observed. 'If only you'd left it another week. Now I'm going to have to leave in a hurry with all sorts of messy loose ends lying around.'

Tim hoped fervently he wasn't going to be one of them. He eyed the distance between them speculatively. If she were holding any weapon other than a gun he'd take the risk of being injured and jump her. She was only slight, after all, but a gun more than evened the odds.

She was frowning as she stared at him.

'I can't think of any way of tying you up without putting the gun down,' she admitted. 'I suppose I'm going to have to call for reinforcements.'

The phone was standing on a small Georgian table a few feet from her. She glanced at it, then keeping her eyes on him moved towards it. When she looked away briefly to step over a box of china, Tim saw his chance. The telephone wire ran from the socket, over a large crate just behind him and snaked across the floor to the phone.

Furtively he reached behind him, grabbed the wire and tugged hard, throwing himself to the floor a split second later. Marcia tripped over the wire and went headlong down onto the floor, the pistol flying out of her hand.

It fell only a few inches away from her and she rolled sideways onto her back and reached out for it frantically.

Moving fast, Tim threw himself on top of her, grabbing her wrist just as she picked it up. He felt the cold, serious sweat of fear as she managed to point it at him briefly, before he tightened his hand over her wrist like a vice and she dropped it again.

He batted it sharply away from them then gasped with pain as she managed to knee him in the groin. She struggled beneath him with surprising strength for such a delicately built woman, twisting like an angry cat as she tried to free herself.

Even so it only took a few seconds for him to immobilise her, with her wrists held over her head and her thighs trapped under one of his. She was wearing a light summer dress under a linen jacket and he ran his free hand swiftly over her body to make sure she didn't have anything on her that she could use as a weapon.

She suddenly stopped struggling and looked up at him from under her long lashes.

'Are you groping me or looking for concealed weapons?'

'Just making sure you don't have any more surprises like that one,' he told her grimly, nodding towards the Luger.

She relaxed in his grasp and laughed softly.

'Pity. The gun isn't loaded – but don't take my word for it.'

Still keeping her pinned to the floor Tim reached

239

out and picked up the Luger.

She was telling the truth.

'Do you think I could sit up? This isn't exactly the most comfortable position in the world.'

Cautiously, Tim released her hands and withdrew his leg. She sat up and massaged her wrists.

'So, what are you thinking of doing now?' she asked him. 'My guess is it won't be phoning the police.'

She was quite right. The reason Tim had been put on the case was because the group wanted to keep the situation under wraps and calling in the police would involve unwelcome publicity.

'I guess I'd better phone the head of the group and see what he wants me to do next.'

'What he's going to want is a discreet cover-up. They won't prosecute because they'll want to keep it from becoming public knowledge.'

She smiled at him bewitchingly.

'But quite frankly I'd rather spare myself the embarrassment of being grilled by both him and the directors of all our sister companies. So why don't I just leave quietly now and leave you to take the credit for exposing me?'

'I don't think so.' Tim's eyes wandered regretfully over her skimpily clad body. 'They're paying me. What they say goes.'

He stood up and picked up the phone.

Marcia rose to her feet and stretched. The light from Tim's powerful torch was coming from directly behind her and he could see the shape of her gorgeous body through the thin dress.

He could also see that underneath it she was completely naked.

He'd suspected it when he'd run his hand over her a minute earlier. His close proximity to her soft, curvaceous body had had its inevitable result, despite his fear of the gun and the pain in his still-throbbing balls.

He fumbled through his pockets looking for the number he needed, just as Marcia moved towards the door.

'Don't leave the room or I'll only have to drag you back,' he warned her nervously. Tim liked fucking women not fighting them and his struggle with her had sent out a lot of confusing signals to his brain.

'I only want to tidy my hair,' she told him, nodding towards her bag which was on a chair by the door.

'Don't move!' he shouted, worried what it might contain. 'Stay right there!'

He strode over to the bag, picked it up and rummaged around in it, while she stood with her hands on her hips, watching him with an amused smile curving her full lips.

It contained the usual female paraphernalia, but nothing she could possibly use as a weapon, so he passed it to her and went back to the phone and plugged it back in. He watched her while the operator connected him.

Raising her hands to her hair meant that her short dress rode up, revealing most of her tanned thighs. The light was still behind her and he could see the sharp thrust of her nipples pushing against the thin fabric of her dress. He swallowed, then his call was connected and he spoke to the group head who, luckily, was still up – even at this late hour.

When he put the phone down she smiled at him.

'What comes next?'

'He's sending some men over to pick you up. They'll be here in about an hour.

She looked thoughtful.

'I wonder what we can do to pass the time?' she purred, then slowly slipped her jacket from her shoulders and walked towards him, hips swaying.

Tim's dick leapt eagerly against his zip at the unmistakable note of sexual invitation in her voice. He knew this was a bad idea. A smart man would keep his distance until the reinforcements arrived and relieved him of his responsibility.

But the memory of their abandoned, dirty sex over the bonnet of her sleek Mercedes was too recent and too potent.

So when she stopped just in front of him and coiled her arms around his neck, her hips pressing arousingly against him, he found his hands sliding towards her breasts.

After all, he reasoned to himself just before he lost the power of rational thought, he could easily overpower her if she tried anything, and it would be a pity to pass up an opportunity like this . . .

A few moments later he was slipping her dress from her bare shoulders. It slithered sexily to the ground leaving her naked except for her high-heeled shoes. He cradled the firm curve of her bottom in one large hand and caressed her breasts with the other, while her tongue slid in and out of his mouth and flicked against his lips.

He screwed her on one of the packing cases, having first thrown both their jackets down so she wouldn't get splinters in her delicious butt.

As he thrust in and out of her, enjoying the feel, taste and smell of her gorgeous body, he wished they had all night – except that he was in his usual state of near exhaustion.

When they'd both finally shuddered into hot, throbbing orgasm, they slid to the floor still entwined and lay there on the bare dusty boards.

The traffic outside had dwindled and only the occasional car passed by, breaking the silence of the night.

Tim glanced at his watch.

'I suppose we ought to get dressed if we don't want them finding us like this,' he said at last.

'Mmm. Do we have to?'

Marcia's searching hand found his satiated dick and squeezed it encouragingly.

'I'm sorry, honey, I think that's it for the night,' he told her regretfully. 'Following you has been virtually a twenty-four-hour job and I'm beat. I don't know where you find the stamina to pursue your social life.'

She laughed softly and continued to cajole his member with a small, determined hand.

It rose hesitantly towards the ceiling.

'Marcia, honey, I really can't,' he protested. 'I'm shot.'

She climbed astride him and guided his dick to the damp, warm entrance to her honeypot.

'Don't be such a defeatist,' she goaded him. 'I'll do all the work.'

She started slowly, increasing the pace as he found reserves of energy from somewhere and began to meet each of her downward movements. She rode him hard, the glorious orbs of her breasts pale gold in the torchlight, bobbing up and down above him.

When at last he reached another earth-shattering climax, he opened his eyes and smiled up at her.

'I'm real sorry that I . . .'

From nowhere, an ornate ormolu clock came crashing down on his head, wielded by her slight, but surprisingly strong arm.

Tim's last conscious thought was to wonder whether she'd used a genuine antique or one of the reproductions.

Jess put the phone down and sat back in her chair, an expression of consternation on her face. Daniel

Moult had just called and told her brusquely that he'd arranged an interview for her at the insurance company the following day.

He'd grown tired of the situation and was convinced that if she was working from the inside she'd soon uncover the perpetrator of the ongoing insurance fraud.

'I had an ad placed about a month ago. We're interviewing five people tomorrow and you're one of them – your appointment is at eleven. I wrote your job application and CV myself and believe me I made you sound good. I'll fax you a copy and a list of the questions you're likely to be asked so you can be well prepared.'

'But . . . but I don't think I can make it tomorrow,' she'd protested miserably, knowing that there was no way she could get through an interview for a high-powered job in insurance.

'Be there or I'll bring in another firm of investigators. You've been dragging your heels on this, Alexa, and that isn't like you. Now I want some results.'

Jess left her desk and went and tapped on Tim's door. She was taken aback when he yelled, 'Go to hell – unless it's very important.'

Nervously she pushed the door open and was horrified to see Tim lying on the sofa with an ice pack held against a massive lump on his forehead.

'What . . . what happened to you?'

'Nothing I'd care to repeat to anyone I don't have to. Will this wait, Jess? As you can see I'm not exactly on top form.'

'I'm sorry Tim – it can't.'

'Well, pour me another Bourbon and take a seat. Help yourself to whatever you'd like.'

Jess glanced at the clock – it was only ten forty-five. She'd never seen Tim in such a bad way. She poured him a Bourbon and herself a mineral water and sat down.

'So what's up that's so important?'

Jess told him.

Tim sat up, groaning and dabbing gingerly at his forehead with the ice pack. He sat for a while, sipping his drink and thinking.

'Alexa will have to come back – just for the interview,' he decided. 'Get her on the phone and explain the situation. Have Martha book the flights. We can't afford to lose the insurance company's business.'

Unable to reach Alexa by phone, Jess was briefly at a loss. Her twin was supposed to phone in during the late afternoon, but sometimes didn't manage to do so until evening, by which time it might be too late to get a flight.

Unwilling to bother Tim again, she acted on impulse and asked Martha to book her on the next flight to Marrakech, then hurried back to the flat to pack an overnight bag.

If she couldn't contact Alexa by phone until this evening, it would save time if she flew out there and updated her on the situation in person. She could stay in Marrakech until her sister returned, holding the fort for her with Will Harper.

Her flight was uneventful – but at least it was on time. The heat of North Africa hit her like a furnace, making her very glad of the air conditioning at Alexa's hotel.

She already knew the room number and went straight to the lifts. Wearing a brunette wig and dark glasses she looked nervously around as she tapped on Alexa's door, praying that her twin would be in and alone.

Alexa opened the door wrapped in a snowy white towel, her damp red hair tumbling around her shoulders.

'Jess! What on earth are you doing here?' she demanded, hugging her.

Jess collapsed thankfully on the bed and they sat and drank icy dry white while Jess put her sister in the picture.

When she'd finished Alexa glanced at her watch.

'I'll have to leave in half an hour if I'm going to make that flight. I'll phone Will and tell him I'm ill. I should be back by this time tomorrow and will appear pale but almost recovered when I see him tomorrow evening.'

'I could see him tonight if you like,' offered Jess. 'I've taken your place with several of your other men and I'm sure no one's suspected anything.'

'I'm very much afraid that Will's too hot for you to handle,' remarked Alexa flippantly. 'He'd eat you alive – we're talking about a man with some very perverse sexual tastes.'

Alexa phoned Will and told him she'd developed a migraine and was unlikely to recover within twenty-four hours, while Jess sat on the bed feeling rather annoyed with her twin.

She'd coped with everything thrown at her to date – and it had been pretty varied stuff. What made Alexa think she couldn't handle an evening with Will? Anyway, she was dying to see something of Morocco in the brief time she was here.

While Alexa dressed she issued Jess with a series of instructions.

'He's bound to phone you tomorrow. Just say you think you'll be okay by evening, but that you're going to sleep the rest of the day. Tell him you'll phone him when you wake up – just in case my flight's delayed.

Whatever you do, don't leave this room, just order anything you need from room service. Marrakech is no place for an innocent like you to be wandering around on your own.'

Of the two of them Alexa had always been the leader. But Jess felt that was no reason for her to talk to her as if she was a complete idiot.

Stay cooped up in a hotel room for twenty-four hours?

Not likely.

She didn't say anything, just waited for Alexa to leave, then pulled on her wig and went out to explore.

The following morning Jess woke up feeling very pleased with herself. She'd had a drink in the hotel bar, then eaten in a neighbouring restaurant all alone. True, several men had tried to pick her up, but they'd all been courteous and charming.

She'd just finished having her breakfast on the balcony when the phone rang.

'Hello, darling, are you feeling any better?' The voice was male so Jess assumed it was Will Harper.

'Much better, thank you,' she replied gaily.

'Feel up to a short trip?'

'Where to?'

'The coast. I thought some sea air might do you good. Marrakech can be too hot at this time of year.'

'What time would we get back?' she asked.

'Some time in the late afternoon.'

'I'd love to come. When will we be setting off?'

'In about an hour. I'll pick you up then.'

Jess thought Will was an attractive man but there was a look in his eyes which unnerved her. The drive to the coast was mostly spent in silence, but she didn't mind because there was so much to see from the car window.

'I've arranged a surprise for you,' he told her, parking the car down by the marina, where rows of graceful yachts bobbed gently in the dazzlingly blue water.

'Oh lovely,' exclaimed Jess. 'What is it?'

'We're going to have lunch on that yacht,' he said, indicating a particularly beautiful boat with pristine white paintwork, moored a short distance away.

Jess had never been on a yacht before and had to stop herself running eagerly up the gangplank. Remembering in time that she was supposed to be Alexa, she strolled elegantly and unhurriedly along beside Will and then preceded him onto the boat.

A steward was setting a table which had been placed in the shadow of a striped awning and a couple of the crew were laying out sunbeds.

Jess had to stop herself from clapping her hands together in delight. On one side of her was the bustling quay lined with little restaurants and bars, on the other a vast expanse of open sea. The light reflected from it was dazzling her, even in her dark glasses.

'Would you like to take a look around before lunch?' Will asked her.

'Yes please.'

There was a spacious lounge, a dining room which could seat at least a dozen people, a study and five bedrooms, each with its own en-suite bathroom.

'I always thought it would be cramped on a yacht,' Jess commented as she admired the master bedroom, 'but I've stayed in hotel rooms a quarter the size of this.'

Will, who had been leaning against the door leading into the bathroom, pushed himself upright and came over to her. He pulled her down onto the king-sized bed and began to caress her breasts over her dress.

Jess felt a moment of alarm. When she'd accepted

his invitation for a trip to the coast she'd assumed no opportunity would arise for them to have sex, but now it was obviously on the agenda.

She wondered whether to claim that her migraine was still bothering her, but knew it wouldn't sound like a plausible excuse.

Would Alexa mind if she let Will screw her? Her twin had cheerfully shared all her other men – why should Will be any different?

Her sister's assumption that she wouldn't be able to handle Will still rankled.

His caresses were exciting her, she could feel herself becoming wet as he undid the buttons down the front of her dress and ran his hand over her belly and hips. Throwing caution to the winds Jess reached out to unzip his trousers and was taken aback when he caught her hand, kissed it and laid it back on the bed.

She was even more taken aback when he leant over, opened a drawer in the bedside cabinet and drew out four thick silken cords.

'Will . . . what are those for?' she asked nervously. In answer he wound one round her wrist and began to tie it to the headboard above her head.

Jess had never been tied up in her life and as panic swept over her she started to struggle with him. Laying down the other three cords he gathered her into his arms and began to drop soft, persuasive kisses on her face and neck, murmuring, 'What's the matter, darling? You used to love it when we did this. Sometimes you'd beg me to. Why not now?'

'I . . . I don't feel like it,' murmured Jess into his shoulder as he ran a hand up her thigh and touched her lightly between the legs.

He rubbed her there, softly and arousingly while she felt herself becoming wetter and wetter. Suddenly he slipped two fingers beneath the lacy edge of her frilly white knickers and pushed them deep inside her. Jess was unable to stop herself squirming against him and bearing down on his hand, her breath coming in shallow gasps.

He withdrew his fingers slowly, lingering to caress her clit, then held his hand, glistening with her juices, in front of her face.

'You do feel like it,' he corrected her. 'Just the thought of it is making you hot. Isn't it? *Isn't it*?'

His cold grey eyes held hers compellingly and suddenly the idea of being tied up and helpless while Will screwed her made Jess feel molten inside.

'Yes,' she whispered reluctantly.

He tied her other wrist to the headboard then pulled her dress apart at the front to reveal her lacy white bra and panties. He caressed her breasts over her bra then undid the catch and bent his head to take one hard, pointed nipple into his mouth.

He slipped her panties down her legs then tied her ankles to the corners of the bed, leaving her spreadeagled, the moist pink folds of her sex wide open revealing the throbbing, deep pink bud of her clitoris.

Without warning, Will unzipped his trousers and thrust into her, penetrating her deeply and making her quiver with excitement.

Dimly, through a foggy haze of sexual euphoria, Jess was aware of a distant muted noise and a strange feeling that the bed was vibrating. But as she felt herself being swept along on the wave of a hot, caressing climax she forgot about it.

After being relentlessly fucked for a long time by the indefatigable Will and experiencing two more orgasms which left her weak and drained, she lay gasping on the bed with Will sprawled above her.

He felt heavy and the cords around her wrists and ankles were chafing her.

'Will,' she murmured softly, then when he didn't reply repeated it more loudly. He raised his head to look at her. 'Untie me,' she urged him.

Rolling off her, he untied her, then lay down beside her again. Jess stared at the marks on her wrists and rubbed them gingerly. She was aware that she'd writhed around beneath him, straining at her bonds, but she'd been in the grip of such a sexual frenzy that she hadn't even noticed she was hurting herself.

The muted noise and vibration penetrated her consciousness again.

'What's that noise?' she asked as Will toyed with her swollen nipples.

'The engines, I should imagine.'

'The engines?' she repeated mystified. 'Why are the engines running?'

He rolled onto one side and propped himself up on his elbow, grinning triumphantly down at her.

'Having lunch on board isn't my only surprise. I've hired the yacht for a few weeks – we're going on a cruise.'

Chapter Seventeen

Jess stared at Will in dismay, then jumped swiftly off the bed and ran to the porthole.

They were already out at sea.

'Will, I can't go on a cruise,' she protested desperately.

'Why not?'

'I've got things to do in Marrakech,' she told him lamely. 'And anyway – what about my clothes?'

'One of my staff paid your bill and packed all your things. They're waiting for you in one of the other cabins.'

Jess was completely at a loss. Here she was, trapped on a yacht with a man she'd only just met, completely at his mercy.

'But . . . why?' she asked him.

'Because I've got some business I need to take care of and I wanted you with me. I knew if I asked you to come you'd probably say no. So I've taken matters into my own hands. Lunch should be ready by now. Are you hungry?'

Without waiting for a reply he went into the bathroom, emerging a few minutes later to find her still staring wretchedly out of the porthole.

'Come up on deck when you've dressed,' was his parting shot as he left the cabin.

Jess's mind was racing. What on earth could she do

now? She went into the bathroom and stood under a cool shower, considering the position.

When Alexa returned to the hotel that evening she'd find the room empty and her sister and luggage gone. She might be able to find out where, but even if she did there was precious little she could do about it.

Which meant Jess was very much on her own.

She didn't have much choice, all she could do was continue to pretend to be Alexa, go along with whatever Will wanted, then look for her opportunity to escape.

They were bound to put in at a port sooner or later. If she let him think she accepted the situation and was enjoying the cruise, there was no reason why he'd stop her going ashore.

Then she'd give him the slip.

In the meantime she'd just have to hope that she could cope with him on a sexual level. The bondage she'd just experienced had been wildly exciting, but on another level it had been disturbing.

Already she couldn't quite believe she'd agreed to it. It had made her feel strange to be tied to the bed, her legs wide apart, waiting helplessly for a man she'd only just met to fuck her.

Strange, but at the same time red-hot with breathless, squirming anticipation.

In fact, thinking about it made her feel wet between the legs again, even though she'd just showered.

Buttoning her dress up, Jess determined to behave as coolly in this situation as Alexa would have done.

Will was waiting on deck, sitting at the table under the striped awning and sipping a beer. She smiled brightly as she approached him, then slipped into the chair opposite his.

'A beer – just what I need,' she greeted him. The hovering steward immediately vanished and

254

reappeared a few seconds later carrying one on a tray. 'I hope your cook's good,' she continued, after a refreshing gulp of the icy liquid, 'I'm starving.'

'He should be – he costs enough,' Will commented.

'Will, isn't all this going to set you back a small fortune?' she asked him. 'A lovely yacht like this with a full crew can't come cheap.'

'It doesn't,' he admitted, 'but I've got the money and there'll be plenty more where that came from when I've clinched the business deal I've got lined up.'

The steward placed a stuffed avocado in front of each of them, then retired to a discreet distance.

Jess scooped up a spoonful of hers and let out a little moan of greed.

'This tastes wonderful,' she announced, attacking it with relish. 'So, what's this business deal? I'm looking to invest some of my own money in anything which promises to be lucrative.'

'I'm thinking of going into partnership with some people operating around the Mediterranean,' he explained, 'but to what extent I'm not sure yet. We'll be picking three of them up in Marseilles and they'll spend a few days on board while we iron out the details. If you decide you want in that's fine by me. I was planning to suggest it, but you beat me to it.'

Alexa had kept Jess updated in their daily telephone calls, so she knew that Will hadn't told her twin that he'd embezzled the money which was paying for the cruise she'd unexpectedly found herself on.

If she could get him to confide that, then maybe she could do what Alexa had planned and persuade him to return the money. She could tell him she had enough for both of them and point out how wildly inconvenient it would be never to be able to return to England.

If she were successful she wouldn't feel such a fool

255

about allowing herself to be kidnapped.

She'd better wait and see what the situation was when they first put into port. If she found his sexual demands too depraved, or felt under threat in any way, she could still escape from him once ashore.

Until then, all she could do was make the best of the situation.

That evening they dined on deck under the stars.

Jess was still feeling somewhat stunned after discovering Will expected her to share the master cabin with him. Sex was one thing, but having him watch her shower and dress had made her very uncomfortable.

Ralph had never just walked in on her when she was performing her ablutions. It was something she felt should be done in private.

She'd been cleaning her teeth at the basin in her bra and pants prior to stepping under the shower, when Will had come into the bathroom, pulled her knickers down around her ankles and screwed her bent over the washbasin.

She'd still had a mouthful of foam, most of which she'd swallowed when she gasped in shock as she felt his rock-hard cock plunging into her.

It had been over very quickly, but she still managed to climax before he pulled out of her and then carried on as if nothing had happened.

It was all a bit much for Jess and when the solicitous steward asked her what she wanted to drink she requested a champagne cocktail. She wasn't accustomed to drinking much and after two of them on an empty stomach felt distinctly tipsy.

It was a beautiful night, warm but with a light breeze. They were surrounded on all sides by the dark, shining sea, reflecting the lights of the yacht back at them. Jess sat there, sipping her drink and pressing her knees together, a hot, lingering pleasure still throbbing between her thighs.

As they ate their starter she exerted herself to make the sort of witty conversation Alexa was so good at, trying not to let Will see that she was in a mild state of shock.

There were more surprises in store.

When the steward had vanished with their plates Will stood up, lifted her onto the table and parted her legs. He eased her silk camiknickers down her thighs, slipped them off and stuffed them in his pocket.

'Will I . . .' she began, then stopped as he bent his head and began to lick and probe his way around her swollen honeypot.

'Will! The steward might come back!' she exclaimed, trying to wriggle back on the table, away from the hot, insistent pressure of his mouth.

He grabbed her by the hips and slid her forward again, raising his head to say briefly, 'He won't unless I ring.'

Jess's head dropped back on her shoulders as she sat there with his tongue flicking over her clit. When his lips closed over it and he sucked hard she moaned aloud.

'Will, please stop,' she begged him, unable to face the mortification of being found by the steward with her skirt up around her waist, her bare bottom in full view and Will's head between her legs.

When he eventually stopped she slipped hurriedly back into her seat then gazed with dismay at the damp stain they'd left on the tablecloth.

Grabbing her glass of wine she hastily slopped some onto the stain, then sat back in her chair, trembling with a combination of lust and nervousness.

She was only able to pick at her main course and, unable to relax, excused herself soon after the meal saying that she felt tired after her migraine and needed an early night.

'Okay – I'll be along later,' he said. 'You should have told me you weren't feeling too good – I thought you seemed a bit tense. Get a good night's sleep and we can spend the day relaxing tomorrow.'

Jess fell into bed, half wishing for the first time that she was safely back in Altrincham with Ralph.

'What do you mean vanished?' demanded Tim blankly. 'Vanished where?'

'On a yacht somewhere in the Mediterranean,' replied Alexa agitatedly. She'd just returned from Marrakech and was exhausted.

Tim let his head fall into his hands in despair.

It really hadn't been a very good week.

The mortification of being knocked out by Marcia still rankled. Luckily he'd regained consciousness and managed to get his jeans back on before the men sent to pick her up arrived. He'd still felt a complete jerk and had had a lot of explaining to do.

Now Jess was missing somewhere at sea.

Alexa had attended her bogus interview, acquitted herself well and then flown straight back to Morocco. Only to find that Jess had vanished.

'Is he likely to hurt her?' Tim asked worriedly.

Alexa was pacing the floor with her arms folded. 'He's not likely to beat her up, if that's what you mean,' she replied distractedly. 'But where sex is concerned Will's always been a bit out of control. Jess isn't going to know what's hit her. I told her to stay in her room – I should have insisted she came back with me, not left her there alone.'

'Don't blame yourself, honey,' he urged her.

258

'Let me make a few calls and see what I can find out.'

Jess had slept well and woke to face the day in a calmer frame of mind.

After all, she reasoned as she made her way up on deck, wearing a red-and-white-striped bikini under a matching T-shirt, Will was hardly likely to harm her with all the crew as witnesses. He was an embezzler, not a murderer. The worst that was likely to happen to her was that she'd experience some bizarre sex, but she could cope with that.

Couldn't she?

The thing to do was go along with it and not let anything throw her.

Will was stretched out on a sunbed reading.

'You look better this morning,' he commented as she sat down next to him. 'I considerately left you to sleep on, despite an overwhelming urge to fuck you awake.'

He leant over and kissed her, briefly fondling her breast as he did so.

'We'll make up for lost time later,' she assured him lightly. 'Am I too late for breakfast?'

After orange juice, croissants and coffee Jess lay down on her stomach on a sunbed and allowed Will to rub her with sun oil. She was taken aback to have him pull her unfastened bikini top from beneath her and toss it over the side.

'You won't need that,' he said carelessly.

Jess had never sunbathed topless and found the prospect of doing so in front of the crew unnerving. But she knew that Alexa would do so without a second thought. There was no one around at present so she reluctantly turned over and allowed Will to oil her full breasts.

As soon as he'd finished she turned over and lay on her stomach. It was pleasant lying in the sun with nothing to do and as none of the crew were visible she lay on her back for a while, keeping her eyes open behind her dark glasses in case any of them approached.

When it was time for lunch she pulled her T-shirt over her head.

'Don't put that on,' said Will, grinning. 'I want to look at you while we eat.'

'I've had enough sun for now,' Jess said reasonably. 'I burn easily and even under the awning it's strong enough to blister me at this time of day. Do you want me out of action with a lobster-coloured, peeling skin?'

'I suppose not,' he agreed. 'Shall we drop anchor and swim later?'

Jess remembered in time that she was a much stronger swimmer than Alexa, who was nervous in deep water.

'Only if I can wear water wings,' she joked. 'I might just hold on to the ladder and tread water.'

In the late afternoon she did just that while Will swam around in the deep blue sea. She wanted to join him, but contented herself staying close to the boat and enjoying the feeling of the cool waves lapping against her.

She was surprised that he didn't initiate sex at some time during the day. He fondled her a lot, keeping her in a state of anticipation, but didn't take it any further.

A wind blew up in the evening so they decided to eat in the dining room.

Jess was wearing a full-skirted, sage-green frock which left her honey-coloured arms and shoulders bare. Will had lain on the bed smoking and watching her dress. He'd refused to let her wear anything under the frock and every time she moved she felt the erotic whisper of the silk slithering over her bare backside and thighs.

When the steward had opened a bottle of champagne and withdrawn, Will sank onto the sofa and patted his lap.

'Come here,' he invited her. As she approached him he unzipped his trousers and took out his cock which looked big, red and very, very hard.

Jess suppressed a shudder of excitement as he lifted her skirts and pulled her down towards him. She helped him guide it into her pussy, which was already swimming with moisture, then sank slowly down onto his knee, wriggling her backside to take him fully into her.

He filled her up completely, making her gasp as she clutched his throbbing member with her internal muscles. She raised her bottom a few inches so he nearly slipped out of her, then slowly lowered herself again.

It felt wonderfully erotic to be impaled on his rod in this position. Anyone looking at them would think she was just sitting on his knee.

After a few minutes, Will insisted they drink their glasses of champagne, then to her horror he rang the bell to summon the steward.

'Will! what are you doing?' she exclaimed, frantically trying to scramble up from his lap.

His arm clamped around her waist like a vice as he replied soothingly, 'Relax, Alexa – he won't know.'

The door opened at that moment to admit the steward, leaving Jess with no alternative but to subside back into Will's lap and try to look unconcerned – no easy matter when her face was bright pink with embarrassment.

She could feel his cock throbbing tantalisingly

inside her as the steward refilled their glasses, then thankfully left the room.

'How could you do that?' she demanded furiously.

'Alexa, darling – stop being such a prude.'

He pulled the front of her dress down and fastened his mouth over one swollen, coral-tinted nipple, lifting his hips to jam his rearing shaft deeper into her.

Slowly but surely, Jess's hot flood of embarrassment gave way to a hotter flood of pure, unadulterated lust.

Alexa was distraught.

It had been three days now since Jess had vanished. She spent most of her time willing the phone to ring and for her sister to be on the other end of the line.

She'd continued to go through the motions of working but her heart wasn't in it. She poured herself another glass of wine and tried to concentrate on the nine o'clock news, but to no avail.

The doorbell rang.

Leaping from the sofa Alexa hurried to the door. A total stranger stood there, tall and lean with fair hair swept back from a long, square-jawed face.

His expression was grim as he stared down at her.

'Hello, Jess. I think you owe me an explanation,' he said in greeting.

Alexa thought fast. This had to be Paul Sears – Tim had told her what had happened and how Marcia had knocked him out and escaped. He was obviously mortified and considered he'd handled the case badly.

She knew that Paul had been shocked to discover his partner had been substituting reproduction antiques for the real thing and even more shocked to discover Jess was working for a private investigation agency.

This was going to take some careful handling.

'Come in Paul,' she invited him. 'Come in and have a drink.'

Jess stuffed her passport and all her money and travellers' cheques into her bag and looked out of the porthole again as the yacht sailed towards Marseilles.

One of the crew, a friendly young Greek with dark curling hair and deep brown eyes, had told her they'd be docking within half an hour.

Will had asked her if she'd like to spend the evening ashore and she'd told him eagerly that she would. She planned to disappear at some stage and get on the next plane home.

Will's sexual demands and the scenarios he wanted her to enact had begun to alarm her.

But not because she found them distasteful.

Quite the reverse, in fact.

However, she was aware that she was being sucked into the dark and murky world of sexual depravity and that she had to get away while she still had the willpower to do so.

She was appalled at some of the things she'd found herself doing – and horrified by how exciting she'd found them at the time.

Alexa had been right – she was completely out of her depth.

It was time to leave and return to her old life in Cheshire. She needed to be back there within a few days ready to attend the pre-term meetings at college. Over the last couple of days the idea had begun to seem quite appealing – she even found herself thinking fondly of Ralph and wondering what he was doing.

For their evening ashore Will had her wear a low cut black dress over a black teddy, suspender belt and stockings.

He'd screwed her on a sunlounger up on deck that

afternoon. She'd spent the entire time as he thrust forcibly in and out of her dreading one of the crew walking past.

But somehow it had added a squalid sort of excitement to the proceedings and she'd ended up writhing beneath him with her legs wrapped around his waist, urging him on to greater efforts.

As they walked around the old port hand in hand trying to decide where to eat, Jess half wished she'd initiated sex while she dressed for the evening. Will had lounged in the bath watching her while she showered. He'd insisted she leave the glass door open so he could see her properly, with the result that the bathroom floor had got very wet. She'd found it a huge turn-on and had been disappointed when he hadn't joined her.

They eventually decided on a restaurant which specialised in Provençal cooking and sat a table outside watching the passers-by.

Jess excused herself as soon as she could, saying she was going to the ladies. A quick check showed her that there was a back door out of there if she didn't mind leaving through the kitchen.

She glanced behind her and was taken aback to see Will entering the restaurant. She dodged hastily into the ladies and waited a few minutes before emerging. When she came out he was just outside, getting some cigarettes from the machine.

She followed him back to their table thinking she'd wait until they'd eaten, then excuse herself again and dodge out through the back door.

He couldn't be getting cigarettes a second time.

Their meal was excellent but she couldn't enjoy it because she was so nervous. Will didn't help, caressing her under the cover of the tablecloth and telling her he'd arranged something special for later.

She tried to find out what it was, but he wouldn't tell her.

It went without saying that it was something sexual.

When they'd eaten she went to the ladies again. When she'd been in there before she'd noticed there was a phone, and while eating decided it wouldn't be a bad idea to make a reverse charge phone call to Alexa and tell her she was safe.

Thankfully Alexa was in.

'Jess! Are you okay? I've been worried sick. Where are you?'

'In a restaurant in Marseilles,' Jess told her cheerfully. 'Just about to do a runner and jump on a plane home.'

Briefly, she brought Alexa up to date. She ended by saying, 'I never thought I'd be glad to get back to Ralph and college. It was only today I realised I need to be back there within a few days – if I want to keep my job.'

'Be careful, Jess – Will's no fool.'

'Well, if I don't make it back by Wednesday, would you mind driving up to Cheshire and taking my place until I do make it?' she ended flippantly.

'Just at college or with Ralph too?' teased Alexa.

'Both, if you like. I'm sure some time with you would do Ralph a lot of good. Okay, Alexa, I'd better go. Hopefully I'll see you tomorrow.'

To Jess's absolute dismay Will was standing by the cash desk a few yards away, paying the bill. Her heart sank. Now what was she going to do? Wait till they stopped for a drink somewhere and try again, she supposed.

He put his arm around her and led her from the restaurant.

'What shall we do now?' she asked brightly.

'Now it's time for your surprise.'

265

They walked through the streets until the area became slightly seedy and there were less tourists and more sailors and locals.

Eventually they entered a dark alleyway and Will stopped outside a tall narrow building with peeling paint and rang the bell. A grille in the door shot open and they were scrutinised before they were able to step into a dimly lit hallway.

'Will, what is this place?' asked Jess nervously. There was a strong smell of perfume mingled with drink and smoke and she could hear the sound of laughter coming from the room at the end of the hallway.

He didn't reply, merely took her hand and pulled her along behind him. The room they found themselves in was expensively and opulently furnished, with red velvet curtains, gilt furniture and a thick, garishly patterned Turkish carpet underfoot.

There were several other people in the room, but all Jess's attention was on the woman approaching them.

She was so immensely fat that it was hard to tell how old she was. Her bleached blonde hair was piled up on top of her head and threaded through with feathers and pearls.

Chins like a pile of crumpets rested heavily above a flashly fake ruby necklace – or at least Jess assumed it was fake. Her enormous bosom rose bolster-like from a boned scarlet dress and her plump arms and hands were laden with more ruby jewellery.

Jess stared at her wide-eyed as Will stepped forward to speak to her in a low voice. After a brief conversation the woman led them to a crimson velvet sofa and asked them what they'd like to drink, before withdrawing.

Jess gazed around the room in confusion. There were half a dozen other women present, all of whom were exceptionally attractive. They all darted looks at the newcomers and after catching Jess's eye, one of them smiled provocatively. They were also, for some reason, in varying states of undress.

Was it a club of some sort? She wasn't sure, but there was a decadence about the atmosphere of the place which made her half excited, half uneasy.

A pretty Eurasian girl deposited their drinks on the table. She was wearing a black Chinese silk robe with a pattern of pink lotus flowers over a pink silk camisole and camiknickers. As she bent forward Jess could see right down the front of her camisole.

So could Will.

The girl exuded a tangible aura of demure sexuality which was apparent even to someone as unworldly as Jess. Or perhaps she was just better at spotting these things after all her recent experiences.

At that moment one of the men, an affluent looking dark man with a big beaky nose, reached out and pulled the Eurasian girl into his lap and began openly fondling her breasts.

Jess's jaw dropped and she looked around the room to see if anyone else looked as surprised as she felt.

No one did.

She turned towards Will, who was sitting back on the sofa, his legs stretched negligently out in front of him, one arm draped casually along the back of the sofa behind her.

'Will, what's going on?' she questioned him in an undertone. 'Where are we?'

He turned to look at her, amusement glinting in his cold grey eyes.

'You're not normally so slow on the uptake, Alexa. This is a brothel, of course – the finest in Marseilles.'

Chapter Eighteen

Jess felt the blood pounding through her body at twice its normal rate, accompanied by a rhythmic thudding in her ear drums. She turned to look at Will, her eyes wide and round.

'A ... a brothel!' she gasped in amazement. 'Why are we in a brothel?'

'I told you I'd arranged something special for this evening,' he said. 'This is it.'

Jess took a gulp of her drink and tried to get a grip on herself. This couldn't be happening to her – she was a dull, rather dowdy college lecturer from Cheshire. She just wasn't the sort of woman who found herself in a quayside brothel in Marseilles.

She considered making a bolt for the door but rejected the idea as too undignified. Besides which, she was wearing high-heeled shoes, which might make bolting difficult.

Why were they in a brothel? What could he be planning? She didn't know, but whatever it was she could feel herself becoming warm and moist in anticipation.

His hand dropped to her thigh and stroked it persuasively.

'Which one shall we choose? You can decide if you like.'

Jess looked at the men in the room. They all looked

affluent but somehow shady. They were mostly French but a couple of them could have been Arabs – and none of them were her type.

She turned towards Will and said determinedly, 'If you think I'm having sex with any of those men, you're out of your mind.'

He laughed out loud.

'Forget the men, Alexa. I didn't bring you here to sell your luscious body. No, we're going to go upstairs with one of the delectable *belles de nuit*. Which one is it to be?'

Jess tried not to let her jaw drop open.

A threesome.

Why not?

Yet another item on a long list of things she'd never done.

She studied all the girls carefully. None seemed to mind her scrutiny in the least. They all smiled at her and at Will who was also appraising them intently.

'What about the blonde?' he murmured in her ear. The blonde was certainly attractive with her voluptuous figure and gorgeous face.

But Jess was particularly struck by a slender girl with hair the colour of mocha chocolate. She had a full sulky mouth, slanting eyes and a creamy skin. Her short ivory silk slip only half concealed a pair of small but perfect breasts and through the flimsy material Jess could see a tiny pair of panties and a suspender belt. The girl's long legs were sheathed in matching ivory stockings and there was a fine gold chain around one ankle.

Sensing Jess's scrutiny, she smiled a sultry, knowing smile, then bent over to pick up a full ashtray from a table. Her slip rode up revealing the tiny pair of panties and emphasising the alluring thrust of her pert backside.

'What about her?' Jess asked Will, whose eyes were riveted to the girl's bottom.

'Okay.' He beckoned the girl who came to stand in front of them, eyes downcast. He spoke to her in rapid French and she nodded, then looked down at the floor again.

'I'll just fix it with Madame,' he told Jess, then walked across the room to where the hugely plump woman had settled her great bulk on a small sofa.

Madame followed him back and introduced her employee as Chantal. The French girl led them out of the lounge, up a narrow flight of stairs, then along a hallway before showing them into an opulent room where an enormous bed was hung with pale blue silk curtains. There was a thick darker blue carpet on the floor, a couple of armchairs, a table and a chaise longue.

A bottle of champagne was chilling in an ice bucket and Will asked the girl to open it, which she did with the deftness born of long practice.

Jess was sitting in one of the armchairs and Will lowered himself onto the arm, murmuring in her ear, 'It's an intoxicating thought, isn't it – that she'll do anything we ask her to? Absolutely anything.'

Jess was in the grip of such a strong nervous excitement that she was unable to reply. She'd certainly never been with another woman before – she wondered if Alexa had.

Chantal brought them both a glass of champagne and stood silently acquiescent as Will ran his hands lightly over her body. He spoke to the girl in French again and she held out a hand to Jess.

Taking it, Jess allowed herself to be led over to the bed, while Will made himself comfortable in the armchair.

Chantal wound her arms around Jess's neck and

kissed her. Her lips felt much softer and her skin much smoother than that of a man. It was a strange sensation, but very arousing. The girl began to caress her, just her back and shoulders at first until Jess began to relax, then her hips and breasts over her black dress.

Jess allowed Chantal to draw down the zip on the back of her dress and remove it, leaving her clad only in her black silk teddy.

The two women stretched out on the bed while Jess enjoyed the other girl's sensual caresses. It was only when she was fully relaxed that she began to stroke Chantal in turn, gently cupping the small high breasts in the palm of her hand and toying with the hard, round nipples.

Jess pulled one of Chantal's shoulder straps down exposing a creamy white breast. The nipple was the colour of café au lait and Jess was unable to resist taking it in her mouth and sucking gently. The other girl moaned and pulled Jess closer, pushing her mound against Jess's own and rubbing it against her in an arousing circular movement.

While the two women stroked each other, Jess could feel Will's gaze burning into them and could tell he was very turned on.

Both women were now naked to the waist and Jess pulled Chantal's slip down over her narrow hips, revealing the tiny pair of ivory silk panties. A few dark wisps of pubic hair peeped out around the lacy edges of the panties and after tracing with her fingertips the narrow strip of material which ran between Chantal's leg, Jess discovered it was already damp.

A few seconds later Chantal reached between Jess's own legs and began to fumble with the two small buttons which held the teddy closed. Her touch there made Jess feel red-hot and when Chantal succeeded in undoing the buttons, Jess opened her thighs invitingly.

The delicate touch of Chantal's slim fingers made her shudder with lust. She could feel the other girl's hand slipping easily over the slick, swollen point of her clit as she stroked it gently, exerting just the right amount of pressure.

A few seconds later, to her amazement, Jess felt her climax approaching. Her eyes locked with Will's, half in surprise and half in ecstasy as she was swept over the edge into a whirling vortex of pleasure.

She didn't have time to recover before Chantal's dark head dipped between her thighs and she felt a warm pink tongue flicking insistently against her clit.

Jess began to moan in earnest, her hips rotating, as for the first time she enjoyed the erotic pleasure of another woman's tongue delving into her pussy.

She felt the bed move and knew Will had joined them. He lay on one side watching them closely, while he stroked Chantal's rear over her miniscule panties. She was kneeling to one side of Jess with her bottom thrust temptingly in the air towards him as he stroked her.

Slowly, he drew the panties down to the top of her thighs revealing the naked, creamy globes of her buttocks with the shadowy folds of her sex hidden between them. Obligingly she parted her legs without ceasing her oral ministrations to Jess's clit.

Now Will could see a few fronds of damp, dark hair partially concealing her honeypot. With both hands he gently parted her outer lips so he could see her intricate inner folds and the tantalising bud of her clit.

Pushing two fingers inside her he explored her velvety wetness, then swiftly removed his clothes and knelt behind her.

He heard her inhale with satisfaction as he entered her, gripping her by the waist as he began to thrust in and out. The force of his movements made Chantal gasp against Jess's pussy and redouble her efforts with her tongue.

Jess came again, in a series of convulsive shudders which transmitted themselves through Chantal's slender body right to Will's cock buried deep within her.

He withdrew and this time mounted Jess, who was lying on her back, her teddy bunched up around her waist and her head thrown back in a posture of complete abandon.

He screwed her vigorously while she panted and writhed beneath him and Chantal caressed his buttocks and balls from behind. When he came it was with the force of a dam bursting, as he pumped his juices into her in a series of dynamic thrusts.

He rolled off Jess and pulled Chantal down next to him, then the three of them lay there breathing hard on the pale blue bedspread.

After a while Chantal climbed off the bed, removed her panties which were still caught up around her thighs, hobbling her movements, and wearing only her suspender belt and stockings went to pour them more champagne.

Propped up against the bed's enormous pillows the three of them sipped the sparkling wine. Will lazily tipped some over Chantal's breasts, causing her already jutting nipples to thrust upwards and outwards even more.

'Why don't you lick that off?' he invited Jess.

Jess was happy to do so.

When she'd finished, Will trickled some champagne between Chantal's thighs, wetting the silky thatch of her bush. Rolling onto his back he positioned her so she was kneeling above his face and opened his mouth to catch the drops of wine dripping from her, his cock rearing up between his thighs again.

Jess climbed astride him and taking his member in her hand, rubbed it against her clit. Lowering herself she slipped it inside her a couple of inches, then raised her hips and stimulated herself again.

Chantal knelt just above his face so he could lap away at her champagne-soaked bush while Jess continued to tease him. Suddenly she sat down hard, making them both gasp, then began to ride him.

She rose and fell, pleasurably impaled on his bone-hard rod while Chantal sat on his face, pleasurably impaled on his muscular tongue. They caught each other's rhythm and moved on the bed like three separate parts of the same entity, the silence broken only by the creaking of the bed, and their groans of pleasure.

The cool grey light of dawn was filtering in through the window when Jess woke up in a tangle of limbs. She was curled up in Chantal's arms and behind her Will slept with an arm thrown over both of them.

An overpowering urge to empty her bladder made Jess rise from the bed and go into the bathroom. When she'd finished she washed her hands and looked longingly at the deep bath – she felt sticky and sweaty after all the action of the night before.

Swiftly stripping off her stockings and suspender belt she turned the taps on. She was just bending over to swish the water around when she heard a sound behind her. Suddenly she felt her hips seized then she felt the full benefit of Will's early morning erection plunging inside her.

'Chantal!' he called over his shoulder. 'Wake up and come in here – it's bath time.'

Back on the yacht Jess slept most of the afternoon and awoke after a deliciously erotic dream to find

Will caressing her naked breasts. She yawned and pushed her hair out of her face as he said, 'We've got guests. Come and help me entertain them when you're dressed.'

He left the cabin, leaving Jess to stumble her way into the shower and stand under a stinging tepid spray while she reviewed the events of the evening before.

At first she soaped herself languorously, her hand drifting between her legs as she mentally relived being bathed by Chantal.

Suddenly it struck her like a ton of bricks that she shouldn't even be here – she should be back in England by now. What had happened to her determination to escape?

Lost in a tidal wave of sheer, unadulterated lust.

She could tell by the throb of the engines that they were at sea again.

Alexa would be frantic.

When had Will said they were docking again? When they reached Nice, if she remembered correctly.

During the next couple of days, she decided, she'd try to get him to confide in her about the embezzled money and if possible get him to agree to return it.

It was the least she could do after allowing herself to be distracted so easily.

Jess didn't like any of their three guests. If these were Will's potential business partners then he was obviously planning to invest in something shady.

And probably illegal.

One of the men was Tunisian, another French and the third Italian. They were all polite to Jess but she didn't like the way their eyes roamed over her, as if they were mentally undressing her.

It didn't seem to bother Will, in fact she got the feeling he was enjoying it. He sat openly caressing her thigh as they enjoyed pre-dinner drinks up on deck.

The steward hadn't rejoined the yacht when it left Marseilles so his place was taken by Spiros, the young Greek crewman who always smiled shyly but admiringly at Jess whenever he saw her.

He was less adept at serving food and drink than the steward and looked uncomfortable in the starched white jacket rather than his usual T-shirt.

The men became grosser and coarser as the evening progressed and Jess was glad to excuse herself at around eleven when one of them suggested playing cards. Telling the men he'd only be a few minutes, Will escorted her to their cabin.

'Are you really thinking of going into business with them?' she asked them. 'They come across like criminals. And I didn't think much of their manners. Did you see the way they were looking at me?'

'Of course I did. They were all wondering what it would be like to fuck you and envying me because they know I am.'

They were walking along the corridor leading to their cabin. Will stopped and turned to face her.

'They were all imagining you with your legs apart and your hot little pussy quivering, waiting for my cock – just like it is now.'

He pushed her back against the wall and dragged her skirt up to her waist. She was wearing a loose-legged pair of camiknickers and he was easily able to slip his hand inside and feel between her legs.

Jess squirmed angrily away from him. She knew it was true, but she didn't like him any better for spelling it out.

He held her against the wall, his fingers working away insidiously at her clit. Still angry, she reached down and unzipped his trousers, desperate to have him inside her immediately.

His cock sprang out and he held it tormentingly against the slippery entrance to her pussy, before jamming it into her. They screwed ferociously against the corridor wall, until Will started to get cramp in his legs from having his knees bent for so long.

Grabbing Jess around the hips he lifted her so she could fasten her legs around his waist, then continued with his urgent pumping.

They came within a few seconds of each other, then Jess unwound her legs and stood leaning against the wall, shaking. Without a word Will withdrew, zipped himself up and walked away.

'I'm sorry, Alexa honey, but there isn't anything we can do,' Tim said reluctantly. 'We'll just have to wait until she rings again and lets us know what's happening.'

'That's easy for you to say, Tim,' stormed Alexa, 'she isn't your sister.' She turned and strode furiously out of the office.

Tim sighed and returned to the report he was writing. He sympathised with Alexa but it didn't sound like Jess was in any real danger. He could only hope she'd turn up in the next couple of days. Even Alexa admitted that she'd been in high spirits when she'd phoned.

He sighed and tapped out another few lines until he was interrupted by the phone.

'Tim? It's Sherry.'

His capricious ex-wife. That was all he needed.

'Hi, Sherry honey – how're you?' he greeted her warily, steeling himself to refuse her whatever it was she wanted.

He knew that it would be two against one – his dick always sided treacherously with Sherry in the hope of renewing its long-held acquaintance with her sweet, musky honeypot.

'I'm fine, Tim, real fine. Guess what I'm doing.'

'I'm sorry, honey, but I'm too busy for guessing games.'

'You won't be too busy for this one, sugar. I'm lying on my bed wearing only that black silk slip you always liked me in. And . . .'

Something about the tone of her voice, the way it was dripping honey and molasses, with an undertone of excitement, made Tim guess what was coming next.

'And?' he prompted her, hating himself for not terminating the call.

'And I'm not wearing any panties,' she continued. 'I've pulled the slip up to my hips and I'm just touching my smooth, shaven mound with the tips of my fingers.'

Tim groaned, while his dick began to stir excitedly inside his jeans. He knew what this was about.

Sherry was bored and when Sherry was bored, what better way of passing the time than ringing up Tim to torment him?

This wasn't the first time he'd been on the receiving end of one of her erotic phone calls.

He willed himself to hang up on her but somehow was still clutching the phone as she described in graphic detail what she was doing to herself.

Eventually she stopped speaking and began moaning, moans which started slowly, then reached a crescendo as she climaxed at the other end of the line.

When Tim eventually put the phone down he felt like he'd just run a marathon, his chest felt tight, there was a buzzing in his ears and the back of his shirt was soaking wet.

Briefly he considered calling a cab and getting round there fast, but knowing Sherry she'd be out, or no longer in the mood.

Better finish the report.

Will spent most of the next day closeted with their three guests, for which Jess was deeply thankful, because it meant she didn't have to spend much time with them. She saw them at breakfast and lunch and that was more than enough.

The way their eyes travelled over her body unsettled her and she didn't like the compliments they paid her – compliments which bordered at times on the obscene.

In the afternoon Jess went down to the study to see if she could find anything to read. She'd been in there only once before when Will was giving her a tour of the yacht, and she had a vague recollection of seeing some books.

The room was pleasantly cool after the heat up on deck and she chose two paperbacks from a selection on the bookshelf. She was just turning to leave the room when she wondered if there were any more in the cupboard.

The door was locked but she spotted a key lying half under the door. Sliding it out she placed it in the lock and turned it. The door swung silently open to reveal a large suitcase. She opened it and then sank back on her heels in amazement.

It was full of money.

Neatly stacked and banded, the notes were all large denominations.

It must be part of the money he'd embezzled.

But why was it lying around in a suitcase instead of safely in a Swiss bank account?

A sound behind her made her jump. Will was leaning against the door with his arms folded.

Without thinking Jess blurted out, 'Is this the money you embezzled?'

He looked at her impassively, then said, 'So you did know. It crossed my mind that you might. How did you find out?'

Mentally kicking herself for having given the game away so completely and so unnecessarily, Jess tried belatedly to retrieve the situation.

Rising to her feet, she moved towards him.

'Will, if you return the money now, the company have agreed not to press charges. All you have to do is give it back. You don't need it – I have enough for both of us.'

'Who are you working for?' he demanded. 'I'm not stupid, Alexa. I've suspected all along that you turning up out of the blue after all these years was no coincidence. But I thought you just wanted to share some of my recently acquired wealth – it didn't cross my mind that you might be trying to get it back.'

Jess tried to reason with him.

'If the company doesn't have the money back in time for the flotation, then they'll have nothing to lose by calling in the police. Once Interpol are notified you'll never be able to return to England without fear of arrest. There aren't many places you can live without risking extradition – do you really want to spend the rest of your life in South America?'

'You didn't answer my question – who are you working for?' He took a step towards her and grabbed her wrist.

Jess didn't know whether he was planning to shake it out of her or not – but she wasn't about to find out the hard way.

'A private detective agency,' she said hastily, trying without success to free her wrist.

'Being retained by the company?'

'Yes,' she admitted.

'Did they know we knew each other?'

'No, that was pure coincidence. My brief was to get close to you and persuade you to return the money – but when I met you again I decided I wanted us to stay together. So I planned to persuade you to return the money, because then we can live on mine anywhere we choose – rather than somewhere with no extradition laws.'

He looked at her closely.

'You're lying, Alexa. I don't believe you have any money of your own. That tale about your aunt was a total fabrication, wasn't it?'

Jess managed to wrench her wrist free and rubbed it crossly, feeling completely out of her depth – a feeling she'd been experiencing with increased frequency since meeting Will Harper.

'Why is the money lying around in a suitcase anyway?' she asked him. 'Why isn't it in a Swiss bank account?'

'Because, my dear, as soon as I've set up my business deal in the Mediterranean this yacht is heading for South America. As you've so astutely pointed out, I need to be somewhere with no extradition laws by the time Interpol start looking for me.

'The suitcase is destined for our charming guests – my investment in our business partnership. The rest is in the safe, which is where it stays until I reach my new home. I decided that keeping my assets liquid was a better idea than risking having them frozen in some bank account. And no, I don't remotely mind the idea of being an expatriate for the rest of my life. What I do mind is the idea of being poor.'

'So you won't see sense and give the money back?' persisted Jess.

'Why should I? I worked hard for it. The question now is – what am I going to do with you?'

'If you intend to keep the money and there's

nothing I can say to make you change your mind, you might as well put me ashore at the nearest port,' suggested Jess hopefully.

'And have you provide the police with my exact location? Hardly, darling. No, I've got a better idea. I think I'll keep you with me – at least for the foreseeable future. I may let you go once we reach South America, or I may not.'

'You mean you're kidnapping me?' gasped Jess, horrified.

Will reached out and idly caressed one of her breasts.

'I'm not just kidnapping you, Alexa. From now on you're going to be my sex slave. Which means you're going to do absolutely everything I tell you, whether you want to or not.'

Chapter Nineteen

Locked in their cabin Jess considered her options, which didn't take long because she didn't actually appear to have any. She wasn't even sure why Will had locked her up – she was hardly likely to jump overboard in the middle of the Mediterranean.

Surely he wasn't serious about her becoming his sex slave.

Or about taking her to South America.

She wished she was safely back at home.

There was a tap at the door, then the key turned in the lock. Spiros, the Greek sailor who'd taken over as steward, stood there with a tray in his hand. He laid it on the table, smiling at her shyly, but looking puzzled too. 'Tea,' he announced, then more quietly, 'You are locked up – why?'

Jess was at a loss what to reply, so she settled for shrugging and saying, 'He's angry with me.'

He nodded, still looking puzzled.

She took the opportunity to ask him, 'What are they all doing up there?'

'Talking.'

He set out the tea things on the table, saying, 'Is there something you wish now? I will bring you anything you ask.'

Jess fleetingly wished it was in his power to bring her a ride home – by helicopter, perhaps.

There was the sound of footsteps coming along the corridor and Spiros hurriedly left the room and locked the door behind him.

After she'd had a cup of tea Jess searched all Will's clothes and belongings thoroughly. She wasn't sure what she was hoping to find, but it passed the time.

What she did find was a scrap of paper with some figures on. She puzzled over it for a while but was unable to make sense of them so she put it back where she'd found it.

At around half-past six the key turned in the lock again and Will came in.

'Don't you think keeping me locked up is rather over-dramatising the situation?' she greeted him. 'I'm not going anywhere, after all.'

He joined her where she was reclining on the bed, opened her short silk robe and slid his hands inside. He didn't reply, just began to caress her.

Jess felt her body respond and let her head fall back on the pillows. She was half tempted to tell him to go to hell. But she couldn't resist the wave of hot, shivering excitement which was already sweeping over him.

Reaching down, she guided his hand between her legs.

They dined on deck that evening with their three guests. Jess made no attempt to take part in the conversation – it was bad enough having the men looking at her lecherously, without having to talk to them too.

Throughout the evening Will kept caressing her. She tried to discourage him from doing so, but she could tell he was getting pleasure from the embarrassment he was causing her. Over drinks, he kept stroking her thigh, then once they were seated at the table he pushed his hand up her skirt under cover of the tablecloth.

Jess was sure the men could tell what was going on. She kept her legs pressed firmly together but somehow Will's determined hand found its way between her thighs.

She could feel a warm pink flush, half of embarrassment, half of arousal, spreading upwards over her chest and neck, colouring her tanned cheeks.

She was naked under her dress, Will had insisted on that, so it was easy for him to touch her intimately. Clenching her teeth, Jess tried to keep her thighs pressed together, but it was no good – she didn't have the willpower.

She was damned if she was going to let him bring her to a climax under the lustful gazes of their dubious guests. Pushing back her chair she stood up and left the table, walking away out of sight to the other side of the deck.

So she was his sex slave, was she?

Maybe, maybe not.

Will soon followed her and she greeted him by dragging down his zip, sinking to her knees and taking his cock in her mouth.

She heard him inhale sharply as she ran her tongue over the glans, licking and probing, before circling it with long, slow movements.

Cradling his balls in her hands she sucked hard, exerting a seductive pressure with her mouth. The still night air lay warmly around them as she sucked away.

She could hear the faint lapping of the water against the anchored yacht and the occasional bellow of laughter from the men at the table.

But other than that the only sounds were of her own wet mouth on Will's cock and his ragged breathing.

She continued with her erotic ministrations for a long time, until she could tell he was on the point of coming.

Withdrawing her mouth she stood up, moved away

and bent over the rail. Looking behind her she said impatiently, 'Well don't just stand there. Come and fuck me.'

She flipped her dress up to her waist so he could see the smooth globes of her luscious backside gleaming in the moonlight. She heard the deck creak as he covered the short distance between them, then she felt the hard end of his cock probing between her thighs.

He thrust it smoothly into her, his entrance made easy by the copiousness of her female juices. Holding onto the rail Jess jammed her backside urgently into his groin and felt his hands close on her breasts over her dress.

It was a heady and erotic sensation, being screwed over the rail of a yacht, anchored in the middle of the Mediterranean. Looking down into the inky waters and smelling the fresh salt tang of the sea, Jess forgot her plight and gave herself up to it.

Almost at boiling point when they started, Will came quite quickly, but Jess kept him inside her and guided his hand to her clit. She didn't release him until he'd brought her to a breathless climax.

Pulling away, she sank gracefully onto a sunlounger.

'Tell the steward I'll have my coffee and brandy round here, will you? Your guests aren't my idea of ideal dinner companions.'

Driving up the M1 in Jess's Fiat Uno, Alexa kept wondering where Jess was and whether she was okay. It was only seven a.m. but already the traffic was heavy. She'd phoned Jess's college in Manchester the day before to find out when the first pre-term meeting was and had been horrified to discover it was today.

She'd told Tim she was going to have to go up there and take her sister's place.

'After all,' she'd told him, 'the only reason she can't

be there herself is because she's pretending to be me. It's the least I can do.'

Tim had reluctantly agreed. She'd also phoned Ralph and pretended to be Jess, telling him she was coming home tomorrow.

He'd been overwhelmingly pleased.

It was going to be tricky convincing him she was her sister. It was one thing Jess taking her place for the occasional night out with one of her men, or for a brief meeting with one of the agency's clients, but another to keep it up in a domestic situation with a long-term lover.

Jess was neat, tidy and houseproud.

Alexa wasn't.

She had a cleaner for her flat, but she knew that Jess looked after the house in Altrincham herself. The extent of Ralph's contribution was anyone's guess. But probably minimal if he was like most men.

It was going to be difficult not knowing where anything was kept, or what sort of routine her sister followed.

After giving it some thought she'd bought a couple of bandages before leaving London. She'd stop at a service station off the M6 before reaching Altrincham and wind one around her right wrist and hand.

She had Jess's house keys in her bag and she'd packed her clothes in Jess's luggage. As for the rest – she'd just have to play it by ear.

Alexa herself still felt as if she were having withdrawal symptoms from Will. Although she'd been too worried about Jess to pay much attention to them, they were definitely there. Part of her knew she'd had a lucky escape from him, but part of her wished she was in Marrakech having him screw her over and over again.

She couldn't begin to imagine how Jess was coping

with him. But there was nothing she could do about it so there was no point dwelling on it.

When she arrived at the house in the late morning she was surprised to find Ralph waiting for her. She'd assumed he'd be at work.

'Jess, sweetheart – I'm so glad you've come back.' He pulled her into his arms and hugged her tightly before holding her at arm's length. 'You look great – really beautiful. Come inside, I'll make some coffee.'

He noticed the bandage for the first time.

'What's that for? Have your hurt yourself?'

'Nothing to worry about – a minor accident.'

'What happened? Tell me.'

'A taxi I was in was involved in an accident. I just wrenched my hand and banged my head, so I won't be much use around the house for a while. Oh, and if I seem a bit vague about anything that's why,' she told him, hoping that would cover anything strange about her behaviour.

'You shouldn't have driven yourself up. Why didn't you tell me yesterday? I'd have caught a train down and driven you back up.'

'Don't worry – I'm fine,' she told him airily. 'Now, did you mention coffee?'

After lunch Ralph went off to work while Alexa hastily explored the house, opening every drawer and cupboard and trying to memorise the contents.

She unpacked her clothes, grimacing at the contents of Jess's wardrobe, then tried to decide what to wear for the meeting.

As Ralph had already seen Jess since her makeover, Alexa's glamorous appearance hadn't come as a shock to him. But the last time Jess's colleagues had seen Jess, it had been in her previous rather dowdy persona.

She didn't want to shock them too much, on the other hand they might as well get used to it for when Jess got back.

If Jess ever got back.

Pushing aside such worrying thoughts, Alexa took a quick shower. She couldn't face wearing any of her sister's dull clothes, but she dressed quietly in a plain white blouse with a pair of fawn tailored trousers and a black jacket. She kept her make-up to a minimum and tied her hair back with a black ribbon.

Even so, her appearance in the staff room was greeted by amazed stares. Luckily, when Alexa had once visited Jess in Manchester she'd picked her up at the college to go to the theatre, so she knew where the staff room was. What she didn't know was who any of her colleagues were.

She tried to adopt Jess's rather diffident demeanour and hoped for the best. She saw several of the men staring at her speculatively and resisted the temptation to give them bewitching smiles.

The meeting started but she didn't pay too much attention, until she was passed her timetable. She stared at it, puzzled, then without thinking spoke directly to the college principal, a hatchet-faced woman with grey hair.

'Excuse me, I think there must be some mistake. I'm down for one lecture each on four separate evenings – and I've got a nine a.m. lecture on three of those days.'

The principal raised an eyebrow at the interruption and said, 'That's the way the timetable worked out, I'm afraid.'

Looking around the room Alexa asked crisply, 'Who else is working four evenings?' Only a nervous-looking man in his early twenties raised his hand. Alexa turned to the woman next to her and glanced at her timetable – she only had one evening lecture.

She had a dim and distant memory of Jess complaining that she always seemed to get a heavier workload than most of her colleagues and Alexa could see why. The principal was a bully and Jess couldn't stand up to her.

Well, Alexa could.

Glancing around the room again she asked, 'Who's working three evenings?' Two people raised their hands. 'Two evenings?' Several of the staff indicated that they were. 'One?'

She couldn't believe this – most of the staff were only teaching one evening a week and Jess was supposed to accommodate four.

Smiling sweetly at the principal, Alexa prepared to do battle.

And win.

Jess spent the morning on deck sunbathing, well away from where Will was having another interminable meeting with his potential business partners.

He came over towards lunchtime, removed her bikini top without a word and fondled her naked breasts. Her back arched, she was enjoying the caresses when over Will's shoulder she spotted the Tunisian. He stood there openly watching, an expression of undisguised lust on his swarthy features.

Snatching her towel Jess covered herself, hissing, 'There's someone watching!'

'So?' enquired Will unperturbed. 'Let him.' He tried to touch her again but she stopped him and he shrugged and went away, leaving the Tunisian still staring at her lecherously.

To her horror he walked across to her and stretched out a large hand towards her breasts.

'Don't you dare touch me!' she spat, trying to twist

off the sunlounger. At that moment the young Greek steward appeared and somehow interposed himself between them.

'Lunch is served,' he said, then began busying himself rearranging Jess's parasol.

The Tunisian shot him a filthy look, then stomped off, muttering to himself.

'Thank you, Spiros,' murmured Jess.

'Is my pleasure. He is bad, that one – and the others.'

Glancing nervously over his shoulder, the steward hurried off.

After lunch Jess went down to the cabin, where Will followed her. Before she realised what he was doing he tied her wrists to the headboard and arranged her in a sitting position.

Unclipping her bikini top he bent his head and took one coral-pink nipple into his mouth, and tugged on it with his lips.

Immediately, hot squirming little spirals of lust began an insidious, internal tickling within her groin. Jess pulled at her bonds, but to no avail.

'Damn it, Will, untie me,' she urged him.

'Why should I?' he enquired, raising his head. 'I like the idea of you tied up and waiting for me. Don't worry – I'll pay you several visits during the afternoon.'

'My idea of a good time isn't spending several hours tied to a bed,' she protested.

'It makes you hot – don't bother to deny it,' he told her, slipping his hand into her bikini briefs. Jess wriggled her backside up the bed trying to avoid his probing fingers, but he found her clit and stroked it, making her gasp with excitement.

When he withdrew his hand it was glistening with

moisture. 'Like I said – it makes you hot. I'll be back later,' he told her casually and left the room.

She was horribly embarrassed when Spiros came into the cabin a few minutes later, carrying an armful of clean towels. She hastily drew her knees up to cover her breasts and tried to look as if it were an everyday occurrence for her to be tethered to the bed wearing only her bikini briefs.

'What is this?' he asked her. 'Why are you tied like this?'

It occurred to Jess that having a friend among the crew wasn't such a bad idea.

'He doesn't want me to get away,' she said, looking downwards.

Spiros's brown eyes were puzzled and filled with consternation. 'This is no way to treat a lady,' he protested. 'I will untie you.'

'No – don't,' she said quickly, 'it will get you into trouble.'

'This is not good,' Spiros asserted.

'No, it isn't,' agreed Jess. 'Spiros – when do we next put into port?'

'Tomorrow – perhaps six in the evening.'

'Nice?'

'Yes, Nice. You will be going away?'

'I hope so,' replied Jess, 'I want to go home.'

'You should go home,' he said determinedly. 'Such a good lady shouldn't be with such bad men.'

He seemed inclined to stay and talk to her and it was only with some difficulty that Jess persuaded him to leave the cabin before Will came back.

Will kept her tied up until early evening, when he released her so he could watch her bathe and dress. He visited her several times before that, usually just caressing and stroking her until she was burning up with frustration, but twice screwing her vigorously.

While Jess was brushing her hair, Will took something out of the pocket of one of his jackets and left the room, but not before she'd seen it was the scrap of paper with numbers on she'd puzzled over before.

She followed him silently and watched through a crack in the office door while he consulted it before opening the safe.

Of course – it was the combination to the safe.

Retracing her steps Jess returned to the cabin.

The evening was torture. Will left the room at one stage and the Tunisian took the opportunity to touch her breasts, while the other two men exchanged what was obviously a lewd comment. Furious, she slapped his hand away, then stepped quickly back as he made a lunge at her.

Will reappeared just in time, and the man subsided back into his seat, but she didn't like the expression on his face as he continued to watch her throughout dinner.

The sooner she was off here the better.

Alexa returned to her sister's home in Altrincham having successfully reduced Jess's evening commitments at college to two lectures on the same evening.

Ralph was already home.

'Hello, darling – how did it go?' he asked her.

'Fine,' she returned brightly, remembering to hang her jacket up rather than tossing it carelessly down on a chair. Crossing over to the sofa she flung herself down. It was seven o'clock and she was ready for a drink, but she doubted if Jess ever came home and poured herself gin and tonic.

'What are we eating tonight?' she asked him casually.

'I don't know – I've pretty much been living on takeaways while you've been away.'

That suited Alexa. 'We'll have to carry on doing that until my hand's better – unless you want to do the cooking. How about pizza tonight? We could open a bottle of wine to celebrate my return home.'

'Jess . . .' Ralph came to sit next to her on the sofa. 'Are you home for good? I've been out of my mind all summer thinking you weren't going to come back.'

'Let's just see how it goes,' she said, deciding she'd let Jess take care of that one – if and when she managed to get back to England. 'Will you open the wine before you go to get the pizza? I got into the habit of having a couple of glasses in the evening when I was staying with Alexa.'

The meal together was pleasant enough, except that Ralph returned with an anchovy pizza and Alexa hated anchovies. She tried to eat a couple but found them so unpleasant that she picked the rest off and stacked them on the side of her plate.

'Have you gone off them?' Ralph asked her.

'I had some fish last week which was a bit off,' she invented hurriedly. 'I should have mentioned it before you went out.'

They watched TV together for a while then Alexa felt tired after her early start that day and said she was going to bed. She planned to sleep in the spare room because that's what Jess had been doing before she'd left home.

She was unprepared for Ralph to follow her upstairs and take her arm as she was halfway through the spare room door.

'Jess, please come back to our bed. I've missed you so much – I need you so much.'

He put his arms around her and kissed her tentatively. Alexa could feel his erection against her hip and was undecided what to do. On the one hand she was tired, but on the other she was intrigued to know what Ralph was like in bed. It was something she always wondered about the men she knew and had never had sex with.

Why not?

It might make her forget her anxiety about her sister for a while.

And Jess had given her permission.

Discreetly she pressed her hip against his hard-on and then allowed him to lead her into the bedroom. She let him make the running, interested to see how he'd approach it.

He undressed her slowly, inhaling sharply when he saw her black lacy bra and panties.

'I did some shopping while I was in London,' she murmured, remembering the plain underwear Jess used to wear. He caressed her breasts reverently through the flimsy lace, before undoing the bra and cupping her full firmness with his hands. He stroked her hips and belly then eased her panties down her legs.

Alexa caught a brief glimpse of his engorged, purple cock before she felt it pushing against her outer labia, then he was enfolded by her warm wetness as he slithered slickly upwards.

As he thrust in and out of her, Alexa thought fleetingly that it was almost refreshing to be having sex in the missionary position. She found it very enjoyable but all too brief, because Ralph came very quickly.

'I'm sorry!' he gasped as he pumped the last remnants of his sperm into her, 'I just couldn't wait.'

After several months' abstinence she could hardly blame him, but she hadn't come herself yet. She held him cradled in her arms for a few minutes, then squeezed his cock gently with her internal muscles a couple of times.

It was enough to make him hard again.

'Ralph,' she whispered, 'that felt so good – make love to me again.'

He began to thrust in and out, supporting his weight on his elbows. Alexa pulled him down on top of her and wrapped her legs around his thighs, angling her pelvis so each thrust stimulated her clit.

Her excitement grew as he moved faster and when she climaxed she clutched him convulsively, arching her back and crying out.

Ralph seemed gratified by her response and as he kissed her deeply she smiled to herself – it shouldn't take too much work to make an imaginative, inventive lover out of him.

A welcome home present for Jess.

And it would go some way towards alleviating the frustration she felt when she thought about Will.

After dinner, Will and his guests decided to play cards. Jess tried to excuse herself but Will pulled her back down next to him.

'Our friends here want to play for different stakes this evening,' he told her as he shuffled the cards.

'So? Why does that mean I have to stay?'

Will smiled at her wolfishly.

'Because every time I lose a hand they want you to remove an article of clothing.'

'And what happens if they lose?'

'They pay up in money.'

'Forget it,' said Jess dismissively. 'I'm going to bed.'

She stalked out of the room without a backward glance. He caught her up in the corridor.

'I'm very good at cards – I always win. Where's the harm, Alexa? They're on the point of making a deal – this will help it along. When we get to South America we'll be able to sit back and wait for the proceeds to come in. We'll live well off it – you'll see.

All I'm asking for now is a little help with entertaining them.'

Jess thought fast.

She was planning to abandon ship tomorrow when they reached Nice and it would probably help her escape if Will thought she was resigned, or even looking forward, to going to South America with him.

And it was true, he was very good at cards – he always seemed to win.

'Alright,' she said reluctantly, 'but I'm not stripping off completely whatever happens. I'll join you in a few minutes – I need to use the bathroom.'

Once in the cabin she slipped off her dress, under which she was naked except for a suspender belt and stockings. She quickly pulled on a bra, panties, and a slip, then donned the dress again.

She joined the men at the table in the smoke-filled cabin and sipped her drink, trying to ignore the hot, covetous glances they kept sending her.

Several games were played before Will lost a hand and Jess took off one of her high-heeled shoes and placed it on the table. A run of bad luck followed for him and she removed the other shoe, then both stockings.

She unrolled the stockings with her back turned, unfastening the suspenders under her skirt, determined to show as little as possible.

When Will lost another hand and Jess had to remove the suspender belt, she began to suspect he was losing deliberately to keep his guests happy. He won the next few games and she began to relax.

Eventually he lost again.

'Time to take the dress off,' he said, when she showed no inclination to do so spontaneously. He stubbed out his cigarette, his cold grey eyes glittering with excitement.

Slowly Jess stood up, unzipped it and let it fall from her shoulders revealing that she was still decorously clad in her slip, bra and pants.

Her eyes met his and she smiled triumphantly, knowing he'd expected her to be naked under the dress. He sat back and linked his hands behind his head, appraising her watchfully.

She knew he wanted their guests to see her naked and envy him, because he had the use of her shapely body and they didn't. He obviously found it a huge turn-on to have other men lusting after her.

Well, too bad.

One of the men dealt the cards and they continued to play. When Will lost again Jess slowly pulled the slip over her head and tossed it onto the table.

'And that,' she announced, 'is as far as it goes. Goodnight.'

Hips swaying, she left the room in her bra and panties.

Chapter Twenty

The last thing Jess wanted Will to suspect was that she was planning to jump ship in Nice. Accordingly she laid her plans carefully.

The morning after her strip, she woke him early by climbing astride him and coaxing his slumbering cock into an impressive erection. Guiding it between her widely-parted labia she lowered herself slowly until it was deep inside her.

She knew he was awake although his eyes were still closed and she began to ride him, gently at first then harder as her arousal mounted.

She wanted him to believe that she was in his sexual thrall too deeply to want to leave him.

It was half true.

She certainly felt regret that after today, if all went according to plan, she'd never again know the excitement of having him fuck her to a series of gasping, panting climaxes.

Better make the most of it now.

She rode him until she came, then while she was still enjoying the last eddying waves of pleasure, he flipped her onto her back and began to screw her in earnest.

Her legs locked tightly around his waist, Jess lay with her head thrown back and her red-gold hair tumbling over the pillow, raising her hips to meet each of his vigorous thrusts.

When it was over Jess, still naked, made a point of moving provocatively around the cabin and its adjoining bathroom, showing him as much of her body as possible, then bending over to pick up discarded clothes with her legs straight and slightly apart.

Will sat propped up against the pillows, his eyes half closed, smoking his first cigarette of the day.

'What time are our guests leaving?' she enquired.

'As soon as we drop anchor.'

'Good, I won't be sorry to see them go. Besides – I have plans for tonight.'

'What plans?'

Sitting on a homeward bound plane with any luck, thought Jess.

Aloud she said, 'You'll have to wait until tonight to find out, but it involves a bottle of baby oil and the crew staying below deck all evening.' She shot him a seductive look from under her lashes as she spoke.

He grinned at her. 'I think that can be arranged.'

When Jess had dressed she left Will taking a shower and went up on deck to find Spiros.

She needed his help.

During the course of the day, Jess interrupted Will's final meeting with their guests three times to get him to screw her.

His stamina, she thought to herself after the final bout, was really something.

She was on all fours on the dining room table waiting for Will to withdraw so she could climb down. He did so reluctantly, while she pulled her bikini briefs back up and retied her bikini top.

At least when she was back home she'd have all this to remember.

'You're practically insatiable today, Alexa,' he commented, zipping up his trousers. 'Any particular reason?'

'Probably just the thought of having you to myself again tonight,' she replied, scrambling down from the table and wondering if Spiros had managed to do what she had asked.

She certainly hoped so.

A lot depended on it.

In the late afternoon the yacht dropped anchor about half a mile out from Nice. Spiros had told her this was going to happen rather than the yacht sailing into port. Will was obviously taking no chances of her escaping.

At around six, the motor launch carrying Spiros, Will and their three guests left the yacht and headed for the shore, while Jess watched from the deck, having kissed Will a passionate goodbye.

As soon as the launch was at a safe distance Jess went down to the cabin and emerged with a waterproof bag tied around her waist containing money, her passport, a small towel and a change of clothes.

Glancing around to make sure no one was watching, she slipped silently over the side of the yacht and headed for the shore at a different angle from the one taken by the launch.

Will knew that Alexa could barely swim and was afraid of deep water.

But Jess was a strong, confident swimmer who could easily cover the half-mile between the yacht and the shore.

She paced herself but it was a clear, calm evening and the swim presented no problems. She knew just where she was heading – Spiros had given her exact directions.

When she eventually emerged from the water it was onto a deserted sandy beach. The warm evening air was scented by the pine trees which grew between the beach and the coast road and Jess inhaled deeply, glad to back on dry land again.

Stripping off her wet bikini she began to dry herself with the small towel. A sound behind her made her look around, there was Spiros coming towards her carrying her two suitcases.

Hastily wrapping the towel around her where it did a totally inadequate job of concealing her naked body, Jess greeted him warmly.

'Spiros – you made it. Did he suspect anything, do you think?'

Depositing the cases in the sand at her feet Spiros shook his head.

'No. I put your baggages in the boat this afternoon, out of sight like you say. The men they go ashore and I come here. I take Mr Harper back to the yacht in one hour.'

His eyes travelled admiringly over her barely covered body.

'It is right you go home to your family. He did not treat you well, a nice lady like you.'

At that moment the towel slipped, exposing Jess's high, firm breasts to Spiros's heated gaze. She tried to pull it back in position but as she covered her breasts, the towel rose above the silky down of her red-gold bush.

Spiros flushed. Looking into his dark brown eyes Jess saw a hot flare of desire there. She could hear the waves lapping against the coarse sand and the cries of the sea birds overhead as they both stood silently gazing at each other.

She took a step towards him, then they were in each other's arms, the towel crumpled in the sand between them.

Spiros was not particularly tall but he was broad-shouldered and muscular. Running her hands down his back while he feverishly caressed her breasts, Jess sighed with pleasure.

He stripped off his jeans and T-shirt revealing a body honed to iron hardness by physical work.

He pulled her down onto the sand in the shade of a resin-scented pine tree, his massive erection towering up from between his thighs.

He stroked her body gently with his large calloused hands. When he kissed her she tasted the clean salty taste of the sea and pulled him closer, her hand wound in his curly dark hair.

He touched every inch of her body before she became impatient to have him inside her and took hold of his cock. It was very thick and ridged with engorged purple veins, the glans already dripping with moisture.

Jess wondered if she would be able to take all of it, however aroused she was.

She needn't have worried.

Spiros reached between her legs and stroked her clitoris, then slipped two fingers inside her and began to explore the intricate folds of her pussy. His thumb kept up an arousing rhythmic movement along the shaft of her clit as he slipped another finger inside her to join the others.

She could feel her honeypot lubricating and the slippery moisture trickling between her thighs as he moved his fingers around inside her.

The heat in her groin had built up to furnace level, an insistent, demanding heat which only his cock could satisfy.

Not a moment too soon he withdrew his hand and pushed her legs apart, knees bent. Jess felt the warm, rounded end of his cock pressing against her slick private parts, then he slid smoothly in.

Before half his length was sheathed in her tight,

molten pussy she felt he'd filled her up completely.

'No more,' she whispered, as he stopped moving for a moment and then lay in the shadows of the pine tree, the light from the setting sun filtering through the branches.

Resting on his elbows Spiros withdrew a little way, then forged upwards again. Gasping at the feel of him, Jess relaxed her internal muscles until he'd gained another couple of inches.

Withdrawing again, he commenced an erotic rocking motion, his huge cock stimulating every part of her internally.

Sighing, Jess wound her legs around his thighs and pulled him down onto her. He began to thrust in earnest; his tanned, muscular body moving over her paler one while she gasped and writhed beneath him.

Soon she was taking all of him inside her and with each thrust getting nearer and nearer to her climax.

Jess had completely forgotten where she was and that she was in the process of escaping from her abductor.

All that was a million miles removed from lying flat on her back on the coarse sand of a beach in the South of France, while a well-endowed Greek sailor fucked her into breathless ecstasy.

She was unaware of the gritty sand chafing her buttocks and the sharp prick of pine needles on her back, as with a last convulsive thrust, Spiros rode them both to a white-hot climax.

She must have dozed off briefly in the aftermath of their passion. The sound of the cicadas brought her back to reality – that and a sudden awareness, how heavy Spiros felt slumped against her.

She rolled out from underneath him and ran into the sea to rinse the sweat and sand from her naked body. Spiros followed her and they splashed together in the warm water of the Mediterranean.

'I must go now,' he told her, dragging his jeans up over his muscular buttocks. 'I must take Mr Harper back to the yacht.'

Spiros had borrowed a beaten-up old van from a friend of his who worked on the docks and he dropped her at the airport before returning to the quay to take Will back to the boat.

Their goodbye kiss was long, passionate and left her almost too weak to carry her heavy suitcases.

Tim was working late as usual when he heard the door to the outer office open and close. A moment later there was a tap on his own door.

'Alexa, honey – what are you doing here so late? I thought you were in Cheshire.'

'It's not Alexa – it's Jess,' replied Jess wearily, sinking onto the sofa.

'I'm real glad to see you back safely,' said Tim. 'What happened? How did you get away? Does Alexa know?'

'Yes, I phoned her from the airport. She told me that you were working late and to come straight here.'

'Yeah, she phoned me earlier – I told her I'd be burning the midnight oil.'

Jess took out her keys and opened both suitcases. Tim's jaw dropped when he saw what was inside.

Money.

A lot of money.

More money than he'd ever seen in his life.

'Is that the money Harper embezzled?' he asked.

Jess nodded. 'Most of it.'

'How . . . how did you manage that?'

While Will was busy with his potential business partners Jess had been busy herself.

She'd transferred most of the money in the case in

307

the cupboard destined for their guests to one of her own suitcases. She'd then filled the other case with books, adding just one layer of money on top in case anyone opened it to check.

She'd also opened the safe, using the combination on the slip of paper in Will's pocket, and put the money she found there into her other case.

Spiros had obligingly taken them ashore for her thinking they held her clothes, leaving her free to swim unencumbered.

Tim was jubilant – the money could be returned to the company tomorrow just in time for the flotation to go ahead.

Another successful case.

'Alexa couldn't have done better,' he praised her, 'and your sister is one smart operator.'

The strain of recent events at last hit Jess and a wave of exhaustion swept over. She felt her eyelids droop and from a distance Tim's voice saying, 'You're bushed. I'll just lock this up, then I'll take you back to Alexa's flat.'

A few days later Jess drove into college for the first day of the new term.

She knew she looked good in a plain but sexy buttercup-yellow suit, her red-gold hair cascading around her shoulders and her delicate features highlighted by deftly applied make-up.

There was a pleasurable throbbing between her thighs reminding her that an hour ago she'd been bent over the kitchen units while Ralph screwed her from behind with an enthusiasm as unexpected as it was unprecedented.

It had been like that since she'd arrived home and Alexa had returned to London.

She wasn't certain whether it was because he'd

picked up on her own renewed appetite for sex, or his few days with Alexa, or even a combination of both. But whatever it was it was great.

Tim had offered her a permanent job but she'd turned it down. It had been fun for the summer, but now she was ready to return to teaching, confident in the knowledge that after what she'd achieved, there was very little she couldn't handle.

She was happy to be back living her old life.

Admittedly with certain changes . . .

In her flat in Hampstead, Alexa was dressing for the latest undercover role she had to play. She'd just spent a satisfying night with Ned, back in town at last after spending the summer working in Glasgow.

It had been good to see him again.

She still thought about Will, half with regret and half with relief that she'd escaped from his sexual thrall. But now she was back in London she could distance herself from her arousing memories and carry on where she'd left off before going to find him.

Today, she'd started work at the insurance company and would remain there until she'd discovered who was behind the ongoing insurance fraud. She'd studied all Jess's reports and had already drawn a few conclusions.

She didn't think it would take her long.

How she loved this job.

'Miss Holt to see you.'

'Send her in please, Martha,' replied Tim, tiredly.

He could barely keep his eyes open.

Last night Sherry had appeared at his flat wanting comforting, having just lost a role she'd been up for in a new TV series.

He'd obligingly comforted her until about three in

the morning, screwing her a total of five times in the process. It had been great but it had left him barely able to walk and feeling like he had muscles made from pure jello.

Now he had a client to see, but he felt more like stretching out on the sofa for some much-needed sleep.

When she'd phoned to make the appointment she'd mentioned that she worked for Martin Sheppard, one of his regular clients and the owner of a substantial communications empire.

Martha opened the door.

'Mr Preece – Miss Holt,' she announced, then returned to her own office.

Tim could hardly believe his eyes.

She looked like the stuff dreams are made of.

Wet dreams.

A cascade of gleaming, honey-coloured hair framed a lovely sensual face, dominated by slanting green eyes and a full pouting mouth.

Her magnificent breasts thrust provocatively against a close-fitting, black silk jacket. It was so low cut that Tim doubted if she was even wearing a bra underneath, let alone a blouse.

A tight scarlet skirt moulded itself to the alluring curves of her hips and backside and finished several inches above the knees. Her shapely legs were encased in sheer black stockings and her black suede shoes had five-inch stiletto heels.

If Miss Holt worked for Martin Sheppard he couldn't imagine in what capacity.

He shook hands with her and offered her a chair, trying not to stare too obviously at her unbelievable cleavage.

'So what can I do for you, Miss Holt?'

'You can get me out of a terrible mess.'

'What sort of mess?' enquired Tim warily. He didn't know exactly what was coming but he had a feeling he wasn't going to like it.

'I'm afraid I've let myself become involved with a married man.'

'Martin Sheppard?'

She looked down at her hands then lifted beseeching green eyes to his.

'That's right. And now he's blackmailing me . . .'

Headline Delta Erotic Survey

In order to provide the kind of books you like to read - and to qualify for a free erotic novel of the Editor's choice - we would appreciate it if you would complete the following survey and send your answers, together with any further comments, to:

Headline Book Publishing
FREEPOST 9 (WD 4984)
London
W1E 7BE

1. Are you male or female?
2. Age? Under 20 / 20 to 30 / 30 to 40 / 40 to 50 / 50 to 60 / 60 to 70 / over
3. At what age did you leave full-time education?
4. Where do you live? (Main geographical area)
5. Are you a regular erotic book buyer / a regular book buyer in general / both?
6. How much approximately do you spend a year on erotic books / on books in general?
7. How did you come by this book?
7a. If you bought it, did you purchase from: a national bookchain / a high street store / a newsagent / a motorway station / an airport / a railway station / other........
8. Do you find erotic books easy / hard to come by?
8a. Do you find Headline Delta erotic books easy / hard to come by?
9. Which are the best / worst erotic books you have ever read?
9a. Which are the best / worst Headline Delta erotic books you have ever read?
10. Within the erotic genre there are many periods, subjects and literary styles. Which of the following do you prefer:
10a. (period) historical / Victorian / C20th / contemporary / future?
10b. (subject) nuns / whores & whorehouses / Continental frolics / s&m / vampires / modern realism / escapist fantasy / science fiction?

10c. (styles) hardboiled / humorous / hardcore / ironic / romantic / realistic?

10d. Are there any other ingredients that particularly appeal to you?

11. We try to create a cover appearance that is suitable for each title. Do you consider them to be successful?

12. Would you prefer them to be less explicit / more explicit?

13. We would be interested to hear of your other reading habits. What other types of books do you read?

14. Who are your favourite authors?

15. Which newspapers do you read?

16. Which magazines?

17. Do you have any other comments or suggestions to make?

If you would like to receive a free erotic novel of the Editor's choice (available only to UK residents), together with an up-to-date listing of Headline Delta titles, please supply your name and address:

Name..

Address...

....

....

A selection of Erotica
from Headline

FONDLE ALL OVER	Nadia Adamant	£4.99 ☐
LUST ON THE LOOSE	Noel Amos	£4.99 ☐
GROUPIES	Johnny Angelo	£4.99 ☐
PASSION IN PARADISE	Anonymous	£4.99 ☐
THE ULTIMATE EROS COLLECTION	Anonymous	£6.99 ☐
EXPOSED	Felice Ash	£4.99 ☐
SIN AND MRS SAXON	Lesley Asquith	£4.99 ☐
HIGH JINKS HALL	Erica Boleyn	£4.99 ☐
TWO WEEKS IN MAY	Maria Caprio	£4.99 ☐
THE PHALLUS OF OSIRIS	Valentina Cilescu	£4.99 ☐
NUDE RISING	Faye Rossignol	£4.99 ☐
AMOUR AMOUR	Marie-Claire Villefranche	£4.99 ☐

All Headline books are available at your local bookshop or newsagent, or can be ordered direct from the publisher. Just tick the titles you want and fill in the form below. Prices and availability subject to change without notice.

Headline Book Publishing PLC, Cash Sales Department, Bookpoint, 39 Milton Park, Abingdon, OXON, OX14 4TD, UK. If you have a credit card you may order by telephone – 0235 831700.

Please enclose a cheque or postal order made payable to Bookpoint Ltd to the value of the cover price and allow the following for postage and packing:
UK & BFPO: £1.00 for the first book, 50p for the second book and 30p for each additional book ordered up to a maximum charge of £3.00.
OVERSEAS & EIRE: £2.00 for the first book, £1.00 for the second book and 50p for each additional book.

Name ....

Address ....

....

....

If you would prefer to pay by credit card, please complete:
Please debit my Visa/Access/Diner's Card/American Express (delete as applicable) card no:

Signature .... Expiry Date ....